BLUE SCREEN OF DEATH

  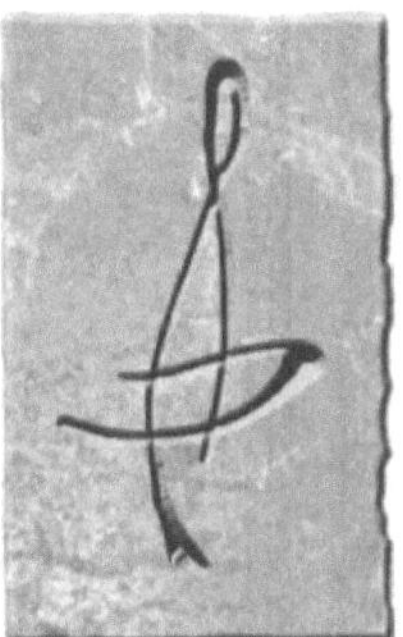

hashtag magic

blue screen of death
control alt delete

HASHTAG MAGIC
BLUE SCREEN OF DEATH

J. STEVEN YOUNG

Chapter 1

Young Colby Stevens sat playing with his new wind-up train and wearing his daddy's favorite watch. While he placed a wind-up engine under the covered bridge of his train set, he pushed around small pieces of tile with symbols on them.

"Abber-cadabber," Colby said. He screeched and giggled.

A blue cat stretched while perched on top of a nearby bookshelf. The cat watched with interest through slitted eyes. The hair on his back began to stand, and his tail, poised in the shape of a question mark, puffed to three times its normal size. He jumped down from the shelf and edged his way to the corner of the bed where he could peek over its edge to look closer at the events as they unfolded. The Russian-blue watched Colby lifting the covered bridge to reveal that his train vanished from the tracks. The young boy's giggle, once playful and exuberant, now twisted in his throat and gurgled as it morphed into a desperate cry.

The cat scattered at the sound of both Colby's call for help, and the thunder of footfalls that approached from downstairs, growing more intense as they scampered to reach the room. Below the cover of the bed, in the shadows, two yellow eyes glowed as the cat continued to observe.

Colby's father listened with interest as his young son finished explaining how he wound-up the wooden train engine before letting it go to travel along the track.

The blue cat watched the boy's first expressions of delight and joy visibly warm his father's heart through the twinkling in his eyes. Then he tilted his head as he further examined the corners of the older human's eyes gather and wrinkle to match the folds in his brow. Worry about the situation and the fear in his boy's voice brought a sudden realization to overshadow an otherwise tender moment.

Jarrod Stevens knew that there was a chance any child he fathered would be gifted, but when his son said his train 'disappeared,' his heart burst with pride and sank to his stomach at once. He reached down to retrieve his watch that had fallen from Colby's wrist.

More feet entering the room caused the blue cat to sink further back into the shadows until the darkness swallowed even the yellow of his glowing eyes.

When asked how he put the train-set together without being able to read instructions, Colby shrugged his shoulders and replied matter-of-factly. "It seemed the right way, mommy. Same when I play with those squiggly-lined blocks."

Jarrod looked to where Colby pointed out several tiles lying on the floor near the train track. His eyes widened at the arrangement of the tiles and the ancient symbols etched on them.

* * *

Colby explained how he just wanted to play with his birthday present and simply couldn't wait until daddy was ready to help put it together.

"Ask Fizzy-Wizzles; he saw," Colby said.

Spirits lifted at the sudden memory of his witness, Colby searched the room in hopes of finding his friend.

Confused, Jarrod looked to his wife who shrugged her shoulders. "Who is Fizzy-Wizzles, son?"

Colby turned around in circles but could not find his little blue friend. "The kitty, he was here, but now he's gone!" Colby started to cry.

"We don't have a cat, Colby." Jarrod patted his son on the head and pushed him toward his nana who arrived to take the boy along.

"Take him downstairs please and distract him," Jarrod said to his mother-in-law. "Give him some licorice as well."

"My little Fart-blossom has magic already?" Nana said.

He gave her a nervous shrug and turned back to the mystery before him while his wife sat down on the edge of the bed beside him.

Colby's Nana gathered him up and took him downstairs with his mother soon following while his father Jarrod stayed behind to search the room.

He looked around, lifting the blankets, checking under pillows, and digging through the toy box. He couldn't find the train anywhere. His attention went back to the tiles lying on the floor.

"Why do you deny what you already know Jarrod?"

The voice came from above him. Jarrod turned to watch the Russian Blue cat leap from the shelf down to the bed and then morph into a little blue man sitting on the edge of Colby's bed.

"Fizzy-Wizzles, indeed," Jarrod said. "Holding out hope I suppose, Fizzlewink." Jarrod gazed at the child-sized yet wrinkled blue man. His hair was as white and puffy as clouds but pulled back neatly into tails alongside his head. "Have you been here long?"

"Long enough." Fizzlewink crossed his legs and squinted at the train track on the floor. "There is a substantial residue there, and you can bet that others will have felt that little parlor trick your boy performed."

Jarrod stared back at Fizzlewink in hopes of hearing what he should do.

"You were warned about this life you wanted for yourself, Jarrod. What did you expect and especially with that woman you chose to play house with." Fizzlewink kept twisting his long left eyebrow. "You were further warned not to have children with your choice in a mate, especially a male child. There will be repercussions."

"I've had time to think about that, my old friend," Jarrod said. He winked at Fizzlewink and grabbed the covered bridge from Colby's playset. "The order will remain, I can prevent a premature resurgence of the Emassa's magic and protect my boy at the same time."

Fizzlewink paced back and forth on the landing. His little legs and feet moved fast and lightly across the floor, all the time he twisted his long white eyebrows that extended several inches from the sides of his cat-shaped head.

"Have you any idea what will happen? Do you forget what happened the last time the wells of power were capped off, forcing a fragile peace between us and our enemies?" Fizzlewink's eyes pleaded with Jarrod to rethink what he planned.

Jarrod shook his head. "They are not exactly enemies, and not all of them feel animosity, Fizz. Things will remain the same for the time being and life will go on as planned in our small community. I have been working on this since the day Colby was born."

* * *

"There will be side effects to this meddling with nature, Jarrod. You can not hope to stem the tide long."

Jarrod stood straight and determined. "No, there will not be side effects. I can do this." Jarrod strode out of the room with Fizzlewink on his heels, though he stopped at the top of the stairs. He raised the covered bridge in the air and over his head. "I will create a shield that shall hold the power at bay until he is old enough to handle it. I have help from an ancient mage."

Fizzlewink stumbled behind the tall man trying to keep up as he ran from Colby's room, up a flight of stairs to a study on the third floor. He watched as Jarrod collected runes, a few objects, and a dusty old book. When he saw the symbol emblazoned on the cover of the heavy-looking leather-bound tome, his eyes widened, and the color drained from his blue face.

"You can't do that, Jarrod. You know what that would mean to you and your little family," Fizzlewink argued. "It isn't worth losing everything."

Jarrod stopped at the landing and looked back at the little blue man. "I have no choice, old friend. I have to protect them as best I can." He began to take the remaining stairs when he stopped and looked back at Fizzlewink. "Look in on them from time to time. Be here to guide my son when he comes of age."

Fizzlewink nodded. "Where will you center this shield?"

"At the school I created for the children of our races to learn and grow. It shall be a final safe place if things go wrong and a place to store what I must take to protect my son."

After watching the little man turn back into a cat and disappear, Jarrod headed down the stairs, pushing his shoulders back and painting a smile on his face.

Downstairs, Jarrod found Colby was placated with a cookie and glass of milk while his older sister Shelly whispered out the back door from the kitchen. Jarrod's mother-in-law glared at him accursedly as she stood by the stove, stirring a pot of something that she likely hoped to pass off as a stew. His wife Aria sat at the table, wringing a handkerchief. Jarrod led them to the living room.

Shelly held a sizable blue cat she found outside on the back porch.

Colby ran to his papa's open arms, tears streaming from his eyes and leaving dark spots upon his light blue shirt. He ignored the words his daddy spoke, choosing instead to fixate on the watch upon his wrist that lit up when he squeezed the buttons. A sudden prick on his foot distracted him from the wristwatch.

"Ouch, papa. Why'd you pinch me?" Colby pulled his foot up to inspect his toes. "It's bleeding."

"Sorry my dear boy, papa must have stuck you with his tools."

Jarrod shoved the red-blotted piece of paper in the fold of his journal and set Colby down on the couch. He leaned in to kiss his son on the forehead and turned away to wipe his eyes. Next, he approached Shelly, his daughter, and gave her a squeeze and kissed her head as well.

"It's time, my dear," he said to Aria. He gathered everyone in the living room and said a few words that no one paid mind to except Nana. They sensed something was wrong, and the children were crying.

Jarrod looked back as he walked out the door and into the night, his wife following behind like an unwilling accomplice to a horrible crime.

Nana held the children back from exiting the house. "Crap on a cracker," she muttered. "Time to lose some memories and magic little ones." She pulled the kids into the house and closed the door.

***

Jarrod and Aria approached the unlit main entry of Escutcheon Academy; the private institution of learning secretly created for the families of magical bloodlines. The secret was that not only did the mundanes, or non-magical humans, not know its purpose, but none of the children accepted for admittance were aware either. Magic users have been in hiding for eons and formal instruction was forbidden by the council of elders in order to maintain a peace within the magical world.

A lone figure stood waiting and unlocked the door to allow Jarrod and Aria inside. Without a word, he locked the doors and escorted the visitors down a series of corridors and stairways. Deep within the bowels of the building, a metal door blocked further procession.

"I've prepared as much as my meager gift allows, old friend," Tiddle said. "The others are waiting in the chamber."

Jarrod patted his friend on the back before placing an open hand on the cold steel door. "It's more than anyone should have done to aid my mad quest." The door began to shimmer as staggered symbols began to glow and rise from the surface of the metal. "You've done well, my friend. I only hope your efforts won't be in vain."

Tiddle squeezed Jarrod's arm then stood back. "We have maybe a decade or so before we find out." He gave Aria an uncomfortable hug before heading back the way they came, disappearing into the darkness.

Making a symbol in the air with his finger, Jarrod cast a spell to open the door and led Aria into the chamber beyond. In the center of the space, he stopped and set his journal down on a simple square pedestal that rose for the floor. Opening the book to the page marked with the blotting of Colby's blood, Jarrod rested his hand on the pages and closed his eyes.

Aria shuddered, though she knew what to expect when she long ago agreed to go through with this plan. "I'm ready; the Emassa help me."

"You remember what this will do to your psyche?" Said a hooded mage in the shadows. "You won't be the same until it comes full circle."

She wrapped her arms around herself. "I will do whatever is required of me to save my children."

Jarrod gazed into his wife's teary eyes and smiled meekly. "I don't deserve you."

Aria laughed in-spite of her mood, but it held no mirth. "No, you don't. But you will deserve every bit of what happens if this plan of yours doesn't work."

Jarrod took the verbal slap. "Let's get to it then." He nodded to the mysterious mage as he approached.

The mage reached out, his arms tattooed with runes, and pricked his own finger. He squeezed a small drop of blood onto the pedestal and began his spell.

A silent whisper and wave of the hands sent a spiral of magic charged mist to encase Aria. The blue hue of light radiating from the wispy tendrils squeezed until eliciting a scream that called back as it echoed off the surrounding walls. When her head went limp, a red glow pushed free of Aria and joined the blue mist, turning it a deep purple.

As the magic pushed free of its prey, allowing Aria to take a breath, the red glow hovered over Aria and began to pull free to stand beside her like a shadow. Aria and shadow regarded one another as the room radiated a purple light that pulsed with Jarrod's every chanted word. Beat by beat, the light matched until a static charge interrupted the spell.

Jarrod looked to his right and spoke the final words of the group spell. He closed his journal, wrapping it in parchment and string, then pushed it into Aria's hands. Turning to her red shadow of light, Jarrod instructed it to take Aria home with the book while placing his wristwatch in Aria's hand. One last kiss on her lips and look into her now glazed-over eyes was all he could spare.

"Go. Now!"

Aria was gone in a swirl of red light, leaving Jarrod to face the form pushing itself through the barrier of purple light encasing the room.

* * *

"Are you changing the deal flesh mage?" the now red man of plasma said.

"I have only added some assurances, brother."

"Brother," the creature spat. "You have no right calling me kin."

"An argument best rekindled when our agreement has been fulfilled," the mage said. His voice betrayed his doubt.

"I will do as I agreed," the spirit said. He turned to Jarrod. "Give me your hand."

Jarrod held out his hand to his brother. "Look after them, brother, I beg you. We can end this war and bring about the power to return all our magic."

The Creature took Jarrod's hand. Energy passed between them, and where the phantom was red plasmatic energy, it now took on flesh. Likewise, Jarrod's flesh melted away and took on a blue tinted energy as they switched places.

Deep laughter resounded from the beast's fleshy voice, and he relished its corporeal sound. "I will do as I agreed. I'll wait until ten years; hence when his power matures, then we shall see what will become of our accord."

Only then did Jarrod realize the meaning of his brother's words. Now having the borrowed flesh of Jarrod, his brother had a decade to plan his own outcome of what was meant to reunite their race.

"You can't-"

The reborn man let go of Jarrod, sending him into oblivion. "I can do as I please."

Jarrod pushed himself against the man borrowing his flesh and released a burst of magically charged energy. Blue light wrapped around Jarrod's brother and squeezed until the pulsing began to increase. Reaching to the pedestal, Jarrod tipped the bowl containing Colby's blood sample. When the magic from his aura reached the sample, the room became flooded with pure white light.

* * *

As the light faded, the man pulled himself from the floor and watched Jarrod's phantasmic lips curl into a satisfied smile.

"Good luck defying my plan with no magic of your own, brother." Jarrod blinked out with the light leaving his brother to scream out in defiant anger.

The newly possessed body turned to see he was the only one that remained in the chamber. "Cowards. I shall have my revenge."

***

A bright light from outside the front of the house brought the Stevens family out of the daze that overtook them. While Nana walked out the front door with Shelly, Colby stayed behind on the couch.

Aria returned home from where she followed her husband and set down a parchment and string wrapped bundle along with Jarrod's watch. She stepped up to the front of the house to observe the figures outside as her memories faded. Aria stood by the window, pouring herself a drink from a tray of assorted crystal bottles filled with various spirits, for the first time.

Colby noticed his father's watch that lay on the table beside the couch and watched as the hands stopped. He reached for it, and it fell to the floor as he touched it. Before Colby could reach down and grab the timepiece, Nana called for him to join her outside. He sobbed as he walked to the front door and followed after his nana.

Aria watched as her mother and two children shuffled down the driveway, looking up at the sky. Aria looked up to see the same swirl of color and light that swallowed the night sky and brightened everything in sight. She raised the glass of liquid courage to her lips and guzzled it down.

Colby watched the dazzling lights swirl across the sky like ribbons stretching from a kite that blew on the winds. He jumped up several times, reaching up his arms to grab hold only to return to the ground empty-handed.

* * *

As the lights began to fade, Colby's eyes started to droop. A bright red and blue swirl of glowing light radiated from his skin for the briefest of moments and was gone as Colby slumped in the arms of his grandmother.

Nana had cataracts, but she still saw the light shimmer across her grandson, and she felt a shudder pass through her as she held the now sleeping boy tight. Her gaze narrowed as she looked first at the boy and then to the sky and then at her daughter, who stood staring back from the large window.

"What was that just then?" Nana said and pointed a bony finger up to her daughter's nose. "Something smells fishy around here."

Aria only stared back at Nana, tears welling in her eyes.

Nana pulled back, eyes wide and mouth quivering. "Is it just my Aria behind those eyes?"

Aria broke down and turned to look at the parcel she left on the end table, not noticing the watch had fallen to the floor and was missing. She took the package to her chest and ran up the stairs leaving her mother at the bottom calling after her.

Colby woke on the couch and then slid down to the floor when his eyes caught sight of his papa's watch. He looked around and saw only the blue cat in the corner, watching him. Colby stuck his tongue out at the feline and pushed the watch into his pocket before running up the stairs.

Fizzlewink watched the boy run past and observed the spell that took hold and surrounded him. It seeped into Colby's body, snuffing out the spark of magic that was the center of his core.

"That will only last so long to hide the boy and block his magic," Fizzlewink thought to himself. "So now we wait until it wears off, and all hell breaks free." He would remain in cat form until the time required he present himself and guide the boy as best he could. He was not looking forward to a decade in cat form.

Chapter 2

It was ten years since the night Colby Stevens first showed magic, but he remembers none of it. Colby grew up on an uninteresting street in an uninteresting neighborhood on the north side of Chicago. He always felt it was uninteresting at any rate. Car-lined streets added an oddly suburban-feeling to this small pocket of the city as high-rise apartments, condominiums, stores, and multi-story walk-ups stood surrounding the area. No, Colby did not see anything strange about his home and why should he, it was planned to blend in with the rest of the city.

On the eve of the tenth year since his magic was taken, Colby got up from the dinner table and took his plate to the kitchen. After finishing dinner, he decided that it was best to retire early in preparation for the next day's festivities.

Tomorrow was not only Colby's birthday, but it was also the first day of summer. The summer solstice was one of the biggest holidays that Colby's grandmother celebrated. She always claimed that it was no coincidence that he was born on such an important day. These two facts combined with some old tale about being the first-born male in five generations, blah, blah, blah. Colby just wanted nothing more than to have magic like his schoolmates.

Before heading off to bed, Colby decided to log into his computer and check his latest attempt at forcing magic. His computer faulted into the dreaded blue screen of death, but this time something was different than the typical segment fault of poor programming and rushed to market software. Strange white symbols appeared on the screen and swirled around on the blue background. He recognized many of the flourishing marks as runes used for magic.

In the center of those symbols was one predominant golden and round symbol that he could not quite make out before a headache began.

Colby closed his eyes from the mounting pain behind them. The dizziness swirled in his head as colors flashed from behind his tightly closed eyelids. His head tilted back and lolled to the side as he slumped and fell from his chair.

From the darkness, his eyes could just barely make out the vision of shapes moving in the distance. Two men, tall and thin, so similar they were indistinguishable from one another. They moved in the shadows of blurry dimness. Except for the glow of each form, they seemed identical. One shone with an aura of blue that sparkled like the Caribbean Sea under the high sun of a bright day. The other he observed as surrounded by reddish darkness that seemed to swallow the light.

They fought and shouted though Colby could not make out what the men said. He strained to hear what the two strange men argued about but could make out only one phrase as he saw the object they each grasped, trying to free it from the other's hands. 'You shall not control the Emassa.' Darkness enveloped Colby, leaving him in the blackness of the void between sleep and wake.

****

* * *

Colby Stevens' dreams were often vivid enough to convince him they were real. So real, in fact, that he made a habit of not consuming liquids after eight o'clock in the evening, for fear of dreaming he was in the bathroom. A wet bed may be a right of passage when you are a little kid. This is not the case when you are waking up to your sixteenth birthday, and you're soaking wet to the bone from head to toe.

He followed his rule the night before, and he did not dream of using the facilities, but he woke up wet all the same. This time he woke wet from the sweat he expelled while running away from something he never imagined before. He was running from a vision of himself. He also did not remember getting into bed. The last thing he had remembered before the strange visions were the blue screen of death on his computer.

Today was supposed to be the best day of his life so far. He was a sixteen-year-old teenager now, and that meant he was no longer a little boy. He could tell that his Nana was trying to make him a favorite breakfast, banana, and peanut butter French toast. Trying to make breakfast, that is since Nana is not the best cook by a long shot. The smell of burned peanuts and scorched banana bread wafted up from the kitchen and assaulted Colby's snot-covered nose as he woke. If the smell had not woken him, the smoke alarms would have.

"Colby dear, come down for breakfast," Nana shouted. "I made your favorite, and it will get cold."

Colby wiped his eyes clean and opened them to find his sister leaning in the doorway of his room. "Are you lost, Shelly?" Colby raised an eyebrow as he looked at his sister's blood-red lips, smoky eyes, and powdered face. She reminded him of a corpse freshly painted for a viewing.

"Why are you all wet? Did you piss the bed?" she asked without seeming to move a muscle in her blank, expressionless face.

Colby got out of bed, dry from the waist down. "Obviously not, I must be getting night sweats or something." He lied, knowing he was running in his dream and that his perspiration-soaked the bedding. He stripped his bed and turned to walk up to his sister, and then closed the door in her face. "Mom still sleeping?"

Shelly laughed, throaty, and without mirth. "Mom is taking off work today. I'm sure her head hurts since she crawled back to bed."

"Sangria Sunday yesterday? Not even the smoke alarms will wake her," Colby said, then sighed and started cleaning up.

"You better hurry and get downstairs before the witch burns down the kitchen, making you that slop," Shelly said from outside the door. "Oh, and happy birthday cheese-curd." Her voice faded with the accompaniment of the clomping made by her two-inch soled shoes as she walked down the hall.

"Thanks, smelly," Colby said.

He hated his sister's nickname for him, but it was not the worst name he gets called. Colby went to the bathroom while dropping his sheets in the laundry chute. After stepping from the shower, he spent several moments before the mirror, checking himself for signs of magic. The aforementioned inspection became part of his morning habit since early childhood, when his daddy would tell him he would become a man soon after he developed his abilities. He did not remember ever hearing his father say that since he has been missing for ten years, but somehow he sensed his father's voice in the back of his mind.

"No signs yet," he told his reflection. "Maybe tomorrow."

Once he finished in the bathroom, Colby got dressed and grabbed his things for school. Before he left his room, he stopped at his bookshelf and reached for the old watch left behind by his father. Colby treasured the watch since the day his father disappeared without leaving a note or trace of where he was going. He never considered wearing the dusty old timepiece before, but today was his special day, and strapping his father's watch around his wrist just seemed right somehow. He donned the weathered old accessory, admiring its jeweled face and 'non-working' quartz timing.

* * *

The watch had not worked for as long as he could remember, but that didn't take away from the desire to keep it close. It was the only familiar piece of his father that remained, and he always felt a deep need to keep it safe until the day he could place it back in his father's hand.

He pushed the pin and set the correct time, then headed for the kitchen. He never paid much mind to the fact the watch never worked. Although Colby had an ingrained ability to take things apart and fix them or make them better, he never dared attempt such with the watch. This morning the unexpected ticking of the timepiece stopped Colby in his tracks.

When had the watch started working, he wondered? Over the years, Colby tried setting it, and it never worked. Every time he attempted to open the back to change the battery, he was unable to remove the plate. He pushed the side button and smiled as the face lit up.

His smile faded as the scattered memory of his last night with his papa flooded his thoughts. A young Colby sat holding his bleeding foot as his father sat him down and kissed him goodbye. The tears welled in Colby's eyes as the feeling of emptiness tightened within his gut from this memory. As Colby dwelled on the emotions, a tingling came over his skin, and a spark jumped from the watch on his wrist.

"What the hell?" Colby snapped out of his emotional tailspin and looked at his wrist. Nothing. He shook his head and cleared the pent-up anger and sadness that mixed his mind into a smoothie of emotions he bottled up inside, then scolded himself for allowing the outburst.

"Keep it within, for without, it harbors dangerous energy," he muttered to himself. He went downstairs playing the mantra over in his head, something his Nana would often tell him when his emotional state became turbulent.

***

The smoke was clearing from the kitchen through a half-open window above the sink as Nana fanned the room with a dishtowel and small cutting board.

"Sit down my little Fart-blossom. Eat up; you're gonna need all your strength today." She picked up a plate and slid it in front of Colby with a broad, toothless smile. "Happy Birthday, Colby."

Nana called him fart-blossom because, as a little boy, Colby had a habit of sitting on people's laps just to let one rip.

Nana must have noticed Colby's silly grin and realized her gums were bare. He held back a giggle as she reached into her housecoat pocket to retrieve her teeth. Once properly seated in her mouth, she flashed Colby a proper smile.

Colby sat down before the plate Nana set out on the counter. He imagined a condemned man in Guantanamo being served better. The blacked toast was oozing a dark roasted brown sludge, all covered in a mountain of syrup and powdered sugar, sliced bananas, and whipped cream. The smell alone was more than Colby could bear, and he dry-heaved.

"Oh dear, that wasn't supposed to happen," Nana said, taking the plate away. "Perhaps it's different with boys. I really don't know."

His grandmother continued mumbling and threw the breakfast away, plate, and all. She paced the kitchen floor, muttering to herself and shaking her tightly permed blue head.

"How do you feel this morning?" she finally asked. "Dizzy, shaky, sweaty…"

"I did wake up all sweaty this morning. Otherwise, I was fine until I sat down," Colby said. He closed his eyes against the visual of the plate that she took away but left an impression he could not shake. "And I dreamt of symbols and runes from a game we play at school."

"Oh blessed be, it's the quickening," Nana said, "I knew it."

Colby looked at his grandma. "I have no magic this morning Nana. I tried."

* * *

Nana started for Colby but was stopped short when Shelly stepped between them. "Sickening, she said sickening. You are probably coming down with something." Shelly glared at her Nana, who frowned back in return. "See … you're making me sick as we speak." Shelly grabbed a fresh banana from the bowl on the counter and tossed it to her brother. "Eat that, safer than the crap the old woman was gonna feed you."

Colby took the fruit and dropped it into his bookbag. It was the first day of summer, but he attended a private academy that held sessions year-round. The sound of the bus coming up the street put an end to any further conversation. Colby jumped up from the counter and headed for the door.

"Gotta run, see you after school, Nannie!" Colby ran out the back, waving his hand.

Shelly went after him at a less frantic pace. She looked back at Nana before continuing toward the door. "You shouldn't fill his head with nonsense."

Nana walked from the kitchen, shaking her finger at Shelly. "What nonsense, Shelly? He is the one, and you know it, my ma told you as much." Nana put her hands on her hips and stared up at Shelly, glaring through half-closed lids. "We should never have hidden the truth of our family magic from him."

"Just because some dusty old ghost decides to keep me awake at night, does not mean she was making any sense."

"You know the gifts our blood carries. Something changed ten years ago, and I feel it in my aching old bones that whatever happened that we can't remember is about to break free."

"We carry a curse. Your magic is unpredictable. Mom's magic is at the bottom of a bottle of booze half the time. And mine, well it is a pain in the ass."

"Well then your magic fits you."

* * *

Shelly stomped around the kitchen before looking out the back screen door. "That mangy cat is back," Shelly shouted. "Stop feeding the strays."

"I still feed you, ya little witch," Nana said as she opened the door and leaned down to retrieve the pathetic looking cat. "Come inside, Fizzlewink. I have some leftover French toast for you."

The tattered blue cat looked up at Nana, sniffed the air, and meowed in protest. He abruptly turned and ran off, following the path taken by Colby.

Nana watched after the strange feline then turned to Shelly and continued their argument. "I said that it was no coincidence that Colby was born on the solstice," Nana explained. "You mark my word; something special will happen to that boy today."

"Is that what the junk in the bottom of your teacup told you this morning," Shelly said as she headed for the back door.

"No, I just mean…Never mind. I just hope he holds that pent-up anger of his in check today, that's all."

Shelly stopped and turned to her Nana before leaving. Her face took a sudden concern that could have melted away the gothic makeup and arrogant façade. "Do you really think one of his fits could cause something…magical?"

Nana looked at Shelly with worry in her eyes. "My dear, I am afraid with the power that boy is about to gain, it could cause a great deal more than we can imagine."

Chapter 3

Colby ran for the bus as it prepared to leave his stop. He nearly made it when the doors closed, and the driver turned his eyes from Colby's with a nasty smile.

"Oh, come on," Colby screamed.

He stopped running and stood there head down, avoiding the sneers and catcalling from the passengers. Once the bus passed, he turned in the direction of his school and began walking. He glared at the back of the bus wishing for it to break down when a loud bang broke his concentration.

* * *

Dark smoke shot from the bus' tailpipe when it came to a full stop as the engine sputtered and died.

Colby caught himself laughing without realizing when his sister's voice sounded in his ear from an approaching car.

"Missed the bus again, cheese-curd?" she asked while watching the bus roll to a stop. "Get in. Bruce will drop you at school on our way past campus."

Shelly watched Colby for signs of anything different about her brother. She wasn't certain, but she thought she saw a slight glow about him.

Colby grumbled and looked past Shelly at Bruce, her on-again-off-again boyfriend. "I can wait for the city bus."

Bruce shook his head and gave Colby a thumb toward the back seat.

Colby climbed into Bruce's overly flashed-up Mustang and pushed the empty fast-food wrappers and cigarette packs aside as he sat. "Thanks, Bruce."

"Hey, no problemo little man, happy birthday," Bruce said.

Bruce rubbed his eyes as he adjusted the rearview mirror from watching Colby mess with his phone to better view Shelly's legs.

Shelly smacked Bruce's hand and fixed the mirror while they drove past the broken down bus. She opened the vanity mirror on her visor to watch Colby as he snickered at those, who moments before, laughed at him when the bus drove off. Shelly smiled at her little brother, but not so he could see.

Colby turned back from his classmates, now exiting the stranded bus, then pulled out and checked his vibrating phone. The screen on his smartphone displayed a strange symbol on it that he did not understand but remembered seeing somewhere before. The symbol was that of two circles, one inside the other. Two semi-circles then surrounded the inner circle. Emanating from the center circle in four separate corners were three rippled lines that looked like rays of energy coming from outside and entered the inner disk. The symbol pulsated.

As Colby touched the screen, a spark jumped from the device, shocking him. "What the…" he mumbled. He looked at the phone closer and saw nothing odd about it, and the image was gone. He looked up to find Shelly glaring at him in the visor mirror.

"You have time for a decent breakfast," Shelly said. "You can grab something at the diner and walk the rest of the way to school from there." She snapped the mirror closed and folder up the visor.

Bruce turned back to Colby and smiled. "Awesome, I'll make you the birthday special."

Colby returned the smile with a half curl to his lip. "Anything is better than what Nana was trying to feed me this morning."

****

They arrived at the diner soon after leaving the broken down bus behind and parked around back in a small lot that nestled behind the building next to the dumpsters. As he exited the car, Colby was greeted by a stench, not unlike that which came from his kitchen when his grandmother cooked. His nose curled at the assault, and his stomach threatened to revolt as his abdomen tightened.

Shelly must have sensed Colby's unease as she gently pushed him in the back door and ushered him to the counter, shoving him into a seat. She poured him a glass of juice and disappeared back into the kitchen.

Colby sat and watched over the open counter as Shelly and Bruce whispered in the kitchen, occasionally looking in his direction and presenting a smile that he assumed was meant to be reassuring. He did not understand what the fuss was all about. Colby had a birthday every year, and they always came and past without notice by any other than Nana, and days later, sometimes his mother would remember. Why was everyone so interested this year?

* * *

Colby began to suspect something, and the only thing he could imagine was that they were planning a party or other surprise. A warm feeling crept up from his stomach at the thought of a surprise birthday party. Could it be that he was going to receive some attention for once, he couldn't help but shake. His nerves took hold as every inch of his skin began to tingle while he lifted the glass of juice to take a drink and calm down. As he began to settle, he lowered the glass toward the counter only to spill it while a plate of bacon, eggs, and hotcakes clattered down in front of him.

Shelly toweled the front of her apron and the counter as she pulled the glass free from Colby's hand.

"Are you all right? I know you hate going to that school, but it can't be all that bad?"

Colby grimaced at the mess he made but noticed again that Shelly was not acting her usual self. Rather than yell or belittle him for spilling the juice, she just poured a fresh glass and walked away.

"It isn't the school. I like the place well enough though I never understood the semi-private nature of admission." Colby was glad for the change in subject or at least a shift in his thoughts. "It's some of the other kids. I don't know what the requirements are for getting admitted because some of the jerks in my classes haven't the brains to make fire from sticks using a lighter."

A clatter of pots and pans in the kitchen preceded Bruce as he came around the counter.

"That is the whole problem with education these days, no standards," Bruce said. "I can't say much about that place, but there was a reason my mother schooled me at home in spite of my dad's wishes. She always feared brainwashing or something if I went to Escutcheon Academy."

Colby was surprised. He assumed everyone from the neighborhood went to Escutcheon Academy, and seeing the look of anger in Bruce's eyes was off-putting.

* * *

Bruce rambled on how his parents fought about his attending the Academy, but his mother would have none of it. She homeschooled him and kept Bruce away from the one place his father wanted him to attend, even though he wasn't accepted. Resentment rolled off Bruce's tongue with every word against the school and his father.

As suddenly as he angered, Bruce straightened up, and a smirk washed across his face. "I heard they do rituals in the basement."

Colby flinched empathetically, feeling for himself the hand of his sister connecting with the back of Bruce's head.

"Don't be stupid. I went there, and we didn't have any cults, you moron." Shelly glared at Bruce, daring him to open his mouth.

Bruce and Colby shared a stifled laugh as their eyes scanned Shelly from head to toe, dressed in her gothic clothes, dark eyes, and black painted nails. If not for the apron, she would seem the perfect fit for some vampire dormitory horror movie.

Shelly threw the remains of Colby's breakfast in a to-go container and put it in a bag with a muffin. She unceremoniously pushed it toward her little brother. "You better get going, and try to keep an even temper today."

Colby smirked at Shelly then gathered his belongings along with the remainder of his breakfast before heading toward the door when he caught a glimpse of some classmates sitting at a table. They were playing a game of Runes. Runes is a game of choice at his school. It was a combination of dominoes and Scrabble, only with mystic runes placed in specific patterns. It was a way of practicing magic before doing a spell. Colby was horrible at the game since he had no magical talent.

Colby paid little attention to the kids' faces or their interactions as his eyes attracted to the symbols on the tiles that lay scattered upon the Formica surface, calling to him. His eyes darted from piece to piece, rearranging their order in his mind while they seemed to glow as his focus shifted between each rune painted upon their surfaces. His focus blurred at the edges of his visual field while his mind concentrated on nothing else but the alabaster stones laid out before each player. Itching at the back of his mind gave him hints at plays he only ever wished he had the ability to create. Where once playing this game frustrated him with a lack of understanding, he now seemed to know instinctively the precise moves to make.

Colby did not stop to wonder at his sudden instincts and knowledge of the runes as he edged closer to the table where the game was playing out. He also did not pause to question his ability to see through the backs of tiles turned away from his sight. He knew every piece on the table and those yet to play. He saw every move that could play out and what the resulting cast would produce.

The boys played their game, oblivious to the approach of the new observer. They were at a standstill, and the timer ticked by as the losing player, perplexed at his predicament, shuffled his tiles expecting to find a winning cast. The answer eluded him, and he prepared, shoulders tight and lips curled, to concede the round and, ultimately, the game. As his hand moved toward his assembly square on the board, ready to fold his prepared constructs, a firm grasp on his wrist stopped his actions.

Colby pulled back the boy's arm and quickly drew seven runes from both the assembly square and the boys' reserve. He aligned the tiles on the board along the bottom of the opponent's most prevalent cast and, using the first three tiles, unraveled the construct, but he did not stop there. From the top of the last tile he placed, Colby extended upwards, connecting the unraveled spell to three adjoining spells using the other four tiles he picked up. With the single casting, Colby unraveled not only the first opposing construct but two more while at the same time expanding upon two constructs of the boy whose stead he now played.

As the final tile was laid, Colby snapped out of his trance and stared down at the board. While the young boy shouted in triumph, Colby turned to the confused looks on the faces of those around him. Colby was among the least competent at the Runes at school, and these boys knew this fact. Colby's eyes flew from one familiar face to the next until they landed upon one of the girls in his classes. A girl he once crushed on.

The girl looked at him quizzically, a curl twitching at the corner of her mouth while small creases formed at the edges of her narrowing eyes.

Colby turned on his heels and ran for the exit of the Diner, running directly into his sister Shelly, who blocked the exit.

"What was that? You have never played anywhere near so advanced a move in Runes," Shelly said. Hands on her hips, Shelly pushed her head forward on her long neck and glared into Colby's eyes.

"I've been writing a program on my computer to help me learn," Colby said. "I gotta go," was all he managed before pushing past her and running full speed for school.

Colby ran directly past his one friend sitting at a booth near the door without even noticing the boy due to his slumped shoulders and ground pointing stare. Once he was far enough away; however, his head lifted but continued his fast pace. What just happened, he wondered. Something in the pit of his stomach churned.

Shelly and Bruce stood at the door, watching Colby rush away.

"I don't think anyone has ever cast a construct like that," Bruce said. "I'll tell you, Shelly, the only thing ever come out of that school I like is you and that game."

Shelly elbowed Bruce in the stomach and headed toward the kitchen. She turned back to watch after her little brother running full out to get away as though scared of something. A curl formed at the corner of Shelly's mouth. The half-smile was replaced by a frown and a wrinkled brow. She was both proud and concerned, thinking about what her grandmother said that same morning.

Bruce bent slightly in the middle and followed after her. "Do you think he can give me some tips? I mean, me and the boys have a regular game, and I usually get my ass taken to the cleaners. With moves like that, I'd become the new laundryman in town-"His last words were cut off by another elbow to the gut.

Shelly turned back and watched her little brother head off toward school, a strange urgency in his step. "I wonder…"

Chapter 4

The halls of Colby's high school were ordinary in the eyes of any other person, but in his eyes, they were dark, scary, and full of terror. As he entered the doors leading down the central corridor, Colby imagined the walls of some dark and musty dungeon. Shuffling onward, he passed classrooms that became torture chambers. Kids stuffed in lockers by bullies were prisoners in cages while the bullies were their 'hoodied' torturers. He remembered well the previous term, while, in his last days of freshman year, he was placed in a similar cage by a similar tormentor.

His torment did not end with entry to the tenth grade. Since the school term began, Colby was subjected to regular shoving, name-calling, and threats. The majority of his troubles came in the form of one person, and as Colby turned down the hall in the direction of his locker, the source of his troubles was there waiting. Jasper Bodine was his torturer's name.

After the fifth grade, Colby's school consolidated, and there were more students in each class. The new students came from a neighboring institute that, for whatever reason, came to join his own. In the beginning, Colby saw it as a way to make more friends, but his wishes soon became quite the opposite.

Before the merging of the schools, Colby was considered a bit different from his friends, but not so much that he was taunted or teased. Once the new kids joined his current classmates, things began to change. Colby was singled out by the new children and called names. He did his best not to draw attention to himself or cause trouble, but trouble always seemed to find him.

The worst of his troubles started when Jasper Bodine returned to the school. At one time, Jasper and Colby were very close friends. They had overnighted at one another's homes and did everything together. They both were friendly competitors for the fastest runners on the school track team. They had been the best of friends until suddenly…they weren't.

Jasper's family moved away without warning, and Colby didn't understand why. He had spent the night only a few days before, having fun and playing video games. When Monday arrived and his best friend did not show up for school, Colby felt a piece of him break away as though he knew he lost something that day.

Two years later, Jasper returned, the same time the schools merged. While others began singling Colby out, so did Jasper. Whenever Colby attempted to talk to Jasper, he became standoffish and insulting. All he would say is that his father forbade him from being friends with the likes of Colby Stevens.

So when they were in sixth grade, Jasper became Colby's worst nightmare. The boy bullied and called Colby names he did not comprehend. He singled Colby out every chance he found and made sure others followed his lead. Colby got ostracized for nothing other than being himself.

* * *

So he preferred hanging out with the girls and being soft-spoken. So he liked to dress well and have manners. So he did exceptionally well at everything in school except magic, but nothing changed, and he was still somehow different, and he could not sense what.

Thankfully in the seventh grade, a new kid joined his school, and Gary Connor became his steadfast new best friend.

To the current day, Colby could not understand what was wrong with him that others, besides Gary, chose to make him their target. He tried to chalk it up to their ignorance or insecurities, but the more he thought about it, the angrier he got. His anger never got him anywhere, except in trouble. Then he thought about what someone like Jasper had that Colby did not.

Jasper Bodine was everything that Colby wasn't. He stood at least 3 inches taller and much broader at the shoulders. To the girls in the school, Jasper Bodine was like a God, where Colby was just like one of the girls. Jasper Bodine knew he was a God to the other kids, and he used it well. Jasper also had magic. It was limited as everyone else, but he had it. Colby did not.

Colby hoped for just once to remain anonymous and ignored, but there was little hope. It was the summer session, and tensions ran high because all the kids wanted to be at the beach or out doing anything but schoolwork. Colby walked down the hall and saw Jasper standing near his locker as the girls ogled him and made passing glances while batting their lashes and pushing out their boobs.

While the girls in the summer session passed Jasper down the hall, his steely blue eyes were only focusing a pointed glare on one person, Colby Stevens.

"Well, if it ain't the cheesy poof," Jasper said, inviting a roar of laughter from his posse of fair-weather followers. "You know the drill poofster. Hand over your homework from last night." Jasper held his hand out to receive the daily tribute and grinned toward his ragtag team of thug wannabes.

Colby expelled a long slow breath as he prepared himself for the usual routine of turning over his homework to Jasper. He began the habit of creating two copies of his assignments. Jasper always received the barely average prepared copy, and being barely average himself; he never caught on. Today he would not be receiving a copy at all.

Colby stopped reaching into his backpack just before his fingers connected with the awaiting sheets of printed essay answers. His mind began replaying the events of countless times being bullied. He saw from the outside while feeling it inside, every humiliating sneer, jibe, name, and the situations he became subjected to since middle school. He finally felt he has put up with enough. Colby held the last of the air he exhaled to produce a single syllable.

"No," he said in a low and determined-yet shaky-voice.

Jasper turned his head from his buddies while his grin twisted into a snarl. "What was that cheesy poof?" Jasper spat through clenched teeth. His outstretched hand curled into a fist as he pulled his arm back, preparing to strike. "You will hand over your homework one way or another, and it better cut the mustard."

Colby leveled his wavering glare and met Jasper's stare, but the crippling fear and desperation behind his eyes were transforming into anger and determination. "I said no, Jasper. Are you as deaf as you are dumb? Unless you're making a sandwich with a yellow condiment, it is cutting the muster, M-U-S-T-E-R."

Colby's eyes twitched, and their normal pale blue irises began to take on a bluer hue as the light began to shine dimly from behind them. "I will no longer yield to your bullying and then handing over copies of homework that earn you subpar grades. Though they're higher scores than you're capable of on your own."

The look on Colby's face sent a subconscious need to back away into the minds of his taunters, and all but Jasper backed off.

Though his expression softened into a look of concern and confusion, Jasper continued to stare down Colby until the flickering of the lights overhead drew his attention.

A buzz filled the air as the fluorescent lights hanging from the speckled ceilings began to flutter. Glittering blue and red sparkles danced across the long white bulbs in the fixtures. Silence fell over the crowd that only moments before watched ass Colby stood up to Jasper.

The buzz grew louder exponentially as the hushed silence joined with whispers of concern and confusion. No one was watching Colby except his only true friend Gary.

Gary observed as a spark chased along Colby's body from his phone to his eyes and then propelled toward Jasper. Gary dove toward Jasper without thinking as the energy Colby expelled passed over them. They landed in a heap just as the wall behind them took the full force of Colby's assault and seemed to absorb it. Gary spared only a moment to watch the last of the glowing fade into the bricks. His confusion over the fact that nothing happened to the walls quickly disappeared as the sound of a scattering crowd drew his attention.

The clamoring of retreating feet and breaking glass finally reached Colby's muddled awareness. He pulled his mind back from the trance state he found himself. The strange light coming from behind his eyes faded, leaving irises bluer than they had once been. He blinked for the first time since his actions were taken over by an unexplained urge to put a stop to the bullying.

Jasper pushed Gary off of him, not knowing what just occurred. He turned and looked at Colby as Gary stepped up and joined his quarries' side. His own eyes reflected the confusion and fear held in those of the two boys who stood across the hall from him. Jasper wiped the wetness from his eyes and spat on the floor at Colby's feet.

"I don't know what you two are thinking, but you'll be sorry." Jasper stepped back and walked away from them, repeating his warning as he quickened his pace toward class. "You wait and see."

Colby watched Jasper jog away. "What a douche," he said and turned to see Gary's concerned face. "What is with you? You look pale, which doesn't look good with your complexion." Colby waited for a snappy comeback, but none followed. "What?"

* * *

When Gary recovered the use of his tongue, he still stumbled over his words, most of which were of the more colorful variety. When he finished his initial barrage of incomplete questions, he said the only thing Colby could understand. "WTF Colby, you just shot sparks out your hands, dude! You shouldn't have done that in front of other people."

Colby blinked and paused a moment before breaking into laughter. "OMG Gary, you totally had me for a second. Shooting sparks from my hands," he laughed. "Come on. We're late for class." Colby turned Gary toward class and started their walk while continuing to chuckle. "Sparks… "

"I'm not joking' Colby. You just… I don't know what it was. Sparks, glowing, flashes, then the lights flickered and broke." Gary paused and shook his head. "You were like, all wizardly or something."

Colby was not entirely certain what Gary was saying. He barely remembered the past several minutes other than confronting Jasper, but he knew he felt different somehow. A sense of triumph, however small, tingled in his chest.

"Don't be weird. It must have been a short in the lights. I don't have magic, let alone any runes drawn. Let's get to class." Colby pushed his friend along and followed, his face awash in confusion. They didn't get far.

Gary took Colby by the arm and stopped him. He pushed his friend toward the entrance of an empty room and moved closer.

"You aren't the only one who is late to bloom," Gary said. "You'd be surprised who else. Is just coming into their magic in this school. By the way, nice playing at Runes this morning."

"Who told you about that?" Colby fixated on the last statement, remembering his interference in the Runes match at the diner.

Gary started walking again. "I was there for breakfast. You walked right past me as you hurried out."

* * *

Before Colby could ask what Gary meant, they were headed back off toward class. The halls they found deserted except for the same girl from the diner, Darla, and another girl who appeared to hang on every word the other whispered. Colby's skin shivered as he watched the girls go silent and turn their eyes on him and smile.

Gary punched Colby in the arm as they passed the giggling girls. As the two shared an uncomfortable laugh, they didn't notice Jasper moving toward them.

Jasper moved in behind Colby and reached forward to hold him in a headlock from behind. As his arm moved into Colby's peripheral, Jasper dropped his arms and tightened up every muscle in his body while beginning to shake. He flew backward and into the lockers along the wall stricken by a force of will as Colby turned to face him.

Colby began to glare, and the light behind his eyes brightened. Only the gruff hands of the Assistant Dean saved him from releasing his anger upon Jasper.

"What is the meaning of this?" the man asked. "There is a zero-tolerance for this type of behavior in this school. You all will be following me to Dean Tiddle's office." He pulled Jasper from the floor and directed Colby and Gary to follow as he led them down the halls.

Chapter 5

The Dean sat behind his desk; his shaggy gray sideburns fluffed out and indistinguishable from the hair jutting out of the large ears that protruded like a chimpanzee's. He glared at the three boys now seated before him from over the top of the thin wire-rim glasses sitting at the end of his pudgy turned-up nose.

Colby looked at the Dean's pursed lips and, combined with the image of something akin to the planet of the apes, let out a stifled grunt.

"You find humor in this situation Mr. Stevens?" the Dean said.

An unsteady stillness overtook the boys as they stared back at the Dean, who sat unmoving behind his desk, eyes fixed directly upon Colby. Moments of silence passed while the Dean kept his gaze locked on Colby before he broke the awkward quiet.

"Would someone like to explain to me what the purpose is behind breaking lights and causing a ruckus?" Dean Tiddle asked.

Jasper pushed forward. "Sir, it wasn't-"

"It was a rhetorical question, Mr. Bodine. Do you know what the word rhetorical means?" The Dean paused a moment as Jasper sat back in his chair and lowered his head. "I am fully aware of what goes on in the halls of my school…normally. Today, however, I am perplexed by the thought of how something so extraordinarily bizarre could transpire beneath my nose and not have seen the clues sooner."

Colby stiffened in his seat. He knew something strange was happening; he felt it deep within his chest, not unlike a stirring of coals in a fire. The heat was growing inside him, but to what purpose he was clueless. Colby spared a sideways glance at Gary, who looked at him shaking his head, indicating he should keep quiet. Was there some truth to what Gary said about sparks and light?

Without looking up, Colby cleared his throat. "I'm unsure what you mean, Mr. Tiddle."

Dean Tiddle stood and walked around the side of his desk. "Do you not, Mr. Stevens? I should think you would be keenly aware of the situation, being as though it centers around yourself." Tiddle walked around and then behind Colby. He placed his hands on Colby's shoulders and pulled him back in his seat. "How long ago did this begin?"

Colby looked up at the Dean while lifting his hands. "Only this morning."

The Dean tittered and walked back around to his seat. "Come now, boy, I was not born yesterday. Far from it." When Colby looked at him more confused, Tiddle sat down and leaned forward on his desk. "I suspect this started after the merger of the two schools, am I right? That is when the mistreatment began?"

Mistreatment, Colby thought. Tiddle was talking about the bullying. A summer rainstorm of relief washed down over Colby. He realized that the Dean was not referring to his bizarre episodes of supposed lights and fireworks.

"Yes, sir, when Jasper returned to school."

"I see," Tiddle said.

Colby could see the look of distaste in Tiddle's mouth as he shook his head slightly back and forth. Perhaps Colby had the wrong impression of the Dean. Tiddle was a man that stayed behind his desk or could be seen glaring out his hallway door spying on trouble makers. His random focuses of wrath seemed to make sense now if what Colby sensed was true. Dean Tiddle had a personal issue with those who came from the other school.

"I'll never understand the decision to merge the two schools into one academy. Everything went to new depths of hell and hasn't much improved." Dean Tiddle leaned back in his chair and looked off into space as he recalled the years before the schools merged.

There were once two schools in the area that provided education exclusively to the families from both sides of the surrounding communities. Kids from the northern side went to the old and now closed school while those in the Buena Park and Lakeview neighborhoods went to Escutcheon Academy.

Only during cross-town Runes tournaments did the schools ever interact, and those events were strictly monitored and often accompanied by trouble. The two schools were rivals for reasons left unexplained, but the Dean spoke as though there was a long bloody war between two factions that had come to an uneasy truce when the schools merged.

"I was once the champion of Runes for this school, long ago before the travesty. I was revered as a hero in these halls."

* * *

The Dean went on to explain the events that led to the joining of two long-time foes as a single institution of learning. Twenty years prior to the merger, there was an upset in the area that caused many families to begin leaving town and even the state. What that unrest was he did not explain, but his wide eyes and hushed tones as he spoke of it added to the mystery while he told his tale.

As fewer students enrolled in both schools, they each became more exclusive and even stopped all inter-academy Runes tournaments. When this happened, Tiddle was no longer seen as a hero and then little more than an acquaintance to those who were once his friends. Only one friend remained faithful, but he went away some time ago, so now Tiddle sat in his office, lording over the School.

The boards of the two schools finally began to discuss a merger openly some five years ago, when things became critical following a previous five years of steadily declining attendance. They refused to start allowing new students that did not fit their strict criteria for acceptance into their academies. Inevitably, they had to choose between what they deemed a pollution of their student body or merging the two institutions into one great place of learning for those found to be suitable.

"What are the criteria for acceptance," Gary asked. "I never understood that part."

Dean Tiddle snapped his eyes shut as though returning from a trance state. "That is the concern of the Board and not a student. All you need know is that behind these walls, you are with those who possess the same spark for greatness."

Jasper stood up and cleared his throat. "What a load of crap. There are only two kinds of people in this school, those who will lead, and those who will follow. I will be a leader, and you two, I will scrape from the bottom of my shoes."

"Shut up, Mr. Bodine," Tiddle said.

"When my father hears-" Jasper was cut off before he could finish his response.

* * *

"What your father will hear is the truth. And though he may dislike hearing it from the likes of me, it will perturb him considerably being made aware of what has transpired here today."

The Dean looked first at Colby and back to Jasper, then folded his fingers as he sat back in his chair. "You two were friends once, best of friends as I recall. What happened that we now find ourselves in this state of open hostility toward one another?"

Colby looked at Jasper to answer. Colby wondered himself what had changed. Besides the fact that Jasper seemed only interested in his popularity and being top dog among the pack, he hung around. Had the schools not merged and the other kids come to be hateful and mean, Colby always felt Jasper would have remained his friend when he returned to their school. The schools did merge, however, and the awful, mean-spirited children of the other side of town came, and they singled out anything or anyone different. Colby began to fester with a rage.

"He follows," Colby muttered between his clenched teeth.

Gary sensed the anger building in his friend and took hold of Colby's arm.

Jasper looked down at Colby and looked at Gary's hand. "Because you are not the same as me. I could never be a friend with the likes of you."

The Dean looked at Jasper. "I would expel 'the likes of you' if it were in my power to do so, but as I do not have such power, I must resign myself to placing you in Saturday detention." His words left curled lips, and a downturned mouth as the bile dripped from every syllable he spoke. "You may go to class, Mr. Bodine, but I would advise against stirring up any more trouble. Your father would not be pleased with any further action I decide to take in this matter. I do have some power."

Jasper stopped before leaving to lean in close to Colby. "This is not the end of it, Cheezy-poof!"

* * *

"Go," the Dean said.

After Jasper swaggered out of the office, smug and grinning, the Dean moved his eyes back to Colby and Gary. "For the life of me, I will never understand his kind."

"Sir?" Colby said.

The Dean shook his head and dismissed his comment. "Power hungry, ignorant to the feelings of others, blind…I think the boy is just confused by that right bastard of a father he has."

"At least he has one," Colby mumbled.

Dean Tiddle's eyes drifted over to Colby, and his heart sank slightly as he truly saw the boy sitting before him for the first time that day. He must be torn between abandonment, hurt, and anger. Tiddle knew those feelings all too well. The Dean stiffened and sat back up in his seat. 'The boy will have to toughen up and deal with life,' he thought to himself.

"Your grades and background will not always save you from the failures or trials you will inevitably face. In spite of your family name and the guarantee of your place in this school, outside these walls you are inconsequential for now. If your education had not been secured long ago…" the Dean stopped speaking and broke eye contact as he turned in his seat. "At any rate, there is yet the matter of those broken lights. Would either of you two care to venture a guess as to how they came to be shattered?"

Gary sat forward, lifting his hand from Colby's arm. It was just then that Colby even realized his friend had been touching him. Before Gary could spout off his wild story of magic and dancing lights, Colby interjected.

"It must have been some sort of short in the wiring, sir. Or perhaps a power surge?"

Gary smirked at Colby. "Power surge…Yeah, that has to be it. When Jasper started harassing Colby to give up his homework and Colby refused, well sparks went flying. Actual sparks."

"I assume this is not the first time Mr. Bodine has made such demands?"

Colby looked down. "No, sir, he's been taking my homework for months now."

"Odd," was the Dean's single word response.

"Sir?"

The Dean looked down at Colby over the top of his glasses. "Odd that you have not been reported for missing assignments, quite the opposite based on your high scores. Equally odd is that Mr. Bodine has consistently received substandard or barely average marks, for it seems as long as he has taken your assignments."

"Well, after the first time, Sir, I began making two versions of my homework, the one I would turn in for myself, and the other I would turn over to Jasper." Colby was unsure how the Dean would take his admission until he heard the undertones of a laugh.

"Although I do not condone the act, and you should have reported it at once, it serves the little upstart right." He took off his glasses and set them on his desk while he pinched the bridge of his nose and frowned. "You will not surrender your homework or create alternate versions for Mr. Bodine or anyone else ever again. Is that clear?"

Colby nodded and saw Gary nodded as well for support.

Tiddle put his glasses back on and looked back at the boys as though reaching a grand conclusion. "There is still the matter of that scuffle in the halls. I can not let that go unaddressed, regardless of the circumstances. You will both serve detention as well," Tiddle declared.

"But it was Jasper who started it. He's been-" Colby said.

* * *

"Now I am well aware of Mr. Bodine's bullying, and it will not be tolerated, but neither will uncontrolled fits of retaliation and wild magic." Dean Tiddle raised his hands before Colby could deny. "I know magic when I see it."

"But I have no magic," Colby said.

"I wouldn't be so quick to discount this, Colby. In the meantime, hall monitors will be tactfully placed to prevent further trouble, and an anti-bullying policy reminder sent out to all parents and guardians." Dean Tiddle looked away from the boys and down to some papers on his desk. "Take yourselves out of my office and get to class."

Unceremoniously dismissed, Colby and Gary removed themselves from the administrative offices.

"That was weird," Colby said. "What was he talking about, saying our education had been secured?"

"The Dean is a bit weird himself, who knows what he meant." Gary shifted his backpack around and pulled out a wrapped box and card. "In all the morning's excitement, I forgot to give you this. Happy birthday." Gary held out the gift, wearing a broad, toothy smile that reflected the joy in his eyes.

Colby could see the excitement on his friend's face. "Thank you." Colby took the present and prepared to open it, but put it in his pack instead. "I'll open it later. We're already late for class." He took a pass from the office administrator and moved aside as Gary received his own. "Let's go."

"Don't make any more lights explode on the way if you can manage," Gary said.

The two boys shared a laugh as they left the office.

Dean Tiddle peered around the corner from the side door entrance to his office and watched as the two boys hurriedly walked off to class. He squinted at Colby and then looked up at the flickering lights. "Surge of Power is more like it." A smile spread across his face as he disappeared back into his office and silently closed the door.

Chapter 6

When Colby and Gary entered the classroom, they headed for their seats in the back, taking a long way around to avoid passing Jasper. Colby smirked as Jasper made excuses to the teacher for not having his assignment completed.

Resigned to accepting an incomplete for not attaining Colby's homework, Jasper went to his seat while narrowing his glare at the two boys taking seats in the back. He paused and turned to move toward the two of them, but was stopped by the teacher's voice.

"Everyone, please take your seats. Now," their teacher said. "We have a very special guest today who is here to discuss a new program and after school club. This new organization will extend the credits received from this class and would be an exceptional addition to any records for those seeking higher education in the subject of archeology."

The classroom noise level rose with murmurs and groans of both interest and dislike of having a guest speaker. The teacher cleared his throat as he advanced on the classroom door, invoking the expected silence of the students. He returned to stand behind his desk and motioned toward the open door.

"Class may I present the distinguished archeologist and famed explorer, Professor Rigel Stark."

The initially forced clapping of the class immediately grew by the raised excitement of the female population of students. The figure that entered the room brought an energy and presence that evoked dreamy eyes and batting lashes from every girl.

Rigel Stark stepped up to the center of the room and smiled at the students before him. He allowed the raising applause and excitement for a few more moments before raising his hands to settle the noise. He stood at least six feet four inches in height, fully muscled and toned, with cappuccino hair in thick locks and piercing bright eyes. He smiled, and his perfect teeth gleamed past his short groomed beard.

"Good afternoon, young ladies...and gentlemen," he said in a resonating baritone voice that carried the hint of an English accent.

Several girls in the class sat transfixed and near drooling. Colby thought it silly and imagined the cartoonish swooning, but he couldn't deny the girls' reason for such behavior. He settled himself back in his chair and cleared his thoughts, focusing on what the man had to say.

Professor Stark introduced himself and shared stories of his most exciting adventures in archeological pursuits. While he spoke, he explained the new club that he was starting for the school, which would include learning the tools and processes of the trade.

* * *

"The club is going to research and plan an archeological dig from start to finish. They are going to go through simulated excavations, where students will solve puzzles and learn skills that apply to life and work. While digging up finds is exciting, the student archeologists will learn to follow relevant procedures during excavation and work together as a group. As the students investigate, they must always remain cognizant of the fact that they may be damaging proof even as they reveal its location. If researchers do not notice that artifacts are similar or related to others, or if they dig too deeply and combine the artifacts from two different layers, valuable data may be overlooked or destroyed. Items found without a proper background can provide minimal or no information about how, why, and when they were used.

"Conducting an archeological dig is not tidy, but it provides mystery and learning that applies to many academic subjects, benefiting the club members throughout all their classes. Digs can illuminate the problems all researchers are challenged by when they must draw inferences on the basis of inadequate evidence. They can help instructors uncover how cultures have evolved over the ages. By using observation and theory, club members will learn interpretive skills in a hands-on approach while having fun with problem-solving."

During the entire time Professor Rigel was speaking, Colby paid little attention. As soon as the man's voice settled in the back of his mind, flashes of his dream and the screen of his phone from that morning filled the forefront of his thoughts. His mind focused on the symbols that would not leave his dreams and played like static behind his consciousness. He absently doodled on his notepad. When the sound of the Professor's voice originated from just behind him, Colby returned his attention.

"In addition, there will be a trip over spring break to an actual dig site at a yet undetermined location," Rigel said as he lifted the notebook from Colby's desk. He looked at the markings with great interest before handing it back to Colby. "Those are very interesting runes, far more advanced than those in the game that is so popular among your classmates. Do you know what they are?"

Colby took his notepad and turned it over on his desk. "They're nothing special, just something I must have seen somewhere."

* * *

The Professor was not convinced. "Perhaps we could explore them in the Archeology Club. Will you be joining us?"

Until that moment, Colby was unimpressed with the smooth-talking dirt sifting man, but something from deep inside his subconscious took over. "Yes, I would like that."

"Excellent," Rigel said and patted Colby on the back before moving toward the front of the class. "We have our first member and as such the President of the club. Sign up sheets will be available on the message board outside this room, and the first gathering will be in one week's time." The Professor thanked everyone for his or her time, and as the bell rang, followed Colby and Gary out of the room. "Will, your friend, be joining as well?" he asked, looking at Gary.

"The name is Gary Connor, and I'm not sure the whole digging thing is for me."

Gary grabbed Colby and hurried down the hall. "Are you seriously joining that club and hanging out with Indiana Jones back there?"

"I don't know why, but for some reason, it made perfect sense at the time," Colby said. He stopped himself from explaining more about the symbols and sudden affinity for Runes. "Maybe it'll be fun, and besides, I need something to add to my college applications."

"Right…" Gary said. "I guess I'm gonna have to join now too. Someone has to keep an eye on you these days."

"What do you mean?"

Gary rolled his eyes. "I'm talking about that little light show you performed this morning." Pulling Colby aside, Gary lowered his voice. "I always wondered if you would be a late bloomer, but I didn't expect something like what you did today."

Colby stared at his friend, his eyes wide, and mouth agape.

* * *

"I shouldn't be telling you this, but we are best friends right, and it looks like we share the same secret." Gary moved closer and whispered into Colby's ear.

A moment had passed before Colby closed his mouth, and his right eyebrow shot up. "Have you been experimenting with drugs or something? There is no magic outside ritual runic stuff or inactive psychic things like Shelly's ghost whispering ?"

"Shush. Keep it down. My parents warned me about letting anyone know about this because of some old threat or something. But if we are both able to work magic without runes, then what's the harm?" Gary searched Colby's reaction for any clue of acknowledgment but found only disbelief and confusion.

"Joking," Gary said. "I'm just joking."

Gary brushed off the uncomfortable situation and started down the hall. "See you at lunch? I have to head to trig."

Colby watched his friend leave. He looked at Gary and squinted, then looked down at his hands before laughing at himself for a moment and stopped. A shiver ran down his spine, and he shook his head. Unsure what to make of the strangeness from that morning, Colby hoped the remainder of the day would level out and return to the usual un-eventfulness for which he was accustomed.

His next class for the day was spent in the English office as an aide. He had little to do and no homework to finish or study, so he decided to open the birthday gift he received from Gary. Skipping past the card and going straight for the gift box, Colby tore off the paper and tossed it into the wastebasket. When he opened the box, he smirked while pulling out the contents.

"A rune making kit," he said.

The irony of the gift at a time when he suddenly became more interested in the game was not lost on Colby. He opened the kit and pulled out a few of the alabaster tiles. Real Alabaster, he realized, not an inexpensive gift. Colby would have to make the most of such a present from his best friend.

Colby set down the tile he held and pulled out his notebook, where he spent the morning doodling symbols from his dreams. Though he was unsure what the new runes were, he felt confident they were valid and would be useful to him at some point. He took out the charcoal pencil and traced a rune on the first tile, beginning his work.

Using the other tools in the kit, Colby traced, chiseled, and painted in the runes on one side of the small stone tiles. He lined up the tiles in front of him and turned around to clean up the debris from carving out the runes on the soft stone. As he cleaned up the mess, he failed to notice a presence in the room and was startled when he heard the deep rumble of someone clearing their throat.

"Professor Stark," Colby said as he turned and found the man hovering over the desk where his new tiles were laid out on display.

Colby watched the Professor begin to reach down toward the runes and rushed over to collect them.

"Sorry, let me put my things away. I was just finished making them and cleaning the mess. I had no other work to do in here so I…I mean, I hope that it won't be an issue, me doing something personal while on aide duty."

Rigel smiled and pulled his hand back as Colby removed the tiles from his reach. "Nonsense, my boy. It is the school's most revered activity. Is it not? You are here because of your magic bloodline."

"I suppose. But I have not shown any abilities."

"Those are the symbols you marked into your notebook if I am not mistaken. Do you understand their use and type?" Rigel tilted his head to the side and glanced sideways at Colby.

"Not yet," Colby said, "but I'm sure I've seen them before, and they might come in handy."

* * *

Colby placed the tiles in a soft velvet pouch that came with the kit. He looked at the clock hoping the bell would ring early and free him from the awkwardness of talking with the odd Professor. He couldn't understand why this man made him feel nervous.

"I think you will find them very helpful indeed," Rigel said.

"Do you know the game?" Colby watched Rigel stiffen slightly.

"I have played it a time or two, but I find it a bit…limiting. I prefer the true use of runes over the practice of a game."

The bell rang, and Colby released the tension in his shoulders and headed out of the office, noticing Rigel watching after him. He understood what Rigel meant by 'limiting'. Did he know what these new runes meant? Colby was too unsure of the man that he only just met to ask his help. He would investigate them on his own later, maybe during detention.

"Good day Mr. Stevens. See you on Saturday as I will be monitoring your detention."

Rigel moved to the door and watched Colby head down the hall. "That boy will need guidance," he said in a whisper.

***

As Colby walked down the hall to his next class, he pulled his pack around to retrieve the birthday card from Gary that he flippantly set aside to go straight for opening his gift. He turned the card over and again admired the thick bond paper and crisp handwritten name on the top. It became apparent to him that Gary spent more than a dollar on the card by the envelope's appearance and the perfectly addressed moniker on its face.

Sliding his finger under the outer edge of the flap, he slid it along the edges, carefully separating the glued paper to access the card within the envelope. As he pulled the card free, he snickered at the stream of glitter and confetti that fell from the outer edges of the folded stock he held in his hand.

The card was thick and had a lump in the portion he held. Colby immediately knew it was one of those musical cards he enjoyed opening and closing to annoy his mother whenever they went shopping. That thought brought back a flood of happy memories, but that was when he was younger and his mother, not so… drunk.

Over the early years, after his father left, his sister and he would enjoy shopping with their mother when she would sober up and take them for an outing as a distraction. While Colby would run for the toys section, Aria would clench her teeth and loudly whisper for him to behave. He would just giggle and flash a devious grin as he disappeared between racks of clothes only to appear minutes later with the noisiest toy he could find.

His sister Shelly would lay in the aisle screaming for ice cream or a new dress. Aria would push the cart past, trying her best to ignore her wicked little witch of a daughter while telling her how she was just like her grandmother.

Colby spent the remainder of the day trying to recall his best memories to maintain his even temper. His emotions flared throughout the day, but the distractions of the tiles and even the odd Professor helped abate his anger. He kept thinking of his birthday gift from Gary, the new club, and new possibilities with his new runes. The effort paid off, and he made it through the final period. It helped that Jasper gave him a wide berth anytime they were in proximity. And Gary was always near, prepared to intercede, like an equalizing presence that was an extension of himself.

On several occasions, though, Colby noticed Professor Rigel Stark following and watching him. Each time it made him shudder, and he would squeeze the velvet bag containing his new rune tiles. Colby had an odd feeling about this Rigel guy. He couldn't place it, but something made him nervous about the man. He needed something else to focus on, he thought while cinching the strings on his velvet pouch. Perhaps a renewed interest in Runes would help, and he knew where to find people to watch playing.

Chapter 7

After school, Gary noticed an edge to Colby's behavior. He was more agitated than normal. Something was bothering his friend, and he seemed different. Gary thought maybe his friend still fixated on the morning's events and not ready to talk about them. So Gary suggested that he and Colby stop by the park on the way home and join in some games of Runes.

"I was thinking the same thing, but I think I'll just watch."

Gary just smirked and led Colby toward the park.

The game of Runes became an intricate part of the community and school over the past ten years. People of all ages could be found playing the game in the parks and cafés around the neighborhood. At the school, the games became a sport of sorts, and there were many tournaments held throughout the year until a school champion was named before the winter break.

Though Colby never entered the competitions anymore, he tried to learn the game over the years and found himself at a complete loss on grasping the intricacies of play. It was not a matter of the rules and objectives he had trouble with; it was the rune symbols and how they made his brain hurt when he tried to study them. His dismal failure in his first tournament years ago was no help in gaining him any confidence.

The rules were not simple. A board could be used but was unnecessary as all the rune tiles became used for play and navigation. While the main action of the game took place in the center area between two players or teams, another area before those players is set aside for staging future moves. The area is used if a player wished to expose possible combinations they have available in an attempt at gaining extra tiles to complete other movements called constructs. A third area is designated for playing restorative and exemption runes.

The object, however, was simple at its core; collect runes and combinations in increasing difficulty until either player or team run out of runes, retires, or is eliminated by a point spread greater than one hundred.

Runes have a blue and red assignment. The player who goes first will play the red side. For the first game in a round or tournament, players will draw a random rune from the draw box, and whoever has the highest value rune will choose to be red or blue.

Each player or team begins to play with twenty random base runes from a draw box. They may also begin with ten personal runes of any class they have acquired through advancing knowledge of the game. Regardless of the number they possess, only ten may be used per match but can be swapped during any following matches.

All rune turns must build a construct consisting of a subject and action. The action must play upon the subject with a minimum of two runes and maximum limit numbering what remaining runes are held by the player. The larger the construct, the more points gained for difficulty. Multiple actions and subjects increase difficulty but must work in the construct in tandem to achieve a valid purpose.

Only advanced runes or basic ones set to connect multiple constructs may be used in a single rune placement turn.

Players may assemble partial casts in preparation for use. Opponents can see and prepare counter casts, not knowing what, how, or when they will be used. Unused casts cost points in each round against the losing player or team. No points are received for pre-casting runes. The advantages of using this move, are that for each rune used, the player may draw a replacement rune from their draw box. An additional advantage may be to force opponents to play counter pre-casts or mislead them to make incorrect assumptions about future moves.

Colby knew the rules, but so often failed to remember them under the pressure of competition. Therefore, he most often chose to watch. Gary quickly found a game to sit in on, leaving Colby to walk around watching other's play.

As he watched a few rounds at various tables, Colby began to feel an itching desire to play. Without realizing, he pulled his pouch of tiles from his backpack. Colby walked down the row of tables, usually reserved for games in the park, and considered assemblies and constructs he did not understand, yet somehow knew would work.

Colby stopped before an empty seat and noticed an old man who sat opposite the free chair. Colby looked at the man and immediately saw his bright blue eyes behind the sagging lids and wrinkled temples.

The man's skin covered his face and neck like a blanket of gathered and puckered leather. His thin and wispy hair layered upon his head and reminded Colby of the first snows of winter that drifted and blew in the wind. His clothing was unremarkable Colby noticed, but he looked back at the man's eyes. They stood against the passage of time and shone bright and clear such as those of a man many decades younger than this old man appeared.

* * *

"Please, sit young man," he said. "Do an old man the honor of some company and a round or two of Runes."

The man extended his bony arm and pointed at the empty seat. As Colby sat, the old man's crow's feet bunched and folded as his jowls pulled up, and thin lips curved into a toothy grin.

Colby thought it strange how a man with such young eyes and all his teeth looking so healthy would have such an outward look of agedness. Perhaps the teeth are implants, he thought. As he looked the man over, he felt a sense about him—energy. Something seemed oddly familiar about the old man.

"The name is Jenkins," he said and smiled, showing more of his teeth. "Brush well and often, and you can keep 'em for a lifetime."

Colby sat back, looking at the man, wondering if he was that obvious in his stare. He must have been because otherwise, the man would be reading Colby's mind, and that was not possible. Shaking off the odd behavior, Colby smiled and began setting up his tiles.

"I'm Colby. It's a pleasure to meet you, Jenkins."

With little left to say, the two began the process of ordering their tiles and preparing the first construct to play after they picked a tile to determine who went first.

They each drew a rune and compared them. Colby put his tile on the table, the Earth rune symbol for silver, worth a respectable value. Then he watched the old man reveal his rune, molten rock a more advanced rune as it combines fire and earth element of rock on a single tile. Jenkins won the right of the first construct.

"You may be red, my boy," the man said to Colby's surprise. He rarely had the opportunity to take the first construct, and for an inexperienced player, it was not the advantage it should present.

* * *

"Are you certain? Your tile is worth much more than mine. I'm happy being blue."

"Nonsense, my boy. You may find being red has just as much to win…or lose as being blue." Jenkins smiled and nodded for Colby to continue and take the first turn.

Not certain what Jenkins meant, Colby thanked him and began preparing by drawing the remainder of his tiles and selecting ten from his new bag of personal runes. These he chose by selecting the ones he liked the most. He didn't know what they were but thought they looked nice.

Jenkins nodded at Colby's selections and proceeded to choose his own, and then they were ready to play.

Colby started out slowly. He placed a few assembled combinations like; fire and sand to make glass, and iron, water, and fire to make steel, and then he placed his first construct. Lift, stone, assemble, water, dirt, repeat, all to create a wall to deflect a possible attack move from his opponent.

Jenkins raised one eyebrow and looked over what Colby had done for his first moves. With little time spent thinking, the old man constructed stone, with crush and wind as well as the same fire, iron, and water combination. His first assembled cast would mean rocks hurtling at the glass Colby created, depending on how or if he used it. The second could mean Jenkins would build a shield or other defense.

The construct Jenkins built, however, confused Colby. It was a line of runes that, when combined, would result in something akin to quicksand. Colby wondered why the man would do such a thing. His confusion must have spread to his face.

"I've just weakened the ground beneath your wall, my young friend." Jenkins smiled at Colby. "You'll have to think ahead in this game as you would chess or any other situation where you may not know what's coming."

* * *

Colby sank in his chair, thinking this was going to be a slaughter. He was out of the old man's league and totally inept at the game, to begin with. What made him think he was going to do well when he sat down? Colby was ready to resign the game when an itching overtook his fingers.

He looked at his hands and scratched at them. The itching turned to a tingle when he touched his runes, thinking to put them away. An idea began to form as he touched several runes. Colby reshuffled his tiles and rethought his previous decision to quit. As he moved the tiles around, they began to make a pattern to him he started to recognize. Before he understood what overcame him, Colby decided on what to play.

Colby laid down a new construct, this time fortifying the ground beneath his wall and lifting it up using seven runes. He gained a bonus and refreshed his used tiles. The game picked up with more interest from Colby. He wanted to win.

Back and forth, the two players went, attacking and defending. Neither player seemed to notice the crowd gathering around them as they each slapped down their runes trying to best one another.

The further along the rounds went, the more aggressive each player became using more tiles and improving upon their constructs or negating their opponent's previous plays.

Colby was gaining points and fast. Then he watched as Jenkins put a move intersecting three others that blocked both of the future places he was prepared to use a construct. He puckered his face and glared at the board.

Colby rested his fingers over the tray that held his personal runes, the ones he made earlier in the day. The tingle returned to his fingertips as he hovered his hand. He looked down at the tiles and focused on one that looked promising. Without more thought, Colby lifted the alabaster stone and put it in a spot that connected three constructs.

He wasn't certain why it felt like the right place to use it, but he laid it down with slow deliberation and looked up at Jenkins.

* * *

A smile slowly crept across the old man's face. "That is some move, my young friend. You have bested me by unraveling my spells and taking the points for yourself. I retire."

The crowd applauded and cheered.

Colby looked at Jenkins bewildered, but said nothing; nor did he take notice to the noisy spectators around them. He didn't know that is what the tile's rune would do, but Jenkins knew what it meant. "There are still more rounds to play."

Jenkins laughed and held his hand out toward the latest tile played. "My boy, if you have more tiles, the likes of this one, I'm afraid I'd lose rather badly."

Colby smiled at the man though he knew somehow the old man let him win. He started to like this Jenkins fellow.

"Until next time?" Jenkins gathered his things and held out his hand to wave.

Colby went to shake the man's hand and watched as he pulled his hand in and strode away. Thinking it odd, but not taking it personal, Colby waved after the old man. Only then did he notice the cheers and clapping from those gathered around his table. Colby shrank back and pushed his tiles into his bag before shrugging off everyone's congratulations, then pulling Gary along with him to leave.

"That was awesome, Colby," Gary said as they walked out of the park.

"I suppose." Colby looked at the ground while they walked. "I'm not really sure what I did."

Gary stopped and grabbed Colby's arm. "You won, that's what you did. When did you figure out the runes so well?"

"I didn't, I just sort of went on autopilot. Then I used one of the new runes I made from the kit you gave me."

61

* * *

Colby showed Gary the runes, and Gary whistled.

"Those are some pretty fancy and obscure runes. I'm not even sure what they all are, but my dad would know." Gary dug through the bag and pulled a few more tiles out. "Why don't you let me take these to show my dad? Maybe he can tell us what they all mean."

Colby grabbed the tiles and put them back in his bag. "I'll give you the notes I used to make them. I'd like to look at the tiles tonight myself. I'll enter them in my computer program."

"What program is that?"

"Something I've been working on for converting hashtags into rune spells."

Gary looked at Colby for a moment, and his eyes lit up. "Cool, like a game or something?."

"Well no, I was hoping it could force my magic, but it doesn't work."

"Well if it starts working, let me know. If you make it a mobile app, it'd be like using a phone as a wand." Gary started off the opposite direction. "See you in the morning, Colby. Happy birthday again."

"Thanks, Gary," Colby said. "See you tomorrow."

Colby turned back toward home as his stomach began to rumble. It was his birthday, which meant a big dinner. With the way everyone acted this morning, maybe there was a surprise in store for him when he got home after all. He only hoped it didn't involve Nana at the stove.

He then thought about what Gary said. Using his phone as a magic wand, the possibilities bounced around in time with Colby's quickening stride. "Hashtag Magic, maybe it could work."

Chapter 8

Colby returned home to the pungent smell of freshly burnt potatoes and fried fish, at least it smelled like fish. One could rarely tell what things started out as when Nana was involved with cooking. Nana was in the kitchen, trying her hand at preparing dinner. She could not cook her way out of a paper bag, but she would do her best to burn said bag to ash.

Colby burst through the door expecting a big surprise. There was none. No streamers. No Balloons. Not even a cake. The only thing he found was Nana and a smell coming from the stove that would melt warts off a toad's ass. No surprise whatsoever, and he would have to suffer another bad meal and resort to the junk food he kept hidden in his room. How would he ever get muscles or grow facial hair being fed like this?

* * *

"Ah, good you're home," Nana said. Her face and hands were caked with clumps of batter and her clothes covered in said batter's constituent ingredients. "I've made fish and chips for dinner in honor of our special guest." She swung around and pointed to the scraggly cat sitting on a stool in the corner, letting loose of several clumps of gooey dough from her fingertips.

The dough sailed across the room toward the cat whose yowl voiced a protest to the culinary assault. The addition of batter clotting the scrawny creatures bedraggled fur did little to improve its appearance, though, with a deft flick of its hind leg, the cat managed to free the worst of the mess.

Colby chuckled as he narrowed his eyes at the somehow familiar-looking cat. "And who do we have here?" Colby asked as he approached their dinner guest. Colby lowered his hand to the cat and received a gentle head-butt and a gurgle that might have passed for a purr.

"Why that is old Fizzlewink, don't you remember him?" Nana said. "He started comin' around here back when you were just out of diapers. Then one day, he ran off and only came around on rare occasions for some scraps and would wander off."

Colby's eyes lit up as he remembered the old tomcat from his earliest memories. "Fizzy-Wizzles," he said and picked up the cat. "Now I remember, I used to dress him up in Shelly's doll clothes."

The cat leaped from Colby's arms and sat back on the stool in a guarded posture.

Nana laughed at the exchange. "Seems ol' Fizzlewink remembers playing dress-up with less fondness than you, Fart-blossom."

Colby sneered at the nickname. "You suppose he can remember that? It was like, nine or ten years ago. An old cat like him, probably he just doesn't like being called Fizzy-Wizzles." Colby scratched Fizzlewink's head as he lifted him onto his lap and sat at the kitchen island.

* * *

"Of course he doesn't remember," Shelly declared as she clomped into the room. "Cats are smooth-brained and don't have memories like people. Maybe he just remembers your smell, Fart-blossom." Shelly reached down to pet the cat that rewarded her with a half-assed swat. "Mongrel."

"He remembers well enough, I expect," Nana said and winked at the frizzy feline. She put a plate down on the counter with a piece of un-battered fish on it.

Fizzlewink took one whiff and dug in as though he had not eaten in days.

"Seems he has no qualms about your cooking," Shelly said as she returned a potato wedge to the basket after sniffing it. "I'm going out," she said and exited the back door.

Nana set out a plate for Colby and herself and sat down for dinner. "How was your day Colby? Anything exciting happen today?" she asked and winked.

Colby stopped scraping the charcoal soot off his fries and looked up at his grandmother in confusion. "What makes you ask that?"

"Someone called from the Dean's office."

Relieved, Colby relaxed and explained how he got into a confrontation with the school bully and received detention after standing up for himself. "All I did was tell him I wouldn't give him my homework, and later he tried to stuff me in a locker."

Nana raised her brow but didn't say what she first wanted, knowing there was more to the story. "Jasper Bodine is a pompous little horse's ass, who's only in that school because of his father's influence. That boy hasn't two cents in his head to spend, only daddy's money." Nana wrinkled her nose and nodded once with a grunt. "What else happened?"

Colby continued his story, leaving out anything deemed 'magical'. His own opinion on what happened was a hallucination at best. Colby told her about the first conflict in the morning and then retold the events of the second one after lunch involving the locker.

"So, you received detention all day this Saturday just for standing up for yourself?" Nana asked.

Colby bit his lower lip. It was his tell, and Nana always knew when he was not sharing the entire truth. "There was this thing with the lights…but I didn't do anything. The lights just started flickering, and some of them broke. The three of us all received detention on Saturday since nobody admitted to breaking the lights. It isn't fair."

Nana's eyes widened when Colby mentioned the lights. She knew something would happen, and this was just the start of strange events to come. She and the cat had shared a moment before Nana said anything more. "Go ahead and finish your dinner upstairs while you start your homework. Old Fizzlewink, and I will clean up in here."

"You mean he'll clean up the scraps of fish," Colby chuckled. "Thanks, Nannie." Colby got up and headed to his room, leaving his dinner behind. Before he left the kitchen, Colby turned back to his grandmother. "Nana, where did my school tuition payments come from?"

Nana spat a bit of a potato wedge from her mouth rather than choke on it. "What makes you ask such a question?"

"Something the Dean said today about an anonymous source pre-paying my fees and tuition, do you know anything about that?" Colby asked. "There are so many things I feel I'm missing for some reason."

Nana shrugged. "As far as I know, the money came from what your father had saved up before…well, you know. Anyway, I wouldn't worry about what that old toad of a Dean said. He has no need to treat any students different based on where their money comes from or what side of town they live, so long as they pay."

Nana grumbled as she fiddled around at the stove. "I never liked that man and told your father he was a leech. Only out for himself." She continued to mumble.

"He knew my dad?"

Nana stopped moving and looked up, then out the window. She did not turn around. "Oh yes…Well, sort of. Anyway, that's old news. Best leave the past in the past and focus on the present." She turned and went to the cupboard and pulled a package from the cabinet. "Speaking of presents…"

Colby smiled when he turned to her and saw that toothless grin. Nana waddled over, carrying a lopsided box, making him smile more. The batter was dripping from her wiry hair and flour peppering her smock, Colby could only guess that the stove won the battle that transpired when Nana attempted to make dinner again. He wasn't going to reconsider tasting it.

The box was sloppily covered with mismatched wrapping paper meant for different occasions. Baby rattles, toy soldiers, balloons, and princesses coated the box at odd angles and were affixed with what amounted to three rolls of transparent tape. As unappealing as the outside looked, Colby was certain he would love what was within.

Nana was not the best at picking out gifts, but she certainly enjoyed giving them. Colby opened the box and was not let down by what he found inside. A set of maracas, a tiny sombrero, a snow globe depicting a scene from somewhere in Mexico he assumed, and another wrapped item.

He opened the final surprise and found a framed picture beneath the wrapping. It was a picture of his dad holding him on his lap as a toddler. On his head, he wore the tiny sombrero and held the maracas that now lay in the box before him —a reminder. Nana gave him the gift of a memory for his birthday.

Colby stared at the image, smiling at the joy he saw in his father's face. His vision blurred from the moisture, gathering in his own eyes. He could not hold back the well of emotion that built beneath the surface. He pushed the picture back into the badly wrapped and poorly given gift box and closed it. It was a gift of memory that burned him intensely.

* * *

He rubbed his eyes and started for the door. "I suppose it's too much to ask for mom to have been home tonight. Perhaps she'll leave me as well. She practically has already."

Colby slammed the kitchen door as he left, leaving lights flickering in the kitchen and a bewildered Nana.

Nana shrugged and wiped the flour from her dress then took a towel to her hair.

"Yup, it's started, hasn't it old boy?" Nana asked the cat as he cleaned the last of the flesh from a piece of fish. "I only wish his mother was in her right mind to help. He knows nothing of our magic history or that of his returning. What was my daughter thinking by keeping such a secret from him."

The cat answered with a mouth filled meow, and then trotted off out the kitchen door when Nana opened it.

***

Colby fell on his bed face first and screamed into his pillow. Why was he letting this get to him? What did he expect? Year after year, his birthday came and went with barely a whisper of acknowledgment. Oh, his mother would remember in a few days like she always did. Apologizing profusely and trying to make up for forgetting things was her way. One day she was zoned out and distant; the next day, she was her old self and totally committed. It was as though his mother was two different people.

He rolled onto his back and stared at the ceiling, then lifted his hands up and began turning them over and under, examining them for what Gary described as sparks. He found nothing.

Rather than dwell in self-pity, Colby huffed and sat up. Since he had the entire evening of his birthday to spend by himself, what was he to do? He thought about playing a game on-line. No, it didn't appeal to him tonight. He could watch some movies. No, he didn't feel like it. He could study his runes. That was something that piqued his interest.

Colby grabbed his bag and pulled out the runes he made from the kit Gary gave him. He sat down on the floor and crossed his legs before dumping the runes out in a pile.

One by one, Colby picked up the small rectangular tiles and turned them in his hand, examining every line and curve. They were fascinating, but he didn't understand why. He pulled out his tablet and took pictures of a few runes and tried to find similar images using the picture recognition feature of his favorite search engine. No results came close.

He set the tablet aside and let out a heavy breath. "Where are you?" he said and looked at the watch on his wrist.

Scratching at his door brought Colby out of his thoughts. Before he could get up to see what it was, a paw poked through the crack where the door was not completely closed. A blue-faced cat pushed through, turning his head sideways until his shoulders were able to push the door open enough to squeeze through. The cat entered and sat down just inside the door.

Fizzlewink looked at Colby and meowed as though to ask permission to enter.

"Well, you're already in. I suppose the scratching was your way of knocking first?" Colby rubbed his thumb against his index and middle finger while clicking at the cat. "Come here, boy."

Fizzlewink looked at Colby's fingers and pushed his head forward a touch. He tilted his head a moment, then ran over and sat down next to the pile of runes.

Colby scratched Fizzlewink's head and was rewarded again with the gurgling purr he remembered from the kitchen. He continued to pet the cat while it batted at the pile of runes, pushing a few of them into line.

Turning his computer back on, Colby brought up his runes library files and added the new symbols into the database before saving the file. Once saved, his

AI began running through possible combinations and saving them. Colby then altered his application code and made a mobile version that he loaded onto his phone. If nothing else, he now had a reference available on his phone.

Colby opened the app and entered a hashtag. **#PlasmaBall**. Nothing happened.

"Well, it looks like it's just you and me kitty. No magic tonight." Colby laid down on his bed and patted it for the cat to join him.

Fizzlewink looked at the runes one last time before batting at another, then jumped up on the bed and curled up behind Colby's bent knees.

Colby turned off his light and closed his eyes. He did not notice the soft glow in the room.

Fizzlewink looked over the edge of the bed at the glowing runes on the floor. He blinked and put his head back down before closing his own eyes. A gurgling purr filled the room.

Chapter 9

Colby awoke the next morning, still reeling from the game of Runes, and the sudden expert playing he performed topped off by remembering his visit from a little blue cat-man in his dreams the night before. He couldn't help but wonder if there were more secrets awaiting discovery with all the odd feelings he is having and the strange things that are beginning to happen to him. The other side of this would be that he is going bonkers and would soon find himself locked away in a padded cell.

The afternoon before, Gary insisted on borrowing Colby's new Rune tiles for the night to copy them and start trying to figure them out with help from his father.

Colby tried to explain he wasn't sure what they were except that he must have seen them somewhere before, but Gary was not entirely convinced. Rather than give up his new tiles, he gave Gary his notepad that he scribbled the runes within.

By the time Colby finished getting ready for school and made his way to the kitchen, Gary was there and already well into his story about Colby's Runes games the day before. Even Colby's mother was sitting at the table and listening with interest to the descriptions of the rune constructs that Colby was able to assemble against his seasoned opponent.

"I'm sure you exaggerate, Gary," Colby said.

His mother turned toward him with glistening eyes and a mixed smile. He could read the lines of worry, coupled with regret in her face, as she got up from the table to hug him.

"Glad you have begun to learn the Runes, my dear," Aria said.

"Glad you finally came home."

Aria leaned back and looked at her boy. "I'm sorry I wasn't here for your birthday dinner. I'll make it up to you. I promise."

"You always do," Colby said and looked away from her.

Letting him go, Aria reached for her purse and keys before heading to the door. Her shoulders hunched, and head hung down, Colby watched the shudder of her torso as she sniffled and held back her tears. He noticed that Nana watched her leave as well, but the look on her face was not one of concern. Her lips were twisted and puckered into a smirk as she glared at her daughter.

"What's wrong with mom?" Colby asked.

Nana turned back and softened her expression as the folds in her wrinkled face loosened. "Who can tell from one day to the next? Perhaps she got a paper cut or is remembering a scene from Old Yeller. The woman snivels at the drop of a hat these days." Nana lifted a brow as her thin lips curled into a crooked smile. "So tell me about these new runes of yours."

Colby grabbed a piece of toast and banana opting to pass on the shell filled, and gray scrambled eggs. "Just something I saw somewhere, I think. I haven't had a chance to figure them all out yet, but my computer app is running through them." Colby grabbed Gary and began to push him toward the door.

"I can help with that," Gary said and pulled a sheet of paper out of his backpack. He handed the paper to Colby. "I looked through them last night and referenced some books I found. They are really old."

"Are they now?" Nana said.

Colby shoved the paper in his bag and pushed Gary out the back door. "Gotta go, Nana. See you later."

The boys ran for the bus, and this time, when the driver turned to see Colby coming, the driver waited when he looked into Colby's eyes. Gary boarded first and headed for a seat while Colby paused to glare at the driver. Something was definitely happening if this guy decided for the first time not to close the door on him and take off. Colby said nothing as he stared until the driver looked away and closed the doors. Feeling confident for the first time that he could remember, Colby headed back to sit next to Gary. He couldn't wait to get to school today. That was most certainly new.

***

Colby walked down the hall toward his locker with an unusual new air of confidence. He stood tall and looked forward in stark contrast to his normal slouch and downcast eyes. He made eye contact with several other students as he passed them in the hall, many of whom watched his Runes game in the park the previous day. The nods of acknowledgment and waves hello were a new development and began to make him feel uncomfortable. As odd as the feeling was for him, Colby refused to show anything less than a confident composure.

He only faltered when he saw Darla, the pom-pom girl, and her friend Rhea, waving their fingers at him.

His blushing face turned away to find Gary smirking back at him.

"Go talk to them," Gary said.

Colby started to protest and make excuses but was saved from speaking the words when Darla and Rhea disappeared around the corner. There was nothing down that hall. Perplexed, Colby went to follow them, but when he turned the corner, they were already gone. Instead, he saw something else that was completely out of place. A scraggly old bluish cat was running down the corridor toward a set of maintenance stairs beyond an open door.

Colby ran after the cat. He thought that the mangy beast followed him to school and somehow got into the building.

"Fizzlewink," Colby said, checking if anyone was watching.

The cat darted down the stairs as if not hearing Colby. Colby approached the open door and stood at the top of the stairs that led down toward the lower basement of the building and stared into the darkness that awaited him. He did not care much for the dark and cared less for venturing into the unknown bowels of the building to chase after a contrary cat. As the moments passed, he inched further onto the landing and past the threshold. The door slammed behind him.

Colby turned, trying to open the door, but it would not budge. He pulled out his phone to place a call to Gary from the favorites app when the bellowing mew of his family cat beckoned him to follow. Begrudgingly, Colby resigned himself to follow the feline into the basement.

Colby edged his way into the darkness that swallowed the little light entering the stairwell from the crack beneath the door. He had bumped his head on many pipes as well as low hanging poles and beams before it dawned on him that he should use his phone as a flashlight.

* * *

He listened in the cold darkness for any hint of a trail to follow as the cat was no longer near enough to track. The echoes of tiny feet padding against the cement floor gave him some bearing, and he continued until his phone's light began to fail and die. His phone was fully charged that morning, so he couldn't understand why it was so low on power. When at last, his phone reached a low point that it shut down automatically, Colby reached a place where he thought to turn back.

A churning in his stomach pushed up against his thoughts to go back in the direction he came as he looked behind him. When he turned back toward the darkness ahead, his pain was replaced by a burning desire to continue forward. Against his better judgment, Colby followed the strange impulse to move ahead into the inky blackness of the shadows beneath the school that already filled him with dread daily.

'Move on,' the voice in his head told him. 'There is much to learn ahead,' it said though he reeled against the madness that began to overtake his every step. Despite the complete absence of illumination, he moved on without impediment. His mind began to make out a faint glow of light and followed it toward the source.

As he walked forward, he realized that it was not the light of natural origin, he was trailing, but something born of magic. It had to be magic because as he reached out his hand toward that light, tendrils of energy danced across his skin and down his pointed hand. The energy leaped out in a suicidal plunge toward the power that fed his own desire to continue onward.

Onward, the thoughts and impulses compelled him. 'Come to us, Colby,' they teased as he stumbled mindlessly through the pitch of black solitude the bowels of the building held. The thrumming of the boiler and scraping of chairs and desks from the floors above provided an acoustic rhythm that supported his every sluggish step. Something wanted him to drive on against every ounce of his protesting will. Drive forward he did, while he listened to the endless drip of water from the leaky pipes adding to the other noises in concert.

He sweated and strained to resist pressing onward, but the compulsion would not let go of his will. When he looked down, he could see the faint violet toned line of energy wrapped around him, pulling him forward. No longer did he need to worry about the light to shine his way, the Magic was taking him where it wanted.

"Where is that damn cat," Colby said to the darkness.

When he was nearing the point of giving up and passing into over-exhausted sleep, Colby's eyes caught the increasingly familiar glow and shape of runes shining in the distance ahead. He pulled himself up to his feet and carried on toward the glistening symbols.

Eyelids drooping, and energy spent, Colby slumped before a dead end. Only a sealed door lay before him and no other way besides turning back. He began to laugh at himself for falling to the sickness of whatever gas was leaking in the basement and cursed his stupidity for not turning back sooner. As he pulled his knees close to his chest, the muffled sound of voices rose over the scrapping echo of his shoes.

As soon as he stopped moving, Colby heard the voices again and began to perk up. Though he could not make out what they said, he knew for certain he wasn't going mad, so his mood continued to lighten.

He slowly crept toward the door, hoping to decipher anything of what was being discussed. Still, he heard nothing that he could interpret, so he leaned in closer to the door. A shiver ran through his body as he approached, and the small hairs on his neck and arms stood up. His body protested his proximity to the door and could sense the power behind it.

Colby pushed on and laid his ear against the door. A buzzing filled his hearing where moments before he heard the muffled voices of what sounded like men arguing. As he pulled back from the door, the buzzing continued, and a purple glow began to emanate from the door in the shapes of runes etched across the surface.

He stood and faced the door and began to step back as the elusive blue and red tendrils of Energy began to flow freely from his hands and into the runes on the door and frame. Colby watched with fascination as the purple glow dispersed, and he noticed that the runes now glowed red along the doorframe and blue upon the door itself.

Reaching out, Colby pushed forward against the protest of power now pulsing from the closed room before him. The energies stopped flowing from his body, and a dull ache formed behind his eyes. His face began to contort under the strain of movement against an increasingly forceful pushback against his approach. With more strength than he thought he had, Colby reached out his hand to touch the central symbol on the door. It protested.

Light filled the hallway in an explosive release of energy that threw Colby off his feet and onto the floor, several paces back from the door. Colby's head hit the floor, and in an instant, he was out cold. The moment he lost consciousness, the runes on the door scattered, and a final burst of light filled the corridor for the briefest of moments, before being drawn directly to Colby's prone form. The light poured into him, causing a momentary spasm that shook his entire body.

Colby regained consciousness the moment his body relaxed from the spasm. He found himself lying on the floor, many feet away from where he last remembered being. He tried to think of how he got where he now sat on the floor, but his mind was clouded and head throbbing. His eyes felt as though something was pushing on them from behind and above, trying to free them from their sockets. The irritating glow of light in the hall was causing him pain though it barely illuminated the wet and musty smelling tunnel of the school's basement.

School, he thought. Lunchtime had to have ended, which meant he was tardy for his next class or worse; he could have missed the rest of the day. He had no idea what time it was and quickly looked at his watch, remembering that it was mysteriously working after years of being non-functional. Less than a half-hour had passed.

Colby hurried back the way he came, heading for the stairs completely oblivious to the faint glow of light that illuminated his way. It was not until he reached the staircase and placed his hand on the railing that he saw the light. He stopped and stared at his hand that gripped the metal rail, squeezing it harder as realization set in. He was glowing.

He raised his hand toward his face to examine it, turning it back and forth to explore every angle. His eyes traced down his hand and wrist along his arm. He looked at his other hand to confirm that it as well glowed, but it was fading.

The ringing of the bell in the halls, only feet above him, brought Colby back from his wonderment. He would think about what was happening later, and he needed to get to class, so he raced up the stairs and out the door.

Chapter 10

Colby burst through the door and slid from the darkness of the basement and into the full light of the hallways above. He stumbled forward, checking his skin for the glowing light that illuminated his passage back to the ground level and found no trace. Not satisfied, he ran to the closest display case to check his faded reflection in the glass. There were no signs that he continued to shine like a glowworm. The last thing he wanted was to appear like some sparkly vampire out of a novel.

With only a few minutes remaining of the lunch hour, Colby headed toward the cafeteria to find Gary. He ran through the halls, ignoring the complaints and swearing as he pushed past other students milling about between classes. When at last he neared the lunchroom, he slowed his pace to a quick walk and scanned the room for Gary after not finding him in their usual spot.

Gary was sitting at a table on the far side of the room. Colby spotted him through the thinning crowds as the students began getting up and taking their trays away to leave for their next classes. He was sitting with Darla and Rhea, the girls from the hallway before Colby made the journey into the dark, dank corridors below the school. Gary was all smiles and enjoying the attention that Rhea was giving him.

No sooner had Colby begun his approach, Darla cut off mid-conversation and turned in his direction. Her lips parted slightly, exposing her sparkling white teeth as her glossed-red mouth curved up into a smile that caused Colby to stumble.

Colby recovered quickly but not so that Darla hadn't noticed. Her smile broadened, and her nose crinkled while her giggle escaped glossy red lips. Colby followed the tiny wrinkled nose to gaze into Darla's bright green eyes that shone like emeralds in the rays of sunshine streaming in through the windows. A foot connecting with his shin was the only indication he had been standing next to the table, staring down at Darla. A few seconds passed, and he shook the odd tingling and foggy thoughts from his mind. He looked back at Darla through slightly squinted eyes, watching the glow around her fade away, along with a compelling presence he felt moments before.

Darla's smile faltered.

"Where have you been?" Gary asked, smirking at his awkward friend, gawking down at the pom-pom girl.

"What…Oh, I um…I was checking on something," Colby said after a moment of silence.

He turned to Gary and frowned, his ankle stinging. Before he could say more, the bell rang, and the remaining students in the room all got up at once and began filing out of the cafeteria. Colby stiffened when Darla walked by and winked at him as she passed, brushing his shoulder with her fingers. He turned and followed her every move as she melted into the throng of bustling teenagers rushing from the room. Confusion racked his brain.

"Hey! Earth to Colby," Gary said. He snapped his fingers in front of Colby's face several times before getting through. "Oh brother. Come on, we need to get moving."

"Ya, sure," Colby said.

"Dude, if I didn't know better, I'd say you were glowing."

Colby stopped in a panic and began checking his hands and arms. He couldn't find any trace of the iridescent shine he carried in the darkness of the basement.

Gary laughed at his friend. "I'm talking about Darla, you spaz. You don't actually glow." Gary looked again at Colby's hands to make certain, then laughed as Colby pushed his hands into his pockets.

"Did you look at those rune descriptions I put together?" Gary asked.

"Not yet," Colby said gladly, acknowledging the change in subject. "I'll check them during my next classes."

"You better, because you'll need them in the tournament this afternoon."

Gary told Colby about signing the two of them up for a team tournament at the Runes games scheduled to take place during an assembly that same afternoon. Colby forgot there was even an afternoon assembly, never mind thinking about there being Runes competitions.

"You did what?"

"Relax. After what you did yesterday with those new Runes, we'll be sure to place for the next tourney!" Gary pushed on ahead while Colby lagged behind.

"Crap on a cracker," Colby muttered, repeating a favorite Nana phrase.

* * *

***

The assembly was in two hours, so Colby had little time to study and understand the meanings behind the new runes he made from visions and using the kit Gary gave him for his birthday. Though he played them deftly in the park the day before, he did so without fully comprehending their meanings or usage. If he wanted to avoid making a fool of himself in front of the entire school, he needed to figure these symbols out and fast.

He spent the next two periods, pouring over the notes Gary made on each rune and what its potential uses might be. He was amazed to find that each rune presented multiple uses and could be moved to the construct space in a single placement to work with or against multiple other runes. These were highly advanced pieces that he suddenly realized he should not likely have in his possession as a barely intermediate player. He would not, however, allow that to deter him from using them if it meant not making a fool of himself or losing terribly to a more seasoned player.

Colby's time to study came to an end when the bell rang, and students and faculty began to head to the gymnasium where the competition was being held. On his way there, Colby stopped by his locker to get his set of runes and waited for Gary to meet him. He watched as classmates walked by, completely ignoring him as though he was not even there. Colby was comforted by the solitude of obscurity as he disliked being pointed out or center of any attention. In school, the only attention he received was that of Jasper Bodine and his posse.

"You ready for this?" Gary said.

Colby jumped and spun around at the sudden voice in his ear from behind him. He slugged Gary in the arm as his friend laughed at the startled expression turned sour on Colby's face. Colby closed his locker and shrugged before falling into step beside his pal and heading to face the spotlight.

As he neared the assembly, Colby found he was not as obscure as moments before in the hall. Students pointed, glared, and whispered as he passed, and he noticed several teachers as well. A few people were among those in the park the previous day and witnessed his playing with deft moves and strange new runes. Word was spreading of his newly acquired skill, and the attention was pushing upon Colby's chest. He wanted nothing more than to shrink away from the gawking and run.

"Come on, we're gonna do great," Gary said. "Stop worrying."

"I'm not worrying."

Gary laughed. "Sure, you're not. I suppose your face is always all puckered up and looking like a cat's ass?"

Colby scanned the bleachers that lined the wall of the gymnasium. They were full of students, faculty, and parents that came to witness the first competition of the summer term. As his eyes darted from face to face, he looked past them and saw a swirling mass of laughing and pointing people. Every finger pointed his direction as the carousel of mock and humiliation spun around him. Colby's hands flew up to his ears, attempting to block out the laughing and shouting.

His moment of panic was interrupted when Gary grabbed his arm. "Dude!"

"I can't do this," Colby said and turned back for the exit of the gymnasium.

"What are you talking about? You just played yesterday. I know you have issues with crowds and stuff, but you can do this." Gary moved around to block Colby's exit. "You played great yesterday with all those people watching."

Colby lifted his arm to his forehead to wipe away the perspiration that was collecting. "That was different. I sat down at the end table far from others, and nobody was watching until later."

"So pretend you are in the park, and nobody is watching."

Colby raised his eyebrow and shook his head. "It isn't that easy, Gary. You might as well tell me to imagine everyone in underwear. It won't work."

* * *

Gary glared out into the gym and looked at the crowd, frowning. "Yuck, I just imagined old lady Mitchell the English teacher in her bloomers. Not pretty."

That solicited a relief-filled chuckle from Colby. "Thanks for sharing the visual… not." Colby turned to scan the crowd. "Everyone is going to expect me to fail."

"Nobody expected you to play at all. How can they expect you to fail?" Gary slowly pushed Colby toward the empty tables set on the floor. "Look, I'll be right there beside you the whole time. We're a team, you know, and we can do this together."

Colby sighed and resolved himself to play if for no other reason than to help his friend. So he made his way to their assigned first table to await the start of their match.

"Do you think it would be considered cheating if I used my new app for help with the runes?" Colby asked.

Gary shrugged. "It shouldn't be an issue. You are allowed notes; nothing says they can't be digital."

Twisting his mouth and smirking, Colby showed Gary the app. "It's not exactly a notes app. It takes hashtags and converts them to rune combinations."

"That's freakin' awesome. Can you beam that to me?"

Colby tapped his phone to Gary's, and wirelessly shared his app.

The other team was a couple of boys he knew but had little interaction with. They sat opposite Colby and Gary, shuffling their personal runes around on the table, making annoying scuffing sounds and glaring at them. Colby wondered if that was some intimidation tactic, or they were just a little dimwitted. Either way, it was doing nothing to improve Colby's already tenuous state.

The tournament began, and Colby chose the ten of his new runes that he and Gary would use in the match. Gary began the opening round with the first move using five runes, forming a spell to move stone and throw it toward their adversary. He then displayed two starters in the assembly corner giving them nine new runes to choose from the draw box. Gary drew the replacement tiles, and the two friends watched as their opponents took their turn.

Colby watched the two boys shuffle their tiles and whisper, sharing conspiratorial grins before placing their first moves. They slapped their tiles down on the table to match his and Gary's same assembly spells and then placed their construct. The construct intersected their own at the Earth element, gaining the points for the repurposing of that tile and taking the lead by twenty points by blocking their opponents and turning their stone throw into a wall of protection.

The game went back and forth for nearly twenty minutes. Neither side gained many advantages in each turn; however, the tile snapping twerps across from Colby were gaining points enough to put them within the range of winning, and Colby began to scan the audience. He watched for people glaring and snickering at his failures. He couldn't win, and he would embarrass himself and Gary.

"Hey, you can get in the game anytime, pal," Gary whispered.

Colby snapped back into the now and looked at the board. The boys they played were now ready for the final move to win if things played out for them. Colby could see several places now that they could place a winning construct, and he did not have the tiles before him to block enough of the openings. He fingered the personal tiles before him and slid a few of them around, wondering where to place one to their advantage.

There were no places to build a complicated enough construct to lessen the gap in their points, and the other team knew this. Colby watched their squinty little eyes as they sneered at him, just waiting to place their game-winning construct. Colby took a deep breath and resigned himself to an early elimination and began sliding the runes below his fingers back toward him when a tingle in his finger drew his attention.

Colby pulled his fingers back and looked at the runes that sat on their end and faced only him. As his eyes focused on them, three of them began to glow to only his eyes. He glanced at the game in the center of the table and knew without thinking where to place them to level the playing field.

"Are you ready to lose?" the pimply-faced boy on the right said from across the table. "We have you now."

Colby held back his irritation at the boy's pompous tone and creeping grin. He tapped a hashtag into his phone app to see if it would help. When his finger touched the screen, a spark cracked and entered his phone. Rather than wrecking his device, the energy activated something within his new program. A rune appeared on the screen.

With a grin forming of his own, Colby snapped the first rune down on the board, joining three of the opponent's constructs. It was a metaphysical rune representing reversal, and in that single tile move, Colby gained the points of all three constructs and a bonus for single tile move as well as turning their spells against them.

A game official called out the move and awarded the points after a moment of disbelief from the opposition and spectators. Silence had fallen over the audience for only a second before hushed whispers rose through the gymnasium.

The boys stared at the unfamiliar rune and began to grin, thinking it was a joke, but soon realized their doom when another official confirmed the move. It was Rigel who stood next to Colby confirming the rune and its usage.

"Very nice move," Rigel said. "Continue your match."

Rigel stepped back but kept his eyes on the game Colby noticed.

The game ended in two more moves with Gary and Colby winning by more than two hundred points. Colby ignored the grumbles and cheers alike from the crowd. He was focusing on winning now as he looked down the next row of tables to find Jasper Bodine playing.

Colby knew that in spite of Jasper's laziness to do his homework, he was far from stupid and quite skilled in Runes. As much as he despised his tormentor, he recognized and also envied his skill at the game. Today he would likely face his long time source of torment if things continued as well as the first round. As that thought played around in his mind, Colby slowed his pace to the next table.

Gary must have seen what put the pause in Colby's steps, he must have thought as his friend pushed him on.

"Worry about that troglodyte later," Gary said. "One match at a time."

One match after the next, Colby and Gary dominated the tournament and advanced from each table to the next taking on the next team. Colby used his runes and mobile app to greatest effect. His new acuity at runes surprised his opponents and the many spectators.

Colby began to relax more with each win, and it was time for the last round. He nearly lost his anxiety over the inevitable encounter with Jasper. He chanced a look at the next table, where his eyes locked with the sharp-edged glare of Jasper.

Colby took the seat across from Jasper without looking at him. He felt a piercing burn of the daggers from Jasper's stare. Colby fumbled to arrange his tiles and prepare for the match. Hands shaking, he knocked his tiles over more than once. As he tried to contain his fear, he pulled his hands away from the table and saw red and blue sparks dancing on his skin.

The entire time, Gary fumbled to restore the dropped tiles onto their staging tray. He tried to calm Colby, but it was no use. The confidence his friend began displaying that same morning was suddenly swept away by the tidal forces of Jasper's presence. Gary prepared for the worst.

Colby shoved his belongings into his bag and ran while shouting that he retired the match. When he made it outside, his hands looked normal. He imagined it from fear of facing Jasper and losing miserably. Not wanting to face anyone, he turned for home, head down and shoulders slumped. When he got home, he went straight to his room without a word. He flopped onto his bed, covered his head with a pillow, and cursed himself to sleep.

* * *

His dreams were once again filled with strange imagery of runes and other odd symbols. Evil ghostly creatures leaped from various electronic devices, their screens casting a bright blue light.

Chapter 11

Colby sat before his computer, hesitant to turn it on the next morning. He was unsure of what might happen. Twice now he saw strange symbols and the blue screen appear. More than once, his dreams were invaded by similar images. That very morning he awoke after such a vivid dream involving his computer screen going blue and symbols dancing around his head as he burned from the inside out. It was happening on his computer at that moment.

The blue screen of death was nothing out of the ordinary, but the usual cryptic errors and segment fault information was replaced with symbols that he never remembered seeing before, and yet somehow, they felt familiar. Since it happened in his dreams and also in real life, Colby was suspicious of the connection. He forced a shutdown and reboot.

* * *

To work up his nerve, he reached into the back of his desk drawer and retrieved a bag of nacho chips that he kept handy in stashes of food items around his room. He never knew when he might be able to stomach the food his grandmother made. Since his mother had decided to go into work, after all, she would be late in coming home and not likely to fix something more edible.

As he licked the last of the cheese-flavored powder from his orange stained fingers, Colby reluctantly pushed the power button on his computer. While the multi-colored logo pulsed on the screen, indicating the operating system was starting up, Colby began to relax. He felt himself a little silly, paranoid even that he would be nervous about his computer being out to get him.

"All clear," he said, releasing his sustained breath. "I think it's time to finish tweaking my hashtag app and make it a full OS." Colby reached out and touched the icon on his screen for the word processor and began his homework. Next, he reluctantly checked his social site and e-mail for comments about his chickening out against Jasper in Runes. He was shocked to find nothing at all. Finding nothing was stranger than anything else going on. It was weird that not a single comment or trolling post was anywhere to find.

At last, Colby decided that it wasn't worth worrying over. He had better things to occupy his time. Time, he decided, to start surfing the web for clues as to what the symbol and runes were that he kept seeing.

His searches kept returning nothing close to what he saw, so he decided to change his parameters. He Googled for ancient symbols and runes. He described the basic layout of the image and finally began to see some results that looked promising. He sifted through all the information until he finally found something similar to what he was looking for.

"Mystic Symbols of Antiquity," Colby said to the empty room.

"Wheel of the Year," Colby heard behind him. He turned and saw his room was still empty.

* * *

"Great now I'm hearing things," he said and turned back to his computer. "Whoa," he screeched as he fell back and out of his chair.

Sitting on the desk in front of the computer screen was Fizzlewink, the cat. For a moment, however, Colby saw something quite different from a cat, but his focus cleared, and all he saw was a mangy old blue-hued tomcat.

"What are you doing up there, you crazy cat. You scared the crap out o' me." Colby picked himself up from the floor and righted his chair before retaking his seat and ended up looking at the cat nose to nose. "Now I'm seeing things."

Fizzlewink just meowed and moved to the side of the desk and stared at the computer screen.

Colby clicked his mouse on the link that first returned when searching for the symbol, and scanned the limited results. "Ok, so no exact matches, so how about the other smaller rune symbols that appeared as well?" Colby found himself talking to the cat, which somehow felt natural and odd at the same time. "What do you think, Fizzlewink?" Colby said, pointing to the computer screen. "These look promising." Colby located a reference to undated and only recently discovered markings on a stone tablet that was located in the ruins of Chichén Itzá.

Fizzlewink turned himself toward the computer screen, bumped his head against it, and began to purr.

"I agree," Colby told the blue cat. "They aren't exactly the same but similar enough to use as a starting point." Colby continued to scan through every link that he could find containing any reference to the strange and unknown symbology that danced around the edges of his consciousness.

With every new web page or image that he found, the level of frustration increased tenfold. Colby could see every curve and swirl of the ruins just out of focus in his mind. They meant something to him, he could feel it deep within, but the answers would not come out of the shadows in his mind. It was as though something was holding them back. In a final moment of pent-up anger,

Colby picked up his tablet and prepared to hurl it at the computer screen when he saw the tendrils of blue forming around his free hand.

Strands of energy licked at his fingers and danced upon his skin. The light they emitted began to grow as the very symbols Colby had been searching for appeared along the edges of the energy lines. He could see them clearly, and they were unmistakable. As he stared at the power emanating from his hand, he saw the barest of a glimpse into the depths of that power. As he took in the sight, he began to rotate his hand and gaze upon the back when the lights in the room began to fade as though the energy was being drained away.

The walls and furniture were melting into nothingness as they became replaced by outlines bathed in the blue and red hues of his power. The symbols surrounded him, and he turned in circles to look at what he realized he was causing.

Only one thought interrupted his wonderment. "How?"

Colby turned back to his hand and saw himself staring back. Nothing as simple as a reflection could describe what he witnessed, he was gazing upon himself, seeing who he really was. The realization began to stir emotions and confusion, and as the feelings blended, the power became erratic. The room began to return to focus and then fade again as Colby spun around to see a blue-faced little man with bulging yellow eyes hovering before him.

"Put that away before you hurt yourself," the creature said, his long white eyebrows furrowed, and long wispy white hair frizzed from the static-charged air. "I said, stop." The creature took Colby's hand in a firm grip.

Colby abruptly let go of the power that sent his tablet and the creature sailing across the room in opposite directions. Colby hit the floor as his body relaxed and slid off the edge of the bed. His eyes fluttered and closed. Complete darkness sent him into a deep slumber while the light glow remaining on his hands faded to nothing.

***

* * *

The crud on his lashes required more assistance than usual to free Colby's eyelids in the morning. Once he opened his eyes to the bright rays of light entering his room through the open drapes, Colby stretched and yawned before gathering the covers tightly around himself and screeching like a prepubescent girl.

"Well, there is something you don't hear every day. Want to try that again, young man, I don't think the dogs in the next county heard you the first time." Fizzlewink stared at Colby and blinked just once before reaching out to hand him a stick of licorice and pointed to a bottle of sports drink on the bedside table. "Eat this and drink that vile juice to replace your electrolytes."

"Say what?" Colby eventually managed as he gathered his wits.

Fizzlewink softened his features into a slight smile and raised his right bushy white brow. "Ah, the boy child has found his tongue. Eat this licorice and drink that," he repeated and pointed again at the orange drink on the table. "The licorice seems to help. I think it has something to do with the anise." Fizzlewink jumped down from the bed and took the chair at Colby's desk.

Colby could not believe what he was seeing. He took up the licorice and began to chew as he came to terms with the fact he saw a three-foot-tall, blue-skinned wrinkly creature with white hair and long wispy eyebrows. The odd animal spoke. He hadn't been dreaming last night after all.

"What are you?"

Trying his best to look insulted, Fizzlewink puffed his chest and tilted his head back to look fully affronted. "I, young man, am a Nefsmari."

"What is a Nefsmari?" Colby asked. He somehow felt increasing comfort with the proximity of this strange little blue man.

Now Fizzlewink was getting perturbed. "A Nefsmari is what I am; it means 'Spirit Teacher' in a modern tongue. In other ancient times, some of my kind were referred to as muses."

* * *

Colby began to relax and sat up to sip the sports drink. "Where did you come from? I mean, have you always been around? Why are you in my room? What-"

"One question at a time please," Fizzlewink said, holding up his hands. "Some questions are more simple than others to answer and take more time than we have at present. I will answer that I have been 'around' for a very long time, but as it pertains to you, I have been close to you since you were about six years of age. As for why I am in your room, your Nana sent me to wake you for breakfast and see you off to your punishment."

Colby was confused. "What punishment?"

"It is Saturday, my boy, and you have a detention to attend, I believe. You have slept two days since your little display of prowess with the Emassa." Fizzlewink handed Colby his pants and shirt from the floor.

"The what?" he asked as he began to dress in frantic movements.

Fizzlewink sighed and headed for the door. "Emassa, it is the hidden energy that enables all things that are explained as magic."

"But I have no-"

"Magic?" Fizzlewink said. "I assure you that is not correct. Your magic has just been hobbled for the last decade. Now it has awoken, and not just for you, but all magic users."

"What are you talking about? How could my getting magic have anything to do with anyone else?"

Fizzlewink shook his head. "That's a long story. Suffice it to say, your magic has awoken, and now things are going to get interesting."

Colby studied the odd creature, walking around him and poking at him with his finger to prove it was real.

* * *

Fizzlewink slapped away Colby's finger. "Do you mind? I am not some melon in the market that you check for freshness."

Colby held his retreated finger with his other hand, holding it close to his chest and pulled back from the blue man. "Sorry."

Colby suddenly realized that the cat was gone. Looking at the door still being closed, he began searching under his bed and in his closet for the animal. "Have you seen my cat?"

Rolling his eyes, Fizzlewink spun himself around on Colby's desk chair as he followed the path of his young charge. "I have."

Colby turned to the blue man. "Where is he?" Colby watched as Fizzlewink motioned his hands toward himself and lowered them along his sides. Colby's eyes grew wide, threatening to pop from their sockets. "You ate him?"

Another roll of his eyes and heavy sigh, Fizzlewink was getting even more frustrated. "I am the cat, boy. Really? Are you that dim, or did you hit your head?"

Colby sat heavily on the edge of his bed, collecting the tilt-a-whirl of thoughts spinning uncontrollably in his mind. He looked again under his bed and back at the little blue man than at his hands. "Did I turn you into that?" he said, pointing at Fizzlewink.

"Oh, for Emassa's sake. Listen, boy. I am the cat; the cat is me. You did not turn your poor handsome cat into the vertically challenged yet equally handsome being before you. You simply unlocked the power within yourself to finally see me as I am." Fizzlewink extended his arms to his sides and tilted his head in a slight bow. "I am Fizzlewink, at your service, young wizard."

Colby blinked at Fizzlewink for several moments as he collected his thoughts. When he finally spoke, he again peppered the blue man with questions. "Why are you here? Are there others like you? Have you always been trapped inside the cat? Did you cause the runes to tingle? When-"

Fizzlewink raised his hand to stop Colby's questions. "I am here to guide you. Yes, there are others, but that is another matter. I choose to appear as a cat, not be trapped inside one. At least not at first."

The blue man jumped down from his chair and approached Colby, who sat back and inched his way farther onto the bed and away from the approaching creature. "Oh, settle down. I'm not going to bite you. I haven't done that since you were a child." Fizzlewink grinned and showed his feline-like teeth. "Now, tell me what you mean about the runes."

Colby hesitantly told Fizzlewink about his dreams of runes and then a sudden affinity with them, though he did not truly understand them. He also replayed the events in the park playing runes, then again in the school tournament explaining how he felt something while touching certain runes, sensing that they should be played at particular points in the match.

"It was as though someone was guiding me." Colby looked at the cat with the hope of an explanation. "You said you were my guide, was it you doing that?"

Fizzlewink held his chin with one hand while he twirled one of his elongated eyebrows between his finger and thumb of the other hand. "I played no part in that as I was not there." Fizzlewink thought for a moment. "The old man you played, perhaps it was him? Or it could be part of your awakening."

"How could I tell?"

"As I said before, there are others. Perhaps it is worth me taking a stroll through the park to find this old man and investigate the matter for myself." Fizzlewink's eyes narrowed as he turned away and spoke softly to himself. "I'd be interested to know who would be interfering."

He walked out the now open door and disappeared from Colby's view.

"But you were at the school…in the basement?" Colby got up from his bed to follow Fizzlewink. The cat-man was already on his way downstairs. "Oh, crap, wait. You're gonna scare the crap outta my Nana."

Chapter 12

Colby chased after the strange blue man and found only the haggard blue cat awaiting him in the hall. "Fizzlewink?" A half-assed meow answered him as the cat turned for the stairs and led him to the kitchen where Nana was attempting to prepare toast and eggs.

"Good morning Fart-blossom, how are you feeling?" Nana asked, setting a plate of rubbery eggs that would have been sunny side up if the sun was black and looked like a Picasso. "I wouldn't have bothered you except I think you would rather not have detention next weekend as well. Besides, old Fizzlewink said it would be safe to wake you today."

"Fizzlewink, the cat you mean?" Colby asked as he watched the Russian Blue preening in the corner. "You spoke with him?"

Nana giggled and turned to collect a plate of fish from the counter and took it over to the cat. "Of course, I speak to him, don't you?"

Colby did not answer, but instead shoveled the contents of his plate into his mouth and forced it down with a glass of milk. He was beginning to think he was losing his marbles. Of course, cats can't talk.

"Mind you, it is much easier to understand him, now that he is meowing in English." Nana patted Fizzlewink on the head as he began to meow.

"She only sees me as a cat, Colby, at least for now. Better get off to school, young man. We can talk more when you return home later." Fizzlewink left the kitchen as Shelly clomped her way into the room.

"Ah, the cheese curd rises," Shelly said. "If you had slept any longer, you would have become aged cheddar."

"That would not be any gouda," Gary answered as he walked in the back door. "Good to see you will be joining me, wouldn't wanna suffer Jasper alone today."

Colby kissed his Nana goodbye and grabbed his lunch as he and Gary left the house and headed for the bus. Still unsure what he experienced earlier, he did not share his morning with Gary. He explained that he was sick with some strain of the flu but was feeling much better. Their ride to school was filled with normal conversation and the commiseration of spending an entire day locked up in the computer lab with Jasper Bodine. Colby was grateful his friend decided to refrain from mentioning the tournament.

***

Colby and Gary made it to school just in time to witness a large black limousine pull away. There, standing on the sidewalk, was none other than Jasper Bodine. Colby and Gary looked at each other, sharing a thought and how obnoxious it seemed, Jasper getting dropped off at school by a limo. Everybody knew that

Jasper had his own car, perhaps he was grounded from using it.

Jasper looked at Colby and Gary and huffed. "Hey there, girls, or should I say hens." He walked off, clucking like a chicken.

Colby turned to Gary. "Sorry for that. I don't know why I let him get to me like that the other day."

"Don't worry about it. The officials ranked us second place, and they reserved the right to call for a rematch."

"Seriously?" Colby said.

"Serial… I mean, isn't that just cray-cray?" Gary enjoyed making fun of the way some girls in school talked.

Colby just rolled his eyes. He and Gary waited for Jasper to enter the school before they approached, they didn't wish to have any further confrontation started this early in the day. Once they finally entered the school, the two boys made their way to the computer lab.

It would seem this is now a new favorite punishment by the Dean as there were at least five other kids in the lab waiting to fulfill their sentence. The biggest surprise, however, was that the Dean himself was not there to oversee the detention. The man sitting behind the desk was the professor, Rigel Stark. Colby forgot that Rigel mentioned he would be monitoring Saturday detention this week.

"Good morning, boys," Professor Stark said to Colby and Gary. "Would you please have a seat in the front row." The professor pulled out a clipboard and took attendance, making sure that all of the students were present. "All present and accounted for, so let's begin the day shall we."

Jasper sighed and sat back in his seat. "What exactly are we supposed to be doing here today?"

* * *

"Well, young man, if you take a moment to close your mouth and open your ears, I will get to that," said Rigel. "It would seem that I have been granted the use of your skills today as my research assistants. You will each find a sheet of paper in front of you that you will use to search out documents on the Internet. Each document must fit the criteria of each line on your list, and you will bookmark them so that at the end of the day, you will print them and return them to me."

"Grunt work," Jasper said. "Don't you have a secretary or something?"

"Actually young man, today I have several of them, so less talk, and more work. We will take a break in two hours."

After many grumbles and groans, the students took their papers and began their work scouring the Internet for information pointed out on their lists. Colby took a few minutes to look around and see what other students were unfortunate enough to be assigned his same fate rather than enjoying a warm sunny summer Saturday. Seated just behind him was the schools' head pom-pom girl Darla. To her left was a foreign transfer student from India, Rhea. Directly behind them was Jasper Bodine.

Gary turned in his seat to look at the pom-pom girl. "Hey, Darla, what are you in for?"

Darla rolled her eyes and answered without looking up from the keyboard as she pecked the keys with one finger. "I got caught putting liquid Ex-Lax in the coffee machine of the teachers' lounge."

Gary laughed. "Seriously? That is some funny sh-"

"Quiet down and get to work, Mr. Connors," Rigel said, hiding a grin. He heard the exchange between the two students and was glad that he thought to bring his coffee in the morning.

The students quickly settled into their assigned tasks and scoured the web for any information that matched the obscure lists the Professor gave to them. During the first break, more than one of them complained that they were having no luck finding anything that matched what he was expecting of them.

"I can find plenty of stuff on ancient cultures and lost civilizations, but nothing that includes a link between each and none with written proof or verifiable existence," Darla complained. "I mean 'hello' …they are lost."

"I know what you mean, Darla," Rhea said. "We have many myths in my country of ancient and lost histories, but I am thinking that these things we search for are very interesting. I never heard of Nibiru before, and the reading is quite…"

"Quite what, Rhea?" Colby asked. He was suddenly on edge about the lists of material the Professor required of them to search. "Rhea?" Colby looked at the girl as she stared at the computer screen before her. Rhea looked as though she was looking directly past the screen, or looking through it.

Colby suddenly became aware of the stop in chatter among the other kids in the room. He looked to the front of the lab to find that the Professor had not returned to the room from his break. Looking back at the others, he watched while they began to lose the color from their faces. The light from their computers flashed across their features, casting patterns across their skin. He turned to look at his screen, already sensing what he would discover. The blue screen of death and in the center was his mysterious symbol.

Fearing he might become nauseous and pass out, Colby looked away from the screen and back at his peers. "Look away from the screen," he shouted at them.

He pulled on Gary's arm, trying to get his friend to snap out of the trance he appeared to be caught in. Colby reached out and flipped the switch on the monitor in front of Gary, but it didn't turn off. He reached down and pulled the power cord from the outlet below the desk, and still, the computer screen displayed the dancing slurry of symbols that kept the others entranced.

Darla was the first to begin shaking with the first signs of convulsions. Then Rhea presented with foam forming at the corners of her mouth while her eyes began to roll back.

* * *

Colby had to do something. He shouted for the Professor but received no response. The hallways were deserted. Colby was alone to help his friends and Jasper. Without thinking, Colby reached out for the nearest computer and was preparing to grab it and throw it to the floor when the blue and red ribbons of energy began to coalesce around his hands. The symbols from the screen leaped out toward his hands, and he backed away from the screen and shouted.

"Stop," he yelled, and the tendrils of energy sped from his fingers and surged into the computers, causing them to reboot. Colby backed away as the lights around his hands winked out in that instant. "What the hell was that?"

"I beg your pardon," the professor asked from the doorway. "What is going on in here?" Rigel stepped into the room and found the students sitting forward in their seats, coming out of some dazed state.

Colby was uncertain what to say, so he lied. "Some sort of short in the wires or something Professor Stark. I was getting a…I needed to sharpen my pencil, and when I turned back, I saw everyone get shocked, and then the computers rebooted or something." Colby sidestepped Rigel as he took his seat to find that indeed, the computers were sitting at a recovery window after an improper shutdown.

Rigel seemed to take Colby's explanation at face value. "Sounds dreadful, are you young folks alright?" Once he was satisfied that everyone was well and not in need of any medical attention, he dismissed the kids early. "That is to say, I have no problem with you leaving early, but your Dean may wish you to make up the time at a later date. If he were to find out, I let you go early, that is." He winked at the students.

"I'll take my chances," Colby mumbled to Gary's agreement. Neither of them wished to spend any more time in the proximity of Jasper. They started their walk back toward the bus stop when Darla and Rhea stepped up to join them.

"Hey guys, we were just thinking that maybe since we have the rest of the afternoon, some pizza sounds good," Darla said as she batted her lashes at

Colby. "Care to join us?"

Colby was not under any delusion that Darla was interested in anything other than someone buying her lunch, but that did not stop his mouth from shooting off before his brain was loaded. "That sounds great." He grabbed Gary's jacket and pushed him along as they escorted the two girls to the nearby diner. He wanted to find out what Darla was after and wondered if she had magic that she used to compel people.

"What do you think her power is?" Colby asked Gary as he guided him along behind the girls.

Gary stopped and looked at Colby wide-eyed.

Colby laughed and pulled his friend along. "You know, we all come from magic families, there has to be some innate gift." Colby glanced at his friend sideways, beginning to suspect there was more truth to his friend's earlier joke about having a gift. "I think she tries to hypnotize people into doing what she wants."

Gary laughed nervously. "You mean like the force or something?"

"Yeah. Like she looks at you and says, 'You will buy me lunch, and perfume, and drool over me', then bats her lashes and whammy you're her slave." Colby laughed, but he glanced back at Darla as she fluttered her eyes back over her shoulder while they walked.

"Your Jedi mind tricks won't work on me," he said to himself but smiled back at her with a wide fake grin.

Colby turned to Gary as they walked behind the girls. "My magic came back the other night."

Gary stopped walking. "Like the other night, when the electricity went out all over the neighborhood?"

Colby frowned. "Fizzlewink didn't mention that."

* * *

"Your cat? Are you still sick?"

"Dude I wasn't sick. I was wiped out from the magic returning. Fizzlewink, he's not a cat, by the way, he told me that was why I was sleeping for three days. He also said magic was waking for everyone."

Gary stood there for several seconds before laughing. "Dude, you are seriously weird. I saw your cat this morning. He was just a cat."

Colby shrugged. "Fizz said that Nana couldn't see his true form yet either. Maybe we need to do a spell or something."

"Are you guys coming or what?" Darla said. "Come on."

"Let's catch up to them," Gary said. "We can talk about your magic cat later."

Chapter 13

Buena Diner was the local hangout for students of Escutcheon Academy, Colby's school. The cool kids mostly hung out there. Colby only ever stopped in to pick up a to-go order or when his sister took him there for birthday breakfast. This time, however, how he found himself ready to dine with the most popular girl in school and her friend Rhea.

The girls pointed toward a booth near the window when they entered and took the menus a server provided while telling them to seat themselves. Colby didn't care where he sat, so he let the girls choose, and the booth by the window afforded the best possible view, according to Darla. And what Darla wanted, Colby was more than happy to go along with…for now.

* * *

After they had given their orders to the server, Darla scooted closer to Colby. "I hear that you're the President of the new Archeology Club," she said. "Rhea and I were thinking of joining, would that be okay with you Colby?"

Colby couldn't understand why Darla felt she had to ask his permission to join. "I don't see why not. It's an open club, and I was only appointed as President since I was the first to say I had any interest."

"That may be, but as the rules of all clubs in the school handbook state, all members must submit official requests before being reviewed by the standing board of any school-sanctioned clubs." Darla looked at Colby and batted her lashes again. "So, since you are the only one currently on the board of the club, I am requesting your review and acceptance." Darla jolted from a kick under the table. "Oh, and Rhea as well."

Deflated but expecting the ulterior motive, Colby realized now why Darla was paying him any attention. "I suppose that would be ok. The first meeting is this upcoming Thursday."

Darla gave Colby a quick and meaningless peck on the cheek and scooted back away from him. "Totes amaze-balls," she said and began whispering with Rhea.

Colby leaned in close to Gary. "What do you suppose they are whispering about?" Colby said.

Gary looked at the girls and then responded from the corner of his mouth. "Silly girl stuff."

Colby was not convinced. He somehow felt that they were conspiring something; he just didn't know what or for what purpose. Darla had never paid Colby much attention, at least not after the schools merged. Before then, they had been friends.

On Colby's seventh birthday, he enjoyed one of the rare occasions when his mother would rise out of her depressed funk. She threw him a birthday party and invited all the kids from his class at school. Before the merger of the two schools, class sizes were smaller, so the ten or so kids at the house were manageable. Even Jasper Bodine was there.

He remembered fondly the day all his classmates joined him at his home. They spent the day playing games, eating candy, cake, and other sweets and junk food. It was one of his best memories that he held onto so tightly it hurt to think of how far apart the friendships became.

As he remembered the day, Colby glanced over at Darla, remembering how they chased each other around the billiards table in the basement and when she finally caught him, Colby pulled her close and kissed her. They both giggled and dashed away in different directions, neither understanding what possessed them to kiss. Colby wondered at Darla, does she even know what she is doing, that she has been doing since then?

Colby snapped back to the present as he felt a push and recognized the scent of Opium perfume.

Shelly put the pizza in the center of the table and squinted at her little brother. "Hey, space cadet, you coming in for a landing or what?"

Colby sneered up at Shelly. "Haha. Thank you, Miss." He dismissed his sister and took up Darla's plate to serve her a slice of pizza. He wasn't doing so after being coerced by her lovely eyes or any hocus-pocus; he simply used the manners he was taught. He elbowed Gary into action to do the same for Rhea.

The four of them sat and talked of earlier days in school before the merger with the other academy once Colby reminded Darla of the party at his house. Rhea and Gary sat listening for the most part since Gary only started at the school a few years back, and Rhea was a recent transfer student. They didn't mind, and Gary enjoyed seeing Colby loosen up and let go of his tension for a change. That did not last.

No sooner were the four enjoying their pizza when Jasper walked into the diner with his group of idiot friends. He started for the counter when he stopped while passing the booth and turned to face Darla. "What are you doing here, and with those two dorks?"

"Jasper, why don't you go piss off?" Colby said in a moment of unexpected bravery.

Jasper turned to Colby, red-faced and seething. "What did you say, cheese-poof?"

Now it was Darla's turn to step in. She got up from the booth and stood directly in front of Jasper, looking up his nose. "Jasper, why is it you think you own everything in this town? Nobody here was bothering you, or even paying any attention to you for that matter." Darla began jabbing Jasper in the chest with her finger as they backed away from the booth. "Is that your problem? You didn't get enough attention as a baby or even now? Does your daddy ignore you, so that's why you take it out on everyone else?"

Jasper started backing away with every word Darla spat at him. She hit a nerve and was dancing all over it. He began to lift his hand as if to strike out at Darla but was stopped by a much stronger hand from behind.

Jasper swung around to face Bruce and Shelly.

"I think it is time for you to leave Jasper," Bruce said. He pushed a bag of food toward Jasper's chest and released his wrist. "Take this and get out."

Shelly pushed up to Jasper and glared down at him while she snarled. "No one messes with my baby brother but me. Got it, ass-hat? Now twirl and dash?" She spun her finger and pointed to the door.

Jasper took the food and headed for the door. "You'll be sorry for this," he said to Shelly before turning back to Colby's table. "You will all be sorry." Then he stormed for the door with his posse on his heels.

"And pull up your pants fool, don't nobody wanna see your skids," Gary added after Jasper was on the other side of the door. "Thinkin' he's some kind of thug, a rich little white boy."

* * *

Colby, pomegranate red from anger and embarrassment, relaxed and finally took in a breath. Only then had he noticed the diminishing glow of blue light fading around his hand. He moved his hand under the table so no one could see. When Darla looked at him oddly, he smiled. "Well, that was fun, eh?" He picked up a piece of pizza and shoved it into his mouth.

"I just don't get him anymore," Darla said as she sat back down. "He used to be so sweet when we were in junior high."

Gary laughed and spat crumbs from his mouth. "Jasper Bodine? Sweet? What parallel universe or wormhole did you fall through?"

Darla and Rhea smiled, but Colby turned ash-faced. "That was something, huh?" Colby said. Though he was calming down, and the tendrils of blue light had dispersed, he was still anxious. "Where did you learn to read someone like that?"

"Ya, Colby's Nana is a gypsy fortune telling witch or something, and I bet she couldn't read Jasper's beads as well as that?" Gary added much to Colby's horror.

That perked up the girls. Darla just waved off the compliment. "I have psych classes, and I've known Jasper for a long time. We were keen on each other in elementary, up until his mother passed away. That's when he changed. His father took him out of school and placed him in that 'other' academy only to return two years later when they merged with Escutcheon."

Rhea finally spoke up and leaned toward Colby. "Tell us more about your Nana. In my country, we revere those who are touched with the gift of foresight."

Colby swallowed and looked at Rhea then Darla. 'What were these girls up to?' he wondered. "She's an old woman who liked to tell stories to scare us, so we'd go to sleep."

"How does scaring a kid make them go to sleep?" Darla asked.

"Exactly," said Colby. "She used to tell us she was a witch, and we came from a family of witches, gypsies, and vampires." Colby paused and saw the look of wonder on their faces. "All nonsense, of course. There's no such thing as vampires."

The girls wanted to hear more though Colby was trying his best to drop the subject. Colby forced a laugh. "Just a loony old woman who likes to tell stories. She used to tell us she had a spell that would turn us into frogs if we didn't go to sleep." Colby tried to think of something else to talk about, but it was Bruce who interrupted.

"Hey, Colby, your mom just called in an order. I told her you were here with friends so you could take it home when you go, eh?" Bruce seemed to sense that Colby was nervous and gave him a wink. "You just let me know when you're headed out, and I'll have it all ready for you."

"Thanks, Bruce," Colby said and relaxed his tense shoulders. "I think we've had enough excitement for one afternoon. Can it be ready in fifteen or so?"

"You got it, kiddo," Bruce said and went back to the kitchen.

Darla seemed somewhat surprised that Colby was preparing to leave. "Are you sure you have to go so soon? I was hoping to get a small cake or something. I know you just had a birthday."

Colby was delighted to hear that Darla knew he had a birthday, but wondered at her motivation. She obviously only suggested having lunch so she could sweet-talk him into letting her join the archeology club. Though she did stick up for him when Jasper showed up, and now she wanted to get him a birthday cake. He was more confused than ever. "Thanks, that's nice, but I'm not much for sweets, and I should probably get that food home for my mom."

Gary started to say something when Colby kicked him under the table. Before Gary could protest, he noticed something outside the window next to their booth. "Hey, isn't that your cat? Still just a cat, I see."

Colby turned toward the window to see none other than Fizzlewink, the gruff and mangy old Russian Blue cat. "What the…" Colby got up from the booth and stepped out to see what the cat was doing there. "What are you doing here?" Colby said between his clenched teeth. "Go home."

The cat looked up at Colby and meowed, being a cat after all. Fizzlewink continued staring while Colby continued to tell him to go.

Inside the diner, Gary and the two girls watched as Colby stood outside, talking to a cat.

"Does he always talk to his cat?" Darla asked, squinting at the strange feline. "Has that cat got white eyebrows?"

"Perhaps he is touched just as his grandmamma is?" Rhea leaned in to see with interest. "I can't see any eyebrows on the cat, but he has oddly large eyes."

Gary grunted and turned back from the scene playing outside. Not only did his best friend make an excuse to leave early from lunch with two lovely young ladies, now he was outside playing Doctor Dolittle. "Oh, he's touched, all right."

Chapter 14

Finally satisfied that Fizzlewink was on his way somewhere other than outside the diner, Colby went back inside to find his mom's order ready and the server bringing his booth their check. He quickly took the check from the table and paid the hostess.

"Did your cat leave?" Gary asked and glared.

Colby let the remark go and picked up the to-go order. "Sorry, I have to go so soon, but my mom will want this food." Colby turned to leave, then stopped and turned back. "See you in school Monday." Without awaiting a response, he left.

Gary sat silently in the booth while he looked at the girls and felt awkward. "So, you guys wanna take this leftover pizza home?"

Rhea smiled and pushed Darla to get up from the booth. "We should probably go as well. Thank you for your company and please thank Colby again for lunch."

As Rhea and Darla left, Gary stood watching them go and sighed. He was startled by the sudden smack on his shoulder.

"So, what was that all about?" Shelly asked. "You boys on a double date or something?"

"Or something?" Gary admitted. "I don't know what has come over, Colby, but I'm gonna find out."

Shelly watched Gary leave and run to catch up with Colby. "You do that."

Colby made his way to the bus stop, relieved to be away from that mounting discomfort of the diner. When he thought he was in the clear, he saw a little blue man who sat waiting on the bench. Colby approached and did his best to ignore his imaginary pest.

"What happened in the diner, Colby," Fizzlewink asked. He noticed that Colby was attempting to ignore him. "I assure you that I am quite real, my boy, so ignoring me will prove useless."

Colby turned to the wrinkled blue prune of a creature and snapped. "What do you want from me? I can't even have lunch with my friends without trouble following me around." Colby huffed and sat next to Fizzlewink on the bench. He put his head in his hands and sighed deeper. "Why is this happening?"

Fizzlewink waited several moments before responding. "What exactly happened in there?"

Colby told the tale of the afternoon from the moment the blue screen of death appeared, then lunch and up to the point where Fizzlewink popped up in the window. "Why were you even there? Don't you have some mice to chase or something?"

"You used your gift," Fizzlewink said. "It's like a beacon to those who know it, and if I sensed it, others would have as well."

"What do you mean when you say 'others'? What are these others?" Colby was confused and upset. Those two emotions combined to become an irritation that quickly headed toward anger. His emotions were reeling, and that was his trigger. His hands began to get warm and tingly as the blue tendrils started to lash out from his fingers. The only thing that distracted him was the sound of Gary shouting from down the street. "Go away, Fizzlewink. I don't need Gary seeing you."

Fizzlewink grunted and folded his arms. "He can't see me yet, Colby. Only my own kind and those with the gift can see me as anything other than a cat. And that is only when I choose to be seen."

Colby turned to argue and faced the cat. "You are driving me crazy, or I am already prepared for the booby hatch."

"Are you talking to that mangy cat or me?" Gary asked as he caught his breath from running to catch up. "What is he even doing here?"

"He is following me like a dog, I think," Colby said.

Fizzlewink growled and swatted Colby before backing down and trotting off toward home.

"Guess he doesn't like being compared to a dog," Colby said and smiled. "Want to hang out and play some video games or something?" he asked Gary.

Gary nodded but kept looking at Colby, waiting.

"What?" Colby asked.

* * *

"I noticed you said there was no such thing as vampires," Gary said.

"And?"

"You didn't say anything about witches."

"I wouldn't call us witches, Gary. Magical discussions have been very limited in my house since I had no magic, and with dad being gone and all…anyway, let's go home. I want to work on my hashtag operating system."

"Your what?"

"I want to expand the functions of my runes app to be like a conduit for magic. Like a magic wand, but not."

"So, you really do have your magic?"

"That's what Fizz says. But I can't control it. Maybe with the help of an app, I can."

Gary said nothing. He just turned away and started walking faster. "Come on; I'll race you home."

When Colby and Gary arrived back home, they found Fizzlewink waiting to greet them. He was sitting atop a parcel left on the front porch.

Colby grumbled under his breath and shooed the freaky little furball away. He lifted the box and saw that it was addressed to him, but there was no return label. He stuck the box under his arm and opened the door. Inside, his mother waited, smiling.

Colby's Nana met them at the door and took the food then led the boys to the kitchen. "What is that package you have there, Colby?" she asked in passing.

Colby set the box down on the kitchen island and looked at it with interest. "It is addressed to me, but I didn't order anything, and there is no return address."

* * *

Nana waddled up to the island. "Well, open it, my boy. Let's have a look."

Colby glanced at his grandmother suspiciously but opened the box quickly. He enjoyed presents and surprises as far back as he could remember. As he began to open the package by first ripping off the brown paper, he flashed back to a much younger time and saw through his six-year-old eyes. A large oblong box appeared before him with a picture of a wooden train printed on the top. Colby shook the images from his mind and returned to the present.

"It's a new tablet," Colby said. He looked at his mother and then at Nana, wondering if they were responsible for this gift, he realized at that moment. He told no one about his recent episode that resulted in his old tablet getting destroyed when it sailed across his room. The many pieces were well on their way to a landfill. He was not going to question a free tablet, so he opened the box and pulled out the latest and greatest model of tablet.

"What OS version is on it," Gary asked, knowing it would not matter. Colby was bound to put his own tweaks on it.

"Doesn't matter, I'll put my own on it," Colby replied. "It's nearly finished."

He loved hacking into his devices to alter their functions and capabilities. Ever since he was little, he would often be found taking things apart to find out how they worked. He managed to put them back together without leftover bits, and they usually functioned much better afterward. Remembering his fondness for rebuilding things, Colby remembered a time when he rebuilt his mother's vacuum cleaner. "Remember when I rebuilt the vacuum, mom?"

"Oh, dear yes," Aria answered. "You always did have to see what made things tick. I had forgotten about that." Aria's smile faded to a look of confusion. How could she have forgotten something so endearing?

Nana laughed loudly and pointed to Fizzlewink. "I bet that old cat remembers as well." She grabbed her sides in laughter. "He never allowed your sister to vacuum his fur again after that episode. His tail was sucked right up that tube, and he took off toward the door with the vacuum rolling right behind him. It was like to suck the crap right out his backside if he hadn't reached the end of the cord and unplugged it."

"Well, at least I didn't try to turn the poor cat into an art project," Shelly added when she entered the kitchen. She opened the top Styrofoam container to sniff at the contents. Grabbing a fried mushroom, she continued. "You covered that cat from head to toe in Elmer's glue."

Aria started laughing again as her eyes brightened at the memory. "I caught you just in time. You had a large tube of silver glitter ready to turn him into a disco ball." Aria looked at the cocktail that she just mixed and decided to pour it into the drain. "I thought about trying to wash that glue out of Fizzlewink's fur, but the idea of trying to bathe a fifteen-pound tomcat… suffice it to say it was days of listening to the odd mew here and there as that poor cat pulled the dried glue-balls free."

Colby and Shelly shared a glance as they both watched their mother pour out a cocktail, something they had never seen since she began drinking after their father disappeared.

"He still has patches of thin fur on his old body," Gary snorted and pointed at the glaring cat in the corner.

Colby caught the look of embarrassment coming from the face of a cat. He mouthed the words 'sorry' to his friend only to watch him turn around and flip his tail then lay down.

"Oh, I haven't laughed like that in a long time," Aria said. "I haven't been involved enough, but that is going to change, I promise."

Colby smiled and hugged his mother.

"So what is going on in school today? You had some kind of Saturday classes?" Aria either did not remember, or Nana did not share the fact that Colby received detention.

* * *

Colby looked at Gary with closed lips. "We had a computer lab with a new adjunct professor. He started an Archeology Club, and I was assigned to be its President."

Aria turned away and tilted her head as she looked at the blue cat in the corner. She saw his big yellow eyes and a tuft of white fur on the top of his head. She shook the image away and lost her smile again while proceeding to remake her cocktail. "What on earth made you decide to join such a club? You don't want to be a relic hunter now, do you?"

Nana started to speak, but a quick look at her daughter interrupted her otherwise wagging tongue.

"I can't explain it, but for some reason, when the Professor spoke to our class, I just connected with the idea of discovering ancient secrets and rummaging around old ruins." Colby explained how he was not even paying much mind and then suddenly felt the need to join the club. "Since I was first to join, Professor Stark appointed me the club President."

Aria took a long drink of her martini. "Well, I will not prevent you from joining any clubs as long as they don't interfere with your studies, but I just don't see you digging around in the dirt for a living." She stared at the watch on Colby's wrist and began to sniffle. She returned to the counter and made another martini.

Colby witnessed his mother's reaction to his wearing his father's watch and promptly removed it, placing it in his pocket. He felt himself cringe for making his mother upset.

Shelly saw the exchange and attempted to relieve the tension. "Of course he could, he used to play in that pile of fertilizer the neighbors had out on their parkway one summer," Shelly offered. "Couldn't keep the little stinker out of the stuff."

Aria was not amused. "I just want it clear that if this 'Club' affects your grades, then I will have to insist you give it up."

* * *

Colby did not understand his mother's aggravation at his being in the Archeology Club. Normally she remained blissfully unaware of what he was doing. The fact that she so quickly turned back to the drink after promising to be more involved was another concern.

Colby turned to Nana. "I suppose now wouldn't be the best time to tell mom I got my powers back?"

Nana burst out in screams and grabbed Colby. She spun him around and hugged him, smothering him in her rather large and sagging breasts.

Colby pushed Nana away so he could breathe. He held a finger to his lips and glanced at his mother, who.

"She's too concerned with her martini to pay us any mind. Fizzlewink told me about your magic awakening. I was just waiting for you to tell me."

"Tell you what," Shelly asked.

Nana shushed her. "We'll talk about it later when Betty Ford over there is taking a vodka nap."

"Well, maybe I should be heading home," Gary said, feeling the swift change in the atmosphere of the crowded kitchen.

Nana pushed the tension aside and picked up the paper from Colby's parcel. "Nonsense young man. I should have mentioned sooner that your parents called to see if you might be able to stay here this weekend. It seems your parents decided last minute to go on a romantic getaway."

"Gross..." Gary and Colby said at once.

Nana just laughed as she folded the paper from the parcel and shoved it in a cabinet drawer already overstuffed with scraps of wrapping. "Anyway, they will drop off some clothes and such on their way past. So you will be our guest now through Monday morning and leave for school from here."

Gary and Colby smiled and ran from the kitchen. They could work on the hashtag magic application all weekend.

"Be back down for dinner at five," Nana shouted. She looked at her daughter sitting at the kitchen table, drinking a fourth martini, and staring at the cat as it followed the boys out. Nana wiped her hands on her apron and waddled over to the table. "You need to snap out of it, child of mine." She grabbed the drink from her daughter's hand. "Sober up. We need to have a chat."

"Don't waste that booze," Aria complained.

Nana downed the cocktail in a single gulp. "Wouldn't dream of it."

Chapter 15

It was still a few hours before dinner, and with the excitement at the Diner, neither Colby nor Gary ate much pizza. Colby left Gary playing on his new tablet and went downstairs for some snacks. The kitchen was empty, which was odd since Nana usually camped out in there the entire day. He went to the fridge and grabbed a couple of sodas, and popped some pizza rolls in the microwave. While he waited, he looked out the window of the back door to see his Nana and mother having a rather animated discussion. As he tried to make out what they were saying, Fizzlewink came running into the kitchen.

"Colby, you better get back up there," the little blue man said.

Colby could see the urgency in his little blue friend's yellow eyes and went running after Fizzlewink as he bounded back up the stairs. When he reached the doorway, Colby immediately knew what was happening. He could feel strange energy now that accompanied the blue screen of death. Colby reached out for his friend's arm since he knew that calling his name would do nothing. As his hand neared Gary's arm, the now-familiar tendrils of blue energy formed around his hand. When Colby made contact, he shook and shared the convulsive fit that rocked through Gary's body.

Gary dropped the tablet on the bed as its screen went blank. His convulsions ceased, and his breathing returned to normal as he began to open his eyes. "What happened?" he said as he watched Colby pick up the tablet and power it off.

Colby looked for Fizzlewink, but the cat-man was not there. Turning to Gary, he looked at his friend's eyes and asked, "what do you remember?" Gary's pupils were dilated.

Gary sat up and moved his neck around while rubbing his temples. "I was thumbing through the apps on your tablet when the screen hung and started to change…then I was surrounded by blue light and looking up at you, hovering over me like a dork." Gary turned to the doorway and froze.

Colby turned to see Fizzlewink coming back. "Where did you go off to?"

"Someone had to get the licorice," he said, handing Colby the black lengths of candy. The overpowering scent of anise filled the air.

"Where do you keep getting this stuff from?" Colby asked, taking it from Fizzlewink.

Fizzlewink just stared back without answering. Before he became pressed to answer, a sputtering noise broke the silence.

"Wha- What the hell is that?" Gary stuttered and pointed to Fizzlewink.

Colby and Fizzlewink looked from Gary to each other in surprise. And Colby looked back at Gary. "You can see him?"

Gary began inching back on the bed and away from Fizzlewink. "Would I be asking if I couldn't see that blue and white bag of wrinkles you're talking to?"

"I beg your pardon young man, are you judging a man by his color?" Fizzlewink teased.

"You are real, or Gary now has the same mental disorder I do," Colby said.

Fizzlewink rolled his bulbous yellow eyes and hopped up onto the bed next to Gary, much to his discomfort. "Of course I am, don't be a…what was it you called him a few moments ago?" he asked Gary.

"Dork," Gary said.

"Yes, don't be a dork," Fizzlewink said. "I think the bigger question is how this friend of yours can suddenly see me as anything other than a cat that has been glued, nearly glittered, and assaulted by a vacuum cleaner." Fizzlewink narrowed his eyes on Gary, who in vain tried to back away against the headboard.

Colby and Fizzlewink replayed the events over and over again, trying to understand what happened.

"Did I infect him or something, Fizz?" Colby asked.

Fizzlewink grumbled. "Don't be ridiculous. You can't 'infect' someone into seeing my kind. The only ones who can see my people are those who have the gift of what you call magic or sixth sense. And even then they have to be tuned to our presence." Fizzlewink thought for a moment before getting right up in Gary's face. "Has anyone in your family line ever claimed to be psychic?"

"Mom and dad always said we had special gifts, and one day mine would develop. I figured it would be bending forks or something."

"Is that what you meant when you said something about having a secret?" Colby asked.

"Yes, but this is more than even I expected. Helping send you signals during Runes matches is one thing, but this-"

"That was you?" Colby said. "I figured it was the old man, but then it couldn't have been unless he was also at the last tournament."

Gary puffed up with pride. "All me. My gift is influencing objects and electronics. I made them whisper to you."

"Huh? I only felt tingling. I didn't hear-"

Fizzlewink huffed his frustration. "Yes, yes…back on topic, please. What can your parents do?"

"I…I can't remember them saying," Gary said.

"Anyone else in the family show power?" Fizz said.

Gary sat back and thought. "I don't have any other family."

"Maybe you can check for more family on the spider web," Fizzlewink said.

"The world wide web you mean," Gary asked.

Fizzlewink frowned and glared back at Gary. "That's what I said. First things first, we need to see what exactly has been sparked in your system, my boy."

"Hold up," Gary interrupted. "Would one of you please explain to me just what the hell is happening." Gary was oddly calm considering the circumstances. He was zapped by his best friend and was conversing with him and a little blue man who apparently is also the family cat. "First you were a cat, now you're a what?"

Fizzlewink looked Gary up and down before turning back to Colby. "You gonna tell him, or should I?" Fizzlewink asked.

* * *

"I don't even know much myself," Colby admitted. "Why don't you just lay it out for us, Fizz."

Fizzlewink rolled his big yellow eyes and sat back. "Reader's Digest version, for now, I suppose."

Colby and Gary sat wide-eyed and enthralled by the condensed explanation that Fizzlewink gave them.

Fizzlewink explained that long ago, his kind was created by people who evolved earlier than modern man. They weren't much different from the neolithic peoples that existed. Except his people had magic and attempted to live separate from the tribes of man.

There were always chance encounters and those who could see them, considered them Gods or Demons, depending on the situation. As time passed, some intermingling of their race occurred, though it was frowned upon. "You see, my kind has certain 'abilities' that were unpredictable when passed on to a human." Fizzlewink looked at Colby.

"Are you saying I'm part Nefsmari?" Colby asked.

Fizzlewink shook his head. "No you are descended from Nefslama, the human-looking people who created my species." He held up his hand to stop questions and then continued to retell how as mankind progressed, his people began to withdraw and live secretly among man. "We decided we had meddled enough with the natural order, at least most of us believed this. Or so I'm told. I wasn't made until much later…but never mind that."

The Nefslama worked to blend in with humanity and attempted to live as normal a life they could. The problem, however, went beyond their abilities as they lived far too long to remain in one place. They moved to protect their secret and protect their families if they interbred.

A Nefslama would fake their death, using their abilities to appear to age as the years passed. Sometimes if they had help, they would seem to die naturally and have someone dig them up later if buried by accident. Usually, they would try to switch the body in the casket if possible. Many a grave robbing was simply a Nefslama assisting another in moving on to another disguised life. This method became abandoned over the years as there was always the chance of cremation by mistake or being placed in a grave without a coffin.

"So your people came back from the dead and dug themselves out. Is this where vampires and zombies come from?" Gary asked. "Then you roamed around living one lifetime then another, like gypsies."

Fizzlewink snorted. "I suppose you could see it that way, my boy. We are most to blame for many a myth or superstition. Zombies, walking dead, Elvis sightings, these are all originated from my people. But we are not the cause of vampires or demons and possession and such, that is the work of the Shizumu."

Fizzlewink narrowed his eyes and began to speak softly. "The Shizumu are among the 'others' I mentioned. They are the enemies of the Nefslama. Shizumu are not like corporeal creatures and live best by using humans as hosts."

"What happens to the humans?" Colby asked.

"Depends on the strength of the Shizumu and how long they stayed within the host," Fizzlewink said. "We call them Shizumu because it means Rider of Body and Soul though we have more colorful names for them as well. If a human is strong enough and the body snatcher does not stay too long, the human can recover."

Fizzlewink explained how this information is all theory as his people know very little about the Shizumu. Much of the information about them and their origin was taboo and not shared with his generation by the elders.

They do not know what they call themselves. There is no true measure of what is too long for a possession to last before damage begins. "We do know that in some cases, there has been a transfer of powers to the human host when a Shizumu has left the body. The left-behind power is partially where witches and warlocks come from in mythology. When someone has either Nefslama ancestry or blood once touched by Shizumu, they can become a carrier of what you call magic."

Colby went ashen after hearing all this information. The color drained from his face, and he began to stutter, something he had not done for many years until recently. "Wha, wha, what a… a… am I?"

Fizzlewink laughed and grabbed Colby by the shoulders. "You are something altogether new. I assure you, my boy, you are not a warlock." Fizzlewink paused. "At least I think not. Anyway, your father was Nefslama one hundred percent, but there may be more since none of my kind could wield the power you do even though it is by accident."

Colby regained some of his color, but more questions were forming behind his glazing eyes.

"Why am I just hearing about all this if it is a family thing. Did my parents know? Shelly? Nana?"

"Yes, but that's a long story, and you're not ready to hear it. Suffice it to say, there was a spell involved, and memories became muddled along with magic being weakened…for everyone."

Fizzlewink stopped him before Colby could begin asking more questions. "We will figure things out as time progresses, and we discover just what you are capable of. First, the thing is to find out what your friend here is all about being as though from what we know, his parents are neither Nefslama or Shizumu directly. Let's check that genealogy site and start from there."

For the next few hours, the three of them searched several family history sites and Gary's on-line photo galleries of family members. They couldn't find anything. It was as though his family did not exist.

"Well maybe it's a good thing your life isn't spread on the web like everyone else," Colby said. "Let's just focus on the fact you have magic like me and see what we can do."

Fizzlewink and Colby watched with amusement as Gary squeezed up and grunted.

"You're gonna crap your pants if you keep that up," Colby said, rolling back in laughter. "It doesn't work that way."

Gary huffed and stopped his experimenting. "OK then smart-ass, how is it done. School me."

Colby held out his hand and focused on one of the books on his shelves. As he tried to move the book to his hand, nothing happened. Colby strained harder and darted his eyes from the book to his hand and back again, but nothing happened. No tingle, no blue or red tendrils, nothing.

"Who's gonna shit their pants now?" Gary sniggered.

Fizzlewink walked over to Colby and gently used his hand to lower Colby's. "You are still developing your power. At first, it will be emotion-driven, I am guessing. We will need to practice."

Colby got up from his seat, defeated, and began pacing when a knock sounded at his bedroom door.

"Boys," Nana said, entering the room. She carried in a large tray of food of which Colby brought home from the diner. The tray also included the pizza rolls he forgot in the microwave and a plate of fish. "I thought you boys might be hungry. You forgot to come down for dinner, so I thought you might be too busy doing homework or something." Nana put the tray on the bed and began to snoop around the room.

Colby, suddenly realizing that they lost track of time and looked at his wrist to check the time. He forgot that he removed his father's watch earlier in the kitchen when his mother noticed his wearing the timepiece. He took the watch from his pocket and began to set it down on his table.

* * *

Nana stopped Colby and reached out to take the watch and replaced it on Colby's wrist. "You should wear this. I think your father would be pleased."

Colby began to resist, but Nana's hands remained firm on his wrist. "I think mother would differ from that opinion. You didn't see how she reacted when she saw it on my wrist."

Nana finished putting the watch back on Colby and tightened it a bit more forcefully than necessary. "Don't you worry about what your mother has to say about this watch, you wear it. Besides, after our little chat, your mother will see things my way."

Nana turned to leave and stopped at the door. "Your mother only thought of your father and became upset at his not being here. She was not upset you're wearing his watch. You come from a strong family, my little Fart-blossom, your mom, is just going through a bad patch."

Colby wiped the moisture from his eyes. "What makes our family so strong?" Colby asked, searching for deeper answers.

Nana laughed and looked at Colby then to Fizzlewink. "Us witches, gypsies, and vampires have our strengths as I have always said." She winked at Fizzlewink then at Colby with a raised eyebrow. She smiled a toothless grin, turned, and closed the door behind her as she waddled out of the room.

"What is she talking about Fizz," Colby asked.

Fizzlewink frowned and picked up the plate of fish. "I have no idea, but something about that old woman has always unnerved me."

Chapter 16

After a weekend of coding and creating his new hashtag magic operating system, Colby found himself looking forward to the first meeting of the Archeology Club. He now understood why he was suddenly drawn to the lure of exploring ruins and discovering hidden secrets or treasures of antiquity. The inexplicable desire to be a part of this new activity was driving his every thought; that is the thoughts that were not spent dwelling on his strange new affliction, magic.

Colby entered the room where the members were told to meet for the archeology club. He found the room empty except for the Professor, who was sitting at a desk in front reading a dusty old book.

* * *

Noticing Colby's presence, Professor Stark closed the old leather-bound book and placed it inside his bag before waving Colby over to a stool. "Colby Stevens, our illustrious club President, welcome."

"I'm not so sure about illustrious, but I'll do my best, Professor Stark," Colby said as he sat down in the indicated seat.

"You'll be great, I'm certain. Please call me Rigel. There is no need for titles among friends and regularly being called professor makes me feel older than I am." Rigel looked down after glimpsing at a flash of light, noticing the sun from the windows reflecting off Colby's watch. "That is a very nice timepiece you have there, Colby. Where ever did you find it?"

Colby raised his arm but pulled it close to his chest as though guarding a treasure. "It belonged to my father," he said.

"Ah yes, Jarrod Stevens. He had quite the reputation among his contemporaries," Rigel said. "I only met him once in passing when he gave a lecture at my Alma Mater."

Colby was immediately intrigued. "You knew my dad? Are you saying he was an Archeologist?"

Confused at the question, Rigel sat back and considered Colby. "You didn't know what your father's profession is?"

Colby shrugged. "We don't talk about him much. I knew he traveled a lot and was an explorer of sorts, but that was always less important than knowing where he last went."

"Your father was…" Rigel started and after watching Colby's reaction to the past tense, changed his words. "He is a great explorer as well, but his most notable achievements are in the field of Archeology and ancient cultures."

Colby perked up at Rigel's sharing knowledge of his father. "What was he like?

Do you know where he last went?"

Rigel held up his hands. "I only met him in the flesh once. He last gave a lecture on the ruins and curses in…Oh, I forget where. I think it was in a chamber…I mean Central America. The Yucatán."

"Chichén Itzá?" Colby asked without knowing why that particular area came to mind.

"Yes, actually it was. But like I said, I only briefly met him as he greeted our class. He was very well respected from what I can tell. My professor at the time was excited beyond reason when your father first agreed to talk, and the weeks leading up to his visit…It was all he could lecture about. Our class spent those weeks learning about every place your father published information on. I still have my notes, I believe, if you are interested in reading them."

Colby was excited in spite of himself. "Yes, I would love that. My mother doesn't speak about dad."

Colby then realized that now he knew what his father did for a living, he could search for more information on-line. He tilted his head and furrowed his brow, trying to recall how he felt as though he held that knowledge all along. Something drove him to this club and the new desire for Archeology. It could not be a coincidence.

Rigel, noticing Colby's sudden change in his stance, got up from his seat and approached him. "What is the matter? Did I say something wrong?"

Colby waved Rigel off and looked up, changing his expression. "No, it's nothing. I would appreciate any notes you are willing to share with me. I also have a place to start searching on-line."

"Anytime, Colby. You may wish to ask your mother about some of his exploits, however. I heard mention over the years in this profession, of discoveries your father made but never published his findings. Perhaps she could shed light on where last he was headed? Perhaps some research or journals left behind?"

* * *

Colby looked at Rigel. "What do you mean? Secret discoveries or locations?"

Rigel just raised his left eyebrow and smirked at Colby. "Word travels fast in this line of work. When someone makes claims to even one colleague but does not publish, it gets around. You don't happen to have any old notebooks of your father's, do you? They would be highly sought after."

More confusion, as well as questions, began to swirl through Colby's already mixed up memories and thoughts. He needed to talk to someone, but somehow he began to feel that Rigel was a bit too desperate in his questions. "I don't think so," he answered. The truth was he had no idea, but he would find out.

Rigel raised an eyebrow and nodded approvingly without taking his eyes off the watch. "It is quite the collector's item, your watch. I have a rather extensive collection myself. If ever you want to part with the piece, be sure to let me know."

Colby frowned at Rigel and moved to take a seat as Gary entered the room. "I don't think I'd ever sell it."

Rigel watched Colby as he took a seat and then welcomed Gary into the room.

Gary noticed the odd exchange between them as he came in. He took a seat next to Colby. "What was that all about?"

Before Colby could answer, Darla and Rhea came giggling into the classroom and settled in beside Colby and Gary in the front row of desks.

During the first meeting of their new organization, the four members and Rigel looked over the list of students who signed up to be accepted among their ranks. They discussed each candidate at length, much to Colby and Gary's annoyance. With each name came a laundry list of pros and cons from Darla and Rhea each. This one was too quiet that one is too loud. Another was far too stuck-up while yet another was far more 'out there' for the girls liking. Gary did not understand what the issues were.

* * *

Colby, on the other hand, knew in a few cases that the girls on the list were likely competition for the attention of 'Professor yummy pants' as he heard Darla refer to Rigel. "So then as it stands, it is just the four of us?"

Darla straightened in her chair. "Yes, and I think that is just the perfect number, don't you, Rhea?"

Rhea, being the obedient Marcie to Darla's Peppermint Patty, agreed without hesitation. "Yes, ma'am."

Rigel watched the debates with reserved humor and chose now to add his two cents finally. "If these applicants are not acceptable, there is still an open list, and perhaps others may wish to join."

"We'll see," Darla said.

Rigel withheld his laugh, knowing what Darla was thinking. "The next order of business, Mr. President," he asked Colby.

Colby looked at the Professor with horror in his eyes. He was unaccustomed to being in charge or making decisions. Colby always followed and did as he was told. The worst was always being bullied and at the mercy of his oppressor, but he realized that he had stood up to that challenge recently. Now it was time to embrace his newfound elevation in status, even with just the four members of this new association of dirt diggers, and take the lead. "I suppose the next thing we should discuss is a trip to a place where we can practice what we learn in this club."

"You mean like an actual archeological dig?" Gary asked.

Colby looked to Rigel for approval, and when he received a nod, he gladdened and regained control of the group. "Yes, of course, we are an Archeology Club, after all. I think we should go somewhere mysterious and exotic."

"King Solomon's Mines," Darla said without pause. "I would love to discover the hugest, most impressive diamond ever!"

The men in the room laughed.

"What is so funny?" Darla asked, and then looked at Rhea, who just shrugged, looking innocent.

As Gary argued with Darla and Rhea over their ridiculous reasoning for wanting to search for a mythical diamond mine, Colby drifted in his mind to images of ruins, deep in the tropical jungles and shrouded in mist. He felt a pull on his desire to be among the ancient structures and walk among the ghosts of the long-abandoned city.

As his mind's eye wandered, Colby came across a small section of a long-ago decimated building. All that remained were three walls. No roof was present, but along the back wall, there was a shin-high bench or altar. As he watched, Colby saw the wall break open to the left of the shin-high bench. The wall opening revealed a hidden area, where the glint of light exposed an object caught by a ray of sunshine.

Colby's vision zoomed in on the space, straining to catch a glimpse of what lay secreted away behind the wall of ages past. As he approached, a dull stinging began to creep into his awareness. The stinging gained in intensity as he pushed himself forward in the vision. He reached out toward the gap in the wall, sensing the beckoning call to be discovered by what lay within. The stinging became unbearable when at last, the vision was gone.

"Dude, what the hell are you doing," Gary whispered between clenched teeth. "The girls almost saw you pulling that wizardly stuff."

Colby looked down to see his hand still swirling with the barest of blue and red tendrils.

"Put that away," Gary said. "And I'll apologize now for the bruise that pinch is gonna leave."

* * *

Colby shoved his hand in his pocket before collecting his thoughts. "Wait, did you pinch me?"

"Ya, and pretty hard too 'cause you weren't snapping out of it. What was going on just then?"

Colby rubbed his arm, where the source of his stinging sensation emanated from. "I was having a vision or something. I usually only have them when I sleep, and rarely ever that real." Colby described the vision to Gary, hoping to figure out where he had seen this place before. It seemed familiar, as though he was once in that very spot in his reality. He continued to rub his arm. "Man, I can't believe you actually pinched me."

Gary laughed. "Ya, well, it was a pinch you required. I haven't seen you so green since your Nana tried to make chicken pizza."

Colby snapped his head in Gary's direction. "What did you just say?" There was urgency in his voice.

"Just that it was a painful pinch you needed." Gary looked at his friend with concern. "What's up?"

"No, the rest of it."

"What? The time Nana made chicken pizza?"

"That's it," he whispered to Gary. "What about Chichén Itzá?" Colby suggested to Professor Stark and the girls.

Darla and Rhea wrinkled their noses. They had heard no tales of rich caches or esoteric places with gold and jewels associated with the ancient Mayan city in the forests of the Yucatan. "There is nothing special about that place; it isn't even very old when compared to Egyptian tombs or lost diamond mines."

Gary rolled his eyes. "Seriously? Archeology is not really about hunting for riches and all that glitters," Gary said, much to the annoyance of the girls. "And you should check your facts on how old it is."

Rigel watched the dance of differences with a smile but decided to cut in. "All this discussion is rather entertaining but equally unnecessary. There will be no trudging through the jungle seeking a mythical diamond mine." He turned to Colby and smiled. "Your President has selected, and if I may say so, has chosen an excellent first site to visit."

Darla looked at Colby incredulously. "What made you choose Chichén Itzá?"

"Yes Mr. Stevens, why Chichén Itzá?" The Professor asked.

Again, Colby felt an odd discomfort in the way he was being questioned. "Well we just mentioned it when talking about my dad," he lied. He was unsure why he did not tell the truth, but far too many things were changing in his life, and though Rigel knew why he chose the place, the man was still an unknown.

"So, how do we pay for this adventure?" Colby asked, changing the subject.

The barest wrinkle formed on Rigel's brow. Realizing the subject was changed, he turned back to the others. "We will need to hope for donations and hold fundraisers."

"We will meet again in a few weeks. At that time, we should have researched our destination and come up with ways to raise funds for the trip." Rigel watched the kids go, happy with himself, for planting the seed with Colby while mentioning one of his father's previous locations.

"Let's see where this leads us," Rigel said to himself.

Chapter 17

Colby sat in his room, going over websites containing information on Chichén Itzá with Gary's help. They spent the last several weeks going over every piece of information they could find, attempting to locate any pictures that resembled the location from Colby's vision. When they found what they were looking for, their search focused on discovering what the significance meant for that particular place.

Fizzlewink for his part was less than useless when it came to 'surfing the webs' as he repeatedly phrased. He focused on creating a lesson plan for Colby and, to a lesser extent Gary, in the art of using the power of Emassa. Though Colby began to exhibit a small amount of control, Gary showed no promise yet beyond the ability to see Fizzlewink for who and what he was.

* * *

"What were you and Rigel talking about when the rest of us arrived for Archeology Club?" Gary asked. "Seems he had you all agitated about something when I showed up."

Fizzlewink was hearing this for the first time. "Who is this, Rigel?" he asked. A glint of suspicion covered his narrowing eyes.

Gary waved Fizzlewink into relaxing. "Just that adjunct professor who came to form a club. He's harmless unless you have a girlfriend or wife, then you need to keep him away from them," Gary huffed. "I mean, I don't get it; it's like the guy is spraying out pheromones or something on a colossal scale."

"He's harmless, eh?" Colby shrugged his shoulders and continued to search for information on their spring break destination, adding his father's name to the query string. "He keeps asking me if I've found any old journals belonging to my dad. Then he starts rambling on about the places my father could have gone when he disappeared." More details of Chichén Itzá appeared on his screen, but nothing about his father. Colby shoved the computer mouse away and spun around in his chair. "What is this guy's deal? I mean, I was six when dad left, and nobody knows where he went." Colby began to glow from his hands and eyes. The blue strands of light began to pulse and gain intensity.

Fizzlewink hopped off the bed and stepped up to Colby. "What are you feeling right now?" Fizzlewink was beginning to understand what kept Colby back from properly gaining control over his magic.

Colby ignored Fizzlewink at first while the tendrils of light lapped along the length of his fingers and snapped out for freedom. The lights in the room began to flicker and dim while the other electronics in the room began to get brighter.

"I feel empty. So much missing, and it frustrates me. I feel I'm reaching out for something."

"Colby," Fizzlewink shouted, seeing the odd behavior of the surrounding sources of power and electronics.

* * *

Colby released the power in an instant as he turned to look at Fizzlewink. "What," he breathed.

"You were pulling directly upon the Emassa." Fizzlewink grinned at Colby as he calmed, and the lights returned to normal. "I have an idea."

Over the following weeks, Fizzlewink practiced with Colby at focusing his emotions, observing how his young pupil was able to harness his magic and direct it using those emotions as a trigger. In each case, he held either his smartphone or tablet, which caused the strange symbols and runes to appear on the screen while the Emassa flowed.

Rather than explain to the boys what these symbols were, Fizzlewink would continue with the tests without the use of the electronics. Though Colby could channel the magic, it was much more difficult and barely energized more than a static spark from sliding in stocking covered feet across a carpet. He also had no way to direct the magic into a spell.

"We have been at this for weeks, Fizz. When are you going to tell us what this is all about?" Colby asked. He was frustrated and drained.

Fizzlewink looked up from his notepad and tossed Colby some licorice. "Eat that and take a break. I think I get it now, but I need a few days to design a final test."

While Colby was glad to have finally some semblance of control over the meager amount of power he could wield, his continuous requirement to dredge up buried feelings was taking a toll. Things he chose to tuck neatly into a vault of ignorance and denial proved to create more confusion and, in several instances, created volatile situations at school, particularly with Jasper.

More than once, Jasper Bodine and his gang of thugs attempted harassing and bullying Colby and Gary. On each occasion, Colby reacted with increasing hostility. One such occasion, Gary was there to talk him down and distract anyone from noticing the blue tendrils of magic forming around Colby's hands. The constant popping of fluorescent lights was being blamed on shorts in the electric system of the building. The good thing was that there was no more detention, as the blame for the original case of broken lighting was attributed to the same faulty wiring.

The first colors of fall were painting the trees by the time Fizzlewink was satisfied enough to begin explaining to Colby what the purpose of the many tests was. "Sit and take out your tablet Colby," Fizzlewink said. "I want you to begin to draw on your magic, but pay attention to the symbols that appear on your screen."

Colby did as he was instructed and immediately observed the symbols begin to appear on the tablet. Since the first time he saw the strange runes, he searched for their meaning but found none. Whenever he mentioned them to Fizzlewink, the secretive little blue cat-man would wave him off or change the subject. Now he sat before the screen of his tablet and watched as the symbols began to swirl upon the display and lift off the surface to materialize into reality.

One after the next, the unknown symbols flew off the screen and began to dance on his hands.

"Are you going to tell me what this means now?" Colby asked Fizzlewink.

Fizzlewink watched the symbols swirl and pulse with energy. "These are the runes our people first used to focus the power of our magic, but they have not been used for ages."

"You don't use them anymore?" Gary asked.

The runes were used to start teaching the fundamentals of harnessing the Emassa, the power between realities where magic comes from. Once the Nefslama became proficient enough, they no longer required the use of the runes and could wield that magic freely.

"It is much like the way children of Earth play with letter and number blocks," Fizzlewink explained. "Except in very complicated magic, we have no need for them beyond teaching."

* * *

"So, the runes game we play at school?" Gary asked. "What is that, then?"

Fizzlewink postulated that they. May have been purposely turned into a game to teach the runes to the students. "Magic was always going to return. Perhaps the faculty continued the game when regular classes in magic were suspended."

"So why do they appear when I channel the Emassa?" Colby asked.

Fizzlewink furrowed his already wrinkled brow and narrowed his long white eyebrows. "That is a question for which I have no answer; however, we can use this to our advantage in your training. There seems to be some affinity between you and your gizmos. This is likely the best way for you to learn focus."

Gary moved closer to Colby and the flow of runes drifting around him. He reached up and touched one of the odd symbols only to have it dissolve upon his finger. His hand began to glow. Gary's instinct reaction was to shake the foreign glow from his hand, and once he did, the blue light flashed free and hit the floor, bursting apart, leaving a sizable puddle of water in its place. "What the…"

"Be careful, Mr. Connors, lucky that is the worst you did. That was the rune for water." Fizzlewink grabbed a towel and tossed it to Gary to soak up the liquid. "I think we found out what you can do."

Gary could channel the runes; he was simply unable to create them as Colby could. Colby continued to create runes, and Gary did his best to draw them as they appeared. They spent all night creating and copying the runes without tiring. Fizzlewink, on the other hand, snored quietly on the bed while the boys continued well into the next morning until, at last, Gary began to wear out.

"I can't go on anymore," Gary complained. "My fingers are cramped from all this drawing, and I'm starving."

"How can you think of food," Colby said. He was energized by discovery and created runes at a furious pace. "How many have we got so far?"

*** *** ***

Gary began pushing through the pages of etchings strewn about the floor around him. "By my estimation, there are around four hundred at least."

"There are many more yet to discover," Fizzlewink said through a yawn. "I think Gary is correct; however, it is time to break and eat something. I can begin filling in the blanks with many of the runes and constructs."

"Constructs?" Colby asked. "Like in the game?"

Constructs are the symbols used to join runes together into functional spells and more complex bending of reality. Fizzlewink emphasized that these construct characters were needed to build upon the basic runes that Colby already revealed.

"Let's go down to the kitchen and see what's on the menu," Fizzlewink said, licking his lips. "I can smell your Nana's cooking up something tasty."

Colby and Gary grimaced at the thought of Nana's culinary catastrophes. "Replace the 't' in tasty with an' n'. The woman burns water, how can you enjoy the mess she cooks?"

Fizzlewink shrugged and headed for the door. "She cooks with love, and that makes it better. Besides, it reminds me of home."

They arrived in the kitchen to find Nana sitting on a stool at the kitchen island, watching as someone else cooked. Aria was at the stove, flipping pancakes and frying sausages. Shelly sat on top of the counter, eating a plate of eggs and glaring at them all.

"Oh, good, you are here. Hungry boys…and Fizzy-wizzles?" Aria said. "I've made quite a spread for us this morning."

Colby could not remember the last time his mother cooked. He could not recall the last time she was out of bed before noon on a Saturday, either. "What's the occasion?" he asked Nana.

*** *** ***

Nana smiled and winked. "Work in progress." She turned and looked at Fizzlewink. "And how about you, fuzzy butt, want some fish?"

The glare from Fizzlewink was enough to cut the snickering down to snorting from Gary and Colby. The boys took their plates and sat at the kitchen table. There they could talk about what they would do next with the knowledge they collected about the runes.

"You will do nothing unless I instruct you," Fizzlewink shouted. "This is dangerous territory until you learn the fundamentals, and even then it is different, being as though only one of you can create the runes. Speaking of which, I still haven't explained the whole computer connection to all this."

"My aren't you the chatty cat this morning," Aria said, putting a plate of fish on the floor in front of Fizzlewink. "Meow meow meow…"

The boys burst into laughter.

Fizzlewink grumbled and sat down before his plate to eat. "Eat your food and then back to work."

After breakfast, the boys and cat went back upstairs, leaving the ladies of the house in the kitchen alone.

"What is with that cat?" Shelly asked. "And what are those mad scientists up to? I swear my computer was acting up all night, and those two are probably to blame." She put her plate in the sink and started to walk out.

"They are learning," Nana said. "Maybe we could just sneak up there and-"

Aria closed the dishwasher door forcefully and turned to leave the kitchen. "You will let this play out as it should mother, no more interfering."

"What's with her?" Shelly asked after Aria stormed from the kitchen past her. "And since when does she get up to make breakfast instead of a martini?"

* * *

"Your mother and I have reached an understanding. And you, little witch, need to get on board too. Your brother will soon need us, and you need to be ready. A spell is lifting, and memories are returning."

Nana got up from the island and left Shelly standing in the kitchen, wondering what the hell was going on. "This nuthouse just keeps getting nuttier." A rare smile crept over Shelly's lips. "It's about damn time."

Chapter 18

Over the following days, Fizzlewink translated the runes while Gary created tables from the runes Colby scanned into the computer. The drawings were of no use without the power of the Emassa fused with them. Neither Gary nor Colby could activate a rune without Colby first pulling it from his tablet or smartphone.

"What is the problem with these runes? I mean, why do I need help from computers?" Colby asked.

Fizzlewink scratched his head and began twirling his eyebrow. "I can only assume that in this situation, the Emassa manifests itself differently for various beings. Since you are something new, from my experience, you have a unique way of accessing power. Nothing is certain with the magic of Emassa. My people have studied it for many millennia and still have only scratched the surface. Besides, it has been a long time since the Emassa has been flowing; perhaps it has changed."

"And what of the blue color and occasionally red? Is there some significance to that?" Colby asked.

Fizzlewink was silent for a moment and then blinked. "No."

Colby did not believe him. "Tell us more about the Emassa and how your people came to use it and eventually ended up on Earth," Colby said.

Fizzlewink started to object, but Colby insisted.

The Nefslama were a race of artisans, scientists, and explorers. They traveled the world long before homosapiens, evolving faster, and building great civilizations. They discovered a source of energy deep within the planet that seemed to be fed from a rift in the fabric of space and time. The Nefslama studied the fracture and experimented with it until they found the full use of the power that lay between realities. They began to channel it and became very powerful and adept at twisting reality.

It took many centuries of study in the beginning before the first of their kind was able to begin rudimentary use of the magic that the Emassa enabled. They developed a system of runes and constructs to combine the various elements of the magic that they created.

Some great mages worked on massive spells that built wonders like the great temples of the world. One spell that they contrived, however, became unstable and eventually destroyed their capital city along with a vast number of their citizens. The survivors scattered and settled all around the globe.

"Some of the Nefslama were mages that practiced magic that was frowned upon. It was one of them who cast the first spell to create the others."

* * *

"The others?" Colby asked.

Fizzlewink nodded. "Shizumu, that is what we later came to call them. They are energy-based life forms and have no need to identify themselves in the way we do, at least not until their energy found a way to steal bodies through possession."

Many Shizumu were created as a by-product of the spells performed to gain more power by some Nefsmari outcasts. They used Emassa to open their magical core in hopes to store more magical energy. What happened was the two halves of the magical soul split, and the more chaotic half tore itself free.

"The mages who did this were eventually killed by those very Shizumu trying to retake their body. It wasn't pretty. Only one of those outcast mages survived but was eventually imprisoned for his many crimes. Still, that same mage managed to create an army of Shizumu and other monstrosities. He used them to start a war with the elders."

The Nefslama came under attack soon after they banished this rogue mage. The Shizumu were vicious and unrelenting in their attacks, absorbing the bodies of any they came in contact with. The Nefslama were able to erect an energy field around their city, but it weakened under the continued assault from the Shizumu.

Nefsmari were created at this time as a means of escape. They have an ability to teleport anywhere they've been or are able to see. That wasn't enough. All but one Nefsmari was further cursed into large goblin-like beasts that canceled magic. They sent these creatures out to hunt down and capture the Shizumu.

Eventually, the Nefsmari managed to subdue and imprison most of the Shizumu within a hidden dimension created especially for these lost souls.

"Like a prison into that rift, the Nefslama traveled through?" Gary asked.

"Not quite. That is, the Nefslama created the prison with magic, making a pocket dimension of sorts."

* * *

Gary looked skeptical. "What was this void place in the rift? Is that where the Emassa comes from?"

"It does emanate from there as far as we understand it, but where it truly comes from is unknown. It was certainly stronger back then."

"So, where is this city the elders settled when they came here?" Gary asked.

Fizzlewink sighed and looked to the floor. "In ruins these days. We lived all throughout the world in ancient times, but mostly in the Yucatan."

"You mean like Chichen Itzá?" Gary asked.

"Yes, that was one city, but all over that region," Fizzlewink said.

"You have got to be kidding me?" Colby said. "An actual lost city like those of legend and myth and your city is where we are going next spring?"

Again Fizzlewink sighed. "This is odd, indeed. I don't believe in coincidences."

"So, what is the deal with you being a cat?" Colby asked.

"I was made early on in our arrival here when the Emassa was flowing like the amazon." Fizzlewink described how he was taken to transforming into a cat, so he might observe the humans of ancient Egypt. "It is only a guise and prevents normal humans from seeing us. Our own kind can still recognize and communicate with us telepathically as you might think of it though it is more complicated than that. The form of a cat is my easiest and first transformation. We all have a particular mold, according to my mother. All my family is aligned with the feline."

Colby had countless questions forming about the lost city, but seeing Fizzlewink's unmasked pain, he chose to reserve them for another time. He would have to remember to inquire about Fizz's family. "But what about all the other Shizumu that got away?" Colby asked. "What were they doing all that time?"

* * *

"They were learning how to survive, I imagine. They became skilled at slipping within the body of a human and attach to their energy. The name we came to call them, Shizumu, basically means soul rider, as I've mentioned."

"What like a possession?" Gary asked.

Fizzlewink nodded. "And that is where the legends of demons and possessions come from Mr. Connors. Only as stories go, they get twisted and convoluted as time passes. It does not help that superstition and evil are most often associated with things that humans do not understand."

Colby wondered about the Nefslama ever being occupied by Shizumu and asked Fizzlewink about what happened when the Shizumu encountered one of his kind.

The Nefslama were considered to be immune to the Shizumu, but only in that, they tended to be ejected if they didn't destroy the body. Colby and Gary, as well as members of their families, were likewise resistant to being possessed through genetic markers passed down in their bloodlines, but it wasn't proven.

Once someone has been inhabited and released, they usually become sensitive to the energies of the universe, and it manifests in various ways. Sixth sense, witchcraft, telekinesis, etc., these things are all among the presumed results of abilities born to survivors and can be passed to descendants.

"What about the Nefslama? What do they pass down to humans they have mated with?" Colby looked at Fizzlewink and waited while the little man contemplated his answer.

"I am not certain since one of the laws the Nefslama laid out when was that mixing their blood with humans was forbidden without Elder approval. I know it happened, but it wasn't talked about." Fizzlewink stared at Colby intensely.

Colby felt there was more to know. Fizzlewink was holding back. "What would happen if someone decided to break that law?"

* * *

Fizzlewink looked away from Colby. "If members of the council found out, the child would be destroyed."

A shudder ran down the length of Colby's body.

Fizzlewink snickered. "Not to worry, my boy, the council was disbanded centuries ago." He patted Colby on the knee as they sat huddled on the floor. "More than one Nefslama has coupled with a human since the council fell apart."

Gary shook his head and looked at Fizzlewink. "I thought you were stuck in the form of a cat or at least looked like one. You mean other people were doing it with animals?"

"Don't be absurd," Fizzlewink said. He curled his lip down and shook his head to break free of the visual imagery. "I am Nefsmari and not mating. Nefslama are the human-looking ancient mages who consort with humans. Some have mated, others used them to store Emassa when they needed to quickly rebuild their reserves."

"What do you mean by building up your reserves? I thought the Emassa was an energy source you could draw on." Colby asked.

Something disrupted the natural flow of power that Fizzlewink could not explain. From the time shortly after the Shizumu wars, the Nefslama could only take a trickle of power from the Emassa that flowed through ley lines on the planet. They learned how to gather that trickle and store it for use later and gathered it in objects. Once they used all that stored up Emassa, they needed to start gathering it once again, that all changed several years ago.

"Are you saying that around the time my father left, the Emassa opened up again?" Colby said. "Did something happen to him, and that's why he disappeared?"

Fizzlewink shook his head. "I do not know what happened to your father as it relates directly to the Emassa flowing free, but soon after he was gone, so was the free flow of energy. It did not go back to the trickle it was, but nor did it flow free to use at will."

Colby had more questions, but Fizzlewink called a halt to the night's lessons in history. "You have a big test tomorrow and should get off to bed."

Colby had no idea what Fizz was talking about, but he was tired, and Gary already left. Tomorrow was another day, sure to be full of more surprises.

Chapter 19

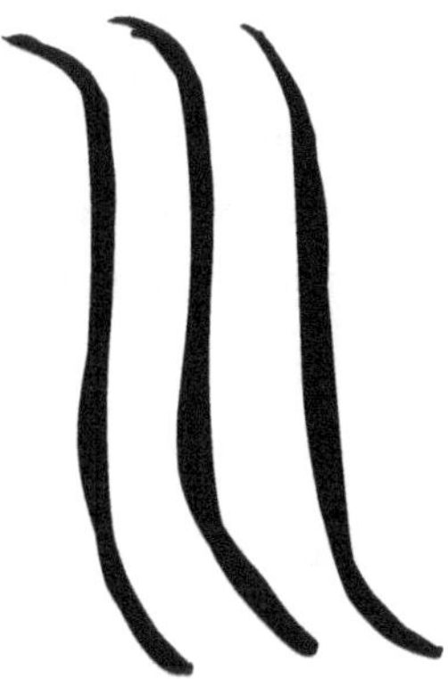

Colby woke the next day to the glaring look from his sister. "What the hell Shelly," he said, gathering up his blankets. He noticed the odd look about her and could not figure out what was different this morning. When he focused on her face, he realized instantly what had changed. "Are you smiling?"

"Get up cheese-curd. You and I have somewhere to go this morning." Shelly continued smiling and left the room.

Fizzlewink charged in the room just as the door was pulled closed behind Shelly. "What was that all about?" he asked.

Colby got up from the bed and pulled out his clothes for the day. He took his towel off the back of his door and prepared to go to the bathroom. "I don't know, but something smells fishy."

Fizzlewink perked up and headed toward the kitchen. "Fish? I'll see you at breakfast."

"No, Fizzlewink, that isn't what…never mind." Colby laughed to himself and proceeded to take his shower, dress, and head down to the kitchen.

Shelly and Nana sat at the counter, staring at Colby while his mother, once again, made breakfast. Though she was sipping what looked to be a mimosa, she was otherwise lucid and clear-headed. Something was amiss.

"What is going on, you're all acting strange this morning and in this family that's an understatement?" Colby hesitated before sitting at the island across from Nana and Shelly. Fizzlewink was blissfully engrossed in a plate of fish and sausage.

"Shelly is taking you downtown today," Aria said. "We completely forgot to take care of this after your birthday, but today is the day." She placed a plate of eggs and sausage before Colby and winked at him.

"And we are going downtown, why?" he asked.

"You need to get your driver's license," Aria said.

"I completely forgot. With everything going on, going to the DMV has been the last thing on my mind."

Fizzlewink stopped eating and jumped up. "Oh no, I completely forgot about that place," he said.

Everyone turned to the loud and unexpected yowls from the frisky feline.

"Thanks for the vote of confidence, Fizz," Colby said. "What is your problem?"

* * *

Shelly looked from the cat to Colby and back. "Should we be helping get a license to drive a multi-ton box of metal around to someone who converses with a cat?"

"Shelly, shut-up," Aria, Nana, and Colby all said.

Fizzlewink finished his breakfast in a hurry and said he was coming with Colby.

Colby finished his breakfast and was preparing to leave when Shelly stopped and closed the door before Fizzlewink followed them out. "I will tolerate many a strange thing and irregular friend, even my increasingly odd little brother, but I will not be seen in public with you toting around that cat."

Fizzlewink appeared next to Colby. "There are some things you need to know about that place."

"What is the big deal? It's just the DMV." Colby said.

"Exactly," Fizzlewink said and began whispering into Colby's ear.

"You say something, cheese-curd?" Shelly said, turning around. The chirp-chirp of the remote unlocking the car meant it was time to go.

"No," Colby said.

His nerves were beginning to become unsettled. He practiced driving all the time. Ever since he received his permit, he drove Nana around, and several times Bruce would let Colby take the wheel of his car. Today he would just take his driving test and make it official, what was there to be worried about? It was a disconcerting look on old Fizzlewink's prune-like blue face that made him start losing his hard-won measure of confidence.

"It's just the DMV," he reassured himself and got into the car.

Colby worried the entire ride down to the Thompson Center, where the DMV was located. Shelly let him out and went to find street parking nearby, telling him to go in and get a number, then hurry up and wait.

Colby entered the building and took the escalators down. As he neared the driver's bureau at the bottom of the moving stairs, another feeling, he did not recognize enhanced the sense of trepidation. Once he got in line, he understood what had Fizzlewink in such a tizzy.

Nearly every worker in the DMV had a reddish glow about them, and as Colby looked closer, he could make out menacing and demonic-looking faces twisting below the surface of their host's skin. He was in 'Demon Central'. These people were possessed.

Colby received his number and a disturbing glare from the man at the greeting desk. He just took a seat when Fizzlewink's parting words this morning popped into his head.

"Stay calm. Don't get emotional. Make your sister ride along during the road test. Leave your gadgets at home. And above all, never look them in the eyes." Fizzlewink stressed that last bit of advice.

Colby looked up to see a man at the counter staring holes through him. He averted his own eyes and looked back at the door, hoping for the first time in his teenage years to see his sister. The relief he felt when she pushed her way in was comforting and annoying both. He felt as though at sixteen, he continued to require a babysitter.

"See something interesting," she snapped at the man behind the counter as she cut the line and moved to join Colby.

The man started to reach for Shelly. "You need to take a number, young lady," he hissed at her.

"You need to keep your hands to yourself and mind your business. I'm here with my brother," she said and dismissed the man with her grimacing snarl.

The man looked away and went back to his business.

* * *

"Jackhole," Shelly grumbled. She turned to Colby and put her smile back on her powdered face. "Are you ready for this little brother?"

"Ya, I guess," he said. "Will you ride along during the test? I mean, these people give me the creeps."

Shelly started to make a smart remark, but then looked around the room and shivered. "I see what you mean. Sure, I'll be your back up, bro."

Nearly two hours had passed before Colby was finally beginning the process of getting his license. He went to the first line and took his written test.

"What language?" the woman barked at him.

Colby looked at her, confused. "Pardon me?"

A raspy, annoyed sigh followed. "What language do you want to take the test in?" she said.

"What language are the street signs written in," he snapped back. He immediately regretted his response but was relieved by the muffled chuckle he heard.

"Cute," she said, glaring and handing him the test. "Complete this and return it to me when you have finished." She pointed to a group of desks and sent him on his way. "Next."

Colby completed the test and received a perfect score before moving on to his eye test. During the test, he could swear that he saw runes and had to focus. It was as though the symbols were trying to alter and confuse him. He steadied his nerves and pushed on, blocking the flow of Emassa that threatened to surface. Once he was finished, he moved on to the line for taking a road test.

Shelly left to pull the car around to the side where the tester would meet them.

While Colby stood waiting for her to drive up, he felt the icy stare of his test administer standing behind him. He gathered his will to push the terror back down and keep it at bay. When Shelly arrived, he let out a breath of relief before walking around the vehicle with the man who would ultimately decide his fate. The future involved Colby's nearly three hours of effort to receive a piece of plastic, symbolizing the fact he could see clearly and pass a simple yet inadequate written test. Now all he had to do was drive the car and remember to use his parking skills and turn signals instead of the signals his Nana preferred to use with her hands. 'That woman should not be allowed to operate a vehicle,' he thought.

"Let's get this over with. I go on lunch break in fifteen minutes," the man said as he entered the front passenger seat. He cleared his throat as Shelly got in the back. "You do not need to be here, miss."

"I will stay with my car."

He raised an eyebrow and made a note on his clipboard. "Enter into traffic and drive three blocks south. Perform a U-turn and drive one block north. You will turn right onto the next street and find a place to parallel park."

Colby performed as instructed though he hesitated at the point where he was told to U-turn. "There are no U-turns here unless a sign indicates, and this is not a wide enough street anyway."

"The instructions were quite clear," the man said and tittered. "Turn left here and find a place to parallel park."

Colby turned and parked the vehicle without any difficulty. He watched as the administrator marked up his test form and scribbled on the bottom.

"You failed," the man said and began to glower at Colby. "Better luck next time." The man began to lean toward Colby.

Colby was confused, wondering what he did wrong. "What do you mean I failed? Because I decided not to fall for your trick and pull a U-turn illegally. You designed the test for failure." Colby was getting upset, and the blue around his hands began to glow and grow stronger than ever before.

"Oh, what do we have here," the man said as his face began to ripple and transform. "You are interesting to me."

Colby began to panic and reached out to the man, touching his wrist.

The man began to shake, and a glow surrounded his body. "What are you?" The red glowing essence began to separate from the man and slide toward Colby. "How are you doing this?"

Shelly watched in shock from the back seat, her eyes darting from Colby to the red glowing thing, to the man, and then to the computer screen in the dashboard of her car. Runes began to appear on the screen, followed by a circular symbol in the center.

Colby reached out to push at the Shizumu and made contact with it. As soon as the energetic pulses of his hand connected with the creature, it began to grin, until the color of Colby's magic changed.

The blue tendrils of energy split to make room for red, and they blended to become rich, intense purple.

Colby pushed on the beast and grabbed hold of the test administrator's wrist. He fought against the revulsion he felt creep across his skin as that same aversion began to feel familiar. He looked up to see the shocked expression on the plasma form of the Shizumu as it was ejected from its host.

A blast of energy and light-filled the vehicle and busted out the back windshield. Car alarms went off in the nearby automobiles. The computer in the dashboard was fried, and the shattered glass from the windshield was blown out the back of the car.

Shelly snapped out of her unblinking stare. "What the hell was that?"

"Yes, what exactly happened here? I felt your power," Fizzlewink said, appearing in the seat next to Shelly, who screamed in surprise.

"You shouldn't be saying anything," she said as the cat began to morph into a little blue man.

Colby and Shelly stared at each other for a moment. Before either could say anything, the man from the DMV came to his senses.

"What's going on here?" he said, looking from Shelly to Colby. "Where am I?"

Shelly jumped in before Colby could mutter a syllable. "You drinking on the job or something? What is your problem?"

The man just looked at her dumbstruck.

"I suggest you just mark that driving test as pass, and we can forget about reporting you," Shelly said.

The man jumped out of the car when they arrived back at the DMV. Colby followed him inside and came back out in short order. His smile spread apart his face, casting a joyful glow. He waved his license in the air as he approached the car, skipping. A moment of accomplishment for him blocked out the strangeness of the events leading up to the acquisition.

"Just get in and drive," Shelly said. Her face was a cross between pissed and freaked out, yet she patted Colby's arm.

Colby accepted the pat on the arm as high praise from Shelly and drove home with his new driver's license and a sister shouting questions in his ear. "When we get home, I'll explain everything."

Chapter 20

Shelly didn't wait until they got home, she insisted on explanations on the drive back. Fizzlewink withdrew and allowed Colby to fill in the details of what was going on since his birthday.

When they arrived home, Colby went straight up to his room with Shelly on his heels.

Fizzlewink was sitting on the bed waiting. "Sit down, both of you, and listen."

"You're a freakin' cat. I'd sooner put you out for the night then take orders from an overgrown talking fur-ball."

* * *

"Sit and listen." Fizzlewink had enough and would be heard.

Without another word or so much as a moan of a complaint, both Colby and Shelly took a seat and waited for Fizzlewink to speak.

"Colby, I think it is about time I helped you remember something you have blocked out for many years. Shelly, this may help explain where this all started." Fizzlewink leaned over and put a hand on Colby's forehead. "Let's go back to when you were a toddler, back to the night your father disappeared." Energy flowed from Fizzlewink and enveloped Colby. "I want you to tell us what you remember."

Colby began to twist in agitation as the night began to replay in his mind. "I was playing in my room," he said. "And you were there, Fizz, except you, were just a talking cat then."

"I was never 'just a cat'," Fizzlewink grumbled. "Please continue."

Colby relayed the memories as they rebuilt in his conscious mind. He sat in front of his little wooden train set after he figured out how to assemble it. Then he sat in the center and began to play with it. During his playing, Colby set a covered bridge over the tracks and waited for the train to pass beneath it. He placed some of his toy Runes tiles beside the bridge after they fell off one of the train cars. When the windup toy scooted along, and under the bridge, Colby shouted 'abber-cadabber', and then waited. The train never exited the opposite side. When Colby lifted the bridge, his train engine was gone, and his head began to hurt. As the pain increased, he was enveloped in blue and red light. His fear caught hold, and he ran around his room, crying.

He told his parents what happened when they arrived, and then there was a funny blue man sitting next to his father. Dad picked Colby up and rocked him and sent him back downstairs with his Nana.

The next thing Colby recalled was walking outside, following his sister and Nana. They were looking up and saw bright swirling lights that took up the entire night sky. The lights swirled and settled, creating a distorted reflection of the ground below.

"I don't remember anything else of that night, just the next morning when dad was gone, and nobody talked about why or where he went," Colby said. He pulled back from Fizzlewink and took the tissue Shelly offered.

"I remember those lights," Shelly said.

Fizzlewink sighed and looked at the two siblings with understanding and a rare expression of empathy. "That is when your father created a spell of protection for you."

"Why would we need a protection spell?" Shelly asked.

Fizzlewink looked away from Shelly and directly at Colby. "The protection was more for Colby's benefit. He caused a sizable shift in the Emassa that night. Something we had not felt in a very long time."

"I thought you didn't know where my father went?"

Fizzlewink shrugged. "I don't know where he went really. I know he performed a spell at that school of yours, but after that, he disappeared. Your mother returned home alone and changed. Your magic was hobbled, and there would be no trace for the others to follow and get to you."

"What could I have done? I was like, six years old."

"You tapped into the Emassa and opened a channel that was felt by anyone capable within a thousand or more miles. No one had been able to draw that much Emassa since before my home was abandoned. And you did so without training, without a second thought, and without help."

"What does that mean?" Gary asked. He walked into the room after having stood in the doorway, listening. He nodded at Colby and Shelly in response to their silent hello and took a seat on the floor next to them.

* * *

"Unclear," Fizzlewink answered. "I can only speak about what Colby's father did to keep those who felt the power from finding him and trying to use him."

Fizzlewink explained how Colby's father broke the rules by having children with Colby's mother. There was something about her; the few elders remaining did not understand. By breaking this edict, he endangered himself and his family, but he loved their mother and his children. When Colby developed his power, it alerted the others to his existence, and they would come looking for him if they could locate the source. Jarrod Stevens cast a spell the likes of which Fizzlewink never before saw, and it deflected the attention away from his family and drew away Colby's power so that they would be safe.

"But why did he leave?" Colby asked.

Fizzlewink shrugged and began twisting his eyebrows. "Like I said, I don't know the power he used or the runes. My best guess is that he sacrificed himself to keep you safe. Though it would seem that he only hobbled your gifts, and they have begun to resurface. No spell lasts forever."

"So, he failed and sacrificed himself for nothing." Colby was torn between the emotions he was feeling. His father did not leave them, for this, he was grateful to learn, but he left without actually taking away the one thing that now placed Colby and everyone he knew, in danger.

"He bought you time, my boy. Precious time." Fizzlewink was trying his hardest to make Colby feel better but was failing.

Shelly was the first to bring a smile to Colby's face. "So then tell us, what will you, who looks like the offspring of Yoda and one of the blue-man group, do to help? Teach us to use the force or something?"

Colby started laughing. "My father was one. I am one, and…my sister is one." He continued to chuckle as Shelly joined him.

Fizzlewink folded his arms and watched the two of them laugh. "I am not Yoda. I am blue."

* * *

Fizzlewink smiled at their change in mood and sensing their desire to learn. "All right, I have hung around this family since that night, keeping an eye on you all. I am not about to shirk my duties and forget the promise I made your father."

"So then can you explain some things to us?" Shelly asked. When Fizzlewink nodded, she scooted closer to Colby. "What's the deal with the DMV worker?"

"Shizumu," Fizzlewink said. "They love places such as that, for reasons that escape me. Anyway, those who work in places such as the DMV are overlooked and afforded an uneasy distance by most who visit. People go to see civil servants and look past them out of nervousness, fear, and unfounded contempt. It matters not the reason, only that Shizumu can occupy such people and go unnoticed."

Fizzlewink spoke about his experiences with the Shizumu. They took control of those who do not have the strength of will to resist them. In the early times, the Shizumu would only possess those nearing death or those who'd lost the will to live. Things changed over time, and the disembodied creatures became more aggressive.

Countless innocents began to succumb to the invasion of the Shizumu essence. Those who fought back failed miserably and paid the ultimate price. They died in flames. If the body rejects the possession, it becomes so heated by fever fighting an infection that does not exist in the blood, but the entire being. Such heat boils the body and ignites the flesh. Spontaneous combustion, to any that knew better, is not spontaneous at all. They had all but disappeared for a very long time. The rumor was that someone imprisoned them somehow. Either way, they were now back.

"Once a Shizumu takes root, it can not be chased off easily," Fizzlewink said. "Exorcisms, holy water, crosses, and the like, those things only cause the Shizumu to retreat into the back of the mind away from the annoyance. If they do leave, however, they soon find another host."

"But Colby separated the thing from that poor driving instructor easily enough,"

Shelly said.

Not easily surprised, Fizzlewink became uncharacteristically agitated. "He what?"

"It wasn't on purpose. It just happened," Colby admitted.

"Tell me exactly what transpired."

Holding nothing back, Colby described what happened at the DMV from the moment he first stepped into the building. He revealed how his skin tingled, and his instincts told him to run, but he fought them down, thinking it was just his nerves getting the better of him.

"There was a distinct aura around many of the people working behind the counters," Colby explained. "I avoided eye contact as you warned though I did try to joke with the lady who gave me my written test." Colby smirked but washed it away when he noticed that Fizz was not amused. "She gave me a similar look."

"Fast-forward little brother," Shelly said.

When they began the driven test, Colby felt more nervous than during his wait inside. It seemed as though the proximity of the Shizumu agitated his power, and the man who administered the test was looking for any reason to trick and fail him. When Colby refused to follow an order that would have been illegal, that is when the conflict began.

"That man just started to stare at me, and I stared back. I saw into his eyes and what lay behind them." Colby shuddered and looked away. "It was a mix of absolute menace and spite, but beyond that, deep within…there was a pleading."

Colby looked back at Fizzlewink. "The red glow of the man began to grow as he spoke with a vibrato voice. It wanted to know what I was." Colby looked at Fizzlewink with the same question. "When I touched his wrist, it was like something within me called to the Shizumu, pulling it loose as though ripping a weed from the ground."

* * *

As his panic mounted, Colby described how he wrenched his hand free from the magnetic pull of the man's wrist, and with it came the essence of the Shizumu. Colby closed his eyes; that is when it happened.

"What happened?" Fizzlewink asked.

"I had my eyes closed, but I could still see the purple light through my eyelids."

Shelly stood up and leaned over Fizzlewink and pointed at Colby. "I'll tell you what happened. Light-bright over there let off a purple flash that propelled the red ghostly thing out the back window of my car and fried out the electronics."

Now pacing the floor and twirling both his elongated eyebrows, Fizzlewink moved from the corner to the wall. He moved from the window to the desk, shaking his head and mumbling incoherently until, at last, he stopped and looked directly into Colby's eyes.

"That is not possible for a single Nefslama alone, a pure-blood. And it has not been accomplished for longer than I care to admit. What you have done will have consequences."

Colby dismissed Fizzlewink's unrest, and warning then puffed up his chest. "I did that guy a favor. I freed him from the demon that subjugated him." Colby pulled back as he watched the blue man begin to boil over. Fizzlewink's face pulled back as his eyes went wide, and his pupils shrank to nothingness.

"You know nothing, insufferable child. You've pulled a burning man from a campfire and cast him into hell. You left him to suffer when he would have preferred dying slowly in that fire, without pain or awareness compared to what awaits him. A Shizumu does not simply give up a host."

"What are you saying?" Shelly asked.

Slapping his hand on his forehead, Fizzlewink turned to Shelly while pointing at Colby. "He's evicted a hornet from its nest, and it will come back, but this time it will bring the rest of the swarm."

The severity of the situation began to settle upon Colby's face. "I can…can I… what can I do?" His eyes pled to Fizzlewink for a solution.

Softness began to return to the cat-man's face as he saw the longing for redemption written across Colby's brow. "I am afraid that I do not have the strength yet, and you have not the control. If the Shizumu played house for any length of time and returns to the host, it is likely the poor man will…Well, let us hope the Shizumu has moved on."

"What about the others? Can they be saved from the squatters taking up residence in their bodies?" Colby asked.

Shaking his head, Fizzlewink sat back down on the bed. "There is nothing we can do now. A reckoning is coming, I fear, and we are not prepared. You have not learned enough yet, and there are no shortcuts."

"Tell us what we can do. This power I have…" Colby looked at his sister, "that we have… It has to be of use or what's the point."

"Before you are ready, you must master your understanding of the runes," Fizzlewink said and grinned with grim acknowledgment of the amount of work ahead. "There are rules to magic and using it."

Chapter 21

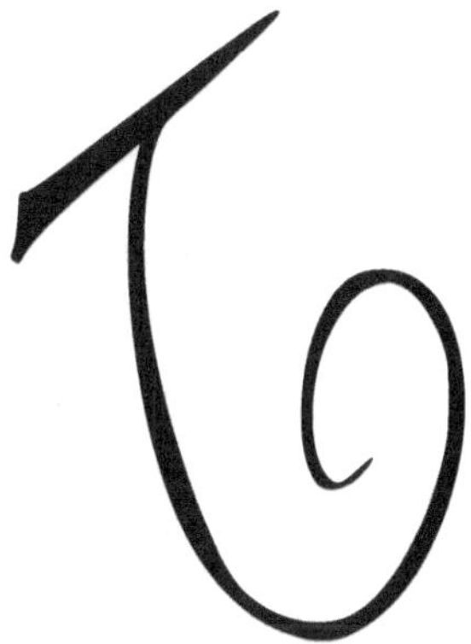

Fizzlewink began teaching the three new Emassa users the true rules of the runes. Unlike the game of Runes played in the school, the use of runes for working with Emassa was even more complicated than Colby imagined. The first thing he had to learn to adjust to was the proper order of placing the runes for a construct to work. In the game, the exact order was less strict than what is required for real spellwork.

The subject in a real rune construct must support the action taken upon it. The construct also requires directions such as duration, timers, triggers, size, and more depending on the intent. The one thing Colby could understand was that the strength of the construct was proportional to the amount of Emassa the wielder put into it when they set the spell.

* * *

Everything he thought he was grasping in the game required relearning, which posed a problem that Colby began to see clearly as Fizzlewink began his instructions of the real runes.

"Who started the Runes game at my school, and why?" Colby asked.

A sly look fell over Fizzlewink's face. "It was started there by your father long ago, at the request of the board that runs the Institute."

Colby didn't know why he wasn't surprised, yet he still wanted more information. "To what end? Specifically, why at just our schools, the two 'private' schools."

Shortly after the Escutcheon Academy started, there was a feud within the council that governed and controlled admittance. Some wanted more liberal policies for enrollment, while the others wanted more restrictions placed on candidate qualifications. The council split, and one faction decided to start a second school, one where only the purest and most influential of the Nefslama descendants were allowed.

The two schools developed disparate curriculums and goals. While Escutcheon continued to follow open and modern practices, allowing mainstreaming of talented yet ordinary humans into her halls, the other school did not. After a time, the separation of those ideals wore on Jarrod Stevens, and he looked for a solution that might help bridge the divide. Thus, the game of Runes was introduced, and the common ground brought an uneasy connection to keep the schools somewhat on the same path.

The Runes games were meant to both teach those descendants who held the gift a rudimentary skill they might one day need, and test those who might hold power to understand them.

"Are you saying that everyone in my school is part Nefslama?" Colby asked. His thoughts went directly to Darla. "I knew it or felt it really."

Tittering and shaking his head, Fizzlewink stretched and licked his wrist before rubbing it behind his ear. "I mentioned the liberal practices of Escutcheon. There are talented and bright students, but not many have the bloodline or enough of it to channel the limited flow of Emassa. The families all have kept their gifts secret, many not even sharing it with their children unless they presented with abilities."

Colby began wondering about those who likely had a connection to the Emassa. Gary, he knew for certain, Darla, highly likely, Rhea, uncertain. And then there was Jasper. Colby shivered. His father had taken him away and put him in the 'Purest' academy, though he returned two years later. And he was extremely talented with Runes, though he was academically challenged or just lazy. Then the thought of playing Runes worried him.

"What happens if I begin using the correct sequencing during a Runes match?" Colby asked.

Brow wrinkled and left eye squinting, Fizzlewink contemplated for a moment. "I hadn't thought of that. Normally I would not think it an issue besides a user of Emassa recognizing the work of another. For you, however, your lack of control and turbulent temper could pose a problem."

"You mean he could activate a spell in the middle of a match, and all hell would break loose," Gary said.

"Indeed. I suggest you play carefully to make certain you always switch the order a bit."

Shelly placed a hand on Colby's shoulder, noticing his mounting worry. "Maybe you should just stop playing to be safe." She knew her little brother and his sudden outbursts when his emotions boiled over. If he played Jasper Bodine again after learning the order of the proper runes, there was no telling what might happen.

As though reading her thoughts, Colby touched her hand. "Jasper is not worth me outing myself."

* * *

"Touching…can we get back to work now?" Fizzlewink was not confident Colby could keep himself in check. He would have to keep an eye on the boy or find some outside help.

***

Lessons began in earnest.

The runes belonged to categories starting from the first level representing the basic forms of physical elements. The second level consists of alterations, binding, and manipulation, as each following odd level contained from the level below. Each level becomes more complex and contains more runes than the previous, and they become more obscure and difficult as they climb the hierarchy.

Colby, Gary, and Shelly's first lessons were to master the basic runes, which was not difficult since they had each learned them in the game played at school. Gary was a natural, plus it helped that his father had been teaching him the basics for a few years. Colby and Shelly, though, were getting frustrated as they progressed into the higher levels of complexity.

"I didn't even like this game when I went to the school," Shelly said. "It was a bunch of nerds and quiet kids that were kinda creepy. No offense, guys."

Colby grunted while Gary just waved Shelly's comment off.

"I get the first level as each rune represents a simple unpaired physical thing. Sure add fire to sand to get glass…Now what?" Colby pointed to his runes. "Am I supposed to then add an action again?"

Gary looked over to Colby's sketchpad. "Yes, add a physical action to take upon the glass. Take multiple actions if you like. You have the glass, now do something with it."

Colby went back to his pad and scribbled some other runes, erasing them as he found they didn't fit based on Fizzlewink's constant tittering. His frustration level was mounting. As brilliant as he was in other things, he just could not wrap his mind around scratching symbols down and lining them up in a particular sequence to create magic.

Gary helped him in matches, as he found out. So he wasn't getting better. Then there were the runes he saw when he had visions in his sleep.

While Colby thought about those runes, he mindlessly drew them on his pad, one long swerve and a curl at the end, then a bisecting dash and two dots. Squiggle, squiggle, slash, curve, dash. Before he knew what was happening, Colby had created a rune construct and was feeding it Emassa.

"Um, Colby…" Gary started to say but was interrupted by Fizzlewink.

"Let go, boy."

Colby looked up in front of him and saw a pane of glass-forming. He panicked at the surprise and tension in Fizzlewink's voice, and he let go. But not without feeding a burst of energy into his creation.

The glass fully formed and then shattered when a force sent the shards hurtling across the room toward the door as it began to open. The glass buried into the wooden door when it opened only inches away from a startled old woman. She stared at the glass daggers, then to Colby, and finally to Fizzlewink.

"What in the Sam hell are you thinking," Nana said. Her eyes, still wide with a mix of shock and anger, narrowed on the little man. "Not under this roof." She looked at the others and stepped aside, then pointed out the door. "Outside with this nonsense and foolishness."

As they began exiting the room, Nana stepped out to block Fizzlewink from leaving. "Not you, cat-man." She pointed back at the glass in the door. "Your fuzzy little butt is gonna clean up this mess."

Fizzlewink looked up. "You see me?"

* * *

"I've always seen you, blurry and glowing, but right now, I almost see your fuzzy ass clear as a pimple on my nose." Nana glared down at him. "Now, clean this up."

Fizzlewink opened up his mouth to argue but changed his mind when he saw Nana shake her head no. When she turned to leave him to his task, he breathed a sigh of relief and motioned his hands to deconstruct Colby's simple spell. Once he finished cleaning up, he peered down the hall, glad to find it empty and the old woman nowhere in sight.

***

Outside in the backyard, Colby, and the others continued to work through the runes various levels and hierarchy, this time just taking notes and talking them out rather than drawing them in sequence in line. Colby didn't want to take any chances, especially out in the open.

Shelly looked over her shoulder, feeling a set of eyes on her back. She saw Nana watching them through the kitchen window. "What we need is someplace to practice that's safe and private. Away from the house and the old battle-ax."

"I can look for somewhere," Colby said. "I'm not getting anywhere with these stupid lines and swirls." He picked up his tablet and began searching the area for any secluded places or old buildings. As he thumbed through his search results, the screen began to distort.

Symbols of strange runes began to dance across his screen. Colby wiped his eyes and looked again. They were gone. "Great, now even my eye floaters are turning into runes."

Colby continued thumbing along when his tablet screen went completely blue, and the runes began appearing on each line down the display. "What the hell." Colby forced his tablet to turn off and put it down. He sat there with his head in his hands.

Fizzlewink walked over to Colby as he exited the back door, watching Nana in the window over his shoulder. "Take heart, young man. It'll come to you when the time is right."

"Seriously…that's the best you can do?" Colby said.

Fizzlewink just blinked at Colby, while Shelly and Gary looked away from their work and watched Colby for signs of Emassa leaking off his hands.

Colby stood up and began pacing. "First I have this weird blue screen of death thing happening which means…I don't know what. Then I have the Northern Lights flying off me uncontrollably like my hands are incontinent or something. I can't grasp these infuriating rules for using runes as Gary can. I have a talking cat trying to teach me some mystical force crap. My sidekicks are Morticia Adams and Steve Urkle."

Throughout Colby's harangue, his hands sparkled and swirled with blue and red ribbons of energy while the others backed away. His hands swung about as he acted out his frustration in overly animated gestures and pointing. He barely noticed when Nana closed the drapes in the kitchen window and disappeared from view.

"All I want is to find out what happened with my dad." Colby pushed his hands down to his sides and stomped his feet in his final act of tantrum. The power, as a gush of water, would burst from a un-kinked water hose, shot from him in a burst of color and resounding boom that shook the trees and ground. Light burst forth and shook leaves from trees and uprooted several plants in the yard. Shingles flew from the garage, and the side windows in Shelly's car burst inward.

Once the dust settled, Colby stood on a patch of glowing earth where once a lush lawn grew. Clumps of dirt and grass were strewn around the yard. The glow faded quickly as Colby took in a breath and exhaled slowly. He looked at the faces of his companions and flushed. Picking up his tablet, he ran into the house through the back door that Nana now held open.

Fizzlewink just tittered and waved his hand to reverse what Colby did to the lawn. "I am not a cat."

* * *

"Easy whiskers," Shelly said and smirked. She looked over at her car, observing the busted windows. "Just great."

"I am so not Urkle," Gary said.

Shelly snickered. "Yes, you are."

Gary threw a clump of grass at her. "Shut-up, Morticia. Nice car."

Chapter 22

No one spoke about Colby's outburst. They figured it best to let it go and focus on continuing their education.

While Shelly learned from Gary the history of what Fizzlewink already imparted, Colby began indexing and correlating the runes and constructs that Fizzlewink taught them. He worked through meals, choosing to eat at his desk, saying he had to finish something on which he was working. It was after Nana threatened to carry him off and bath him herself that Colby relented and stopped his work.

"I'm finished anyway," he said. "I'll have a quick shower and join you all downstairs for breakfast."

* * *

When Colby entered the kitchen, he was greeted by Fizzlewink, Nana, Gary, and Shelly. All of them were sitting together at the table and waiting for him to explain himself.

"What is this, some sort of intervention?" he asked. "Seriously, stop looking at me like that, and where's mom?"

"Sit down and eat. Your mother went into work to catch up on things she has been letting slip," Nana finally said. "Fizzlewink tells me you've been working for days at that computer of yours nonstop. Do you mind sharing what is so important? You should be learning to control your magic."

"Well, I've been doing that," Colby said between bites and chewing. "I was thinking about how we've been forced to deal with the difficulty of learning all these runes and constructs and such." Colby stopped to eat more then continued to speak with his mouth full. "Plus, they take too much time to sequence if you're in a hurry or under duress."

"Go on, Fart-blossom, spit it out," Nana said. "Not the food. Swallow and talk with your mouth empty, please."

Colby smirked and chewed a few more times before swallowing his food and sticking out his tongue, opening his mouth to show it was empty.

"So you know I created an operating system based on the runes and constructs. I built a programming language out of it and downloaded it to my tablet and smartphone."

Colby explained how by using this new program, they could call up the runes they need by simply entering a search word or phrase. Then the runes would appear and build the construct for the spell they needed using an AI running on his desktop computer.

"I call it Hashtag Magic," Colby said with a toast filled grin. He held out his tablet for them to see. "Despite what Fizz said, I found a shortcut to magic."

* * *

Gary smiled and took the offered tablet from Colby's hand. "Now there really is an app for everything." Gary tried calling up a few constructs and watched the symbols appear on the screen. He placed his hand over them, expecting the runes to transfer to his hand, but nothing happened. "Problem computer wizard, the runes just display on the screen."

Colby took the tablet back and handed Gary his phone. "Now try," he said.

Gary re-entered his hashtag on his device and watched as the screen displayed the runes and then emerged through the glass and transfer to his hand. He released the magic and watched as the construct took form.

Everyone watched as the runes became substance and twisted reality. A tiny mouse appeared on the table before them and looked up in surprise just before Fizzlewink leaped from his seat and charged after the rodent. The laughs that followed snapped Fizzlewink out of his current state, and he turned to face them, disappointed that the illusion disappeared.

Fizzlewink frowned at the roar of laughter. "You spend as much time as a cat and see that some things don't wear off on you."

Gary caught his breath. "So why did it work this time?"

Colby detailed how the program worked. The app would connect to a relay, which in turn sent the hashtag runes request to Colby's server for compiling. Through their ability to harness the Emassa, it would transmit the construct back to the requesting device for rendering while siphoning off the required Emassa from the user. It required something personal to be connected with the user, so this was why Gary couldn't use Colby's tablet.

"Best of all, as we learn more runes and constructs, I will enter them into the app. The AI daemon will then attempt to create more complex spells that we can test." Colby waved his arms as he spoke with wide eyes and a broad smile. "I'll update all our devices with the new OS."

It finally occurred to Colby that Nana earlier said, 'Fizzlewink told her', "wait, you said Fizzlewink talked to you… you can hear him?" he said to her.

"I been telling you for years that I'm a witch Colby, of course, I can see and hear him. Well, I could always sort of see him that is." She began collecting dishes and putting food away. "I mean, he still looks like a cat, but he glows, and I can always tell what he's saying even though I hear meowing."

"I could help with that, I think," Colby started.

"NO," Nana and Fizzlewink said at once.

"I mean, I already have a full plate with three of you to teach is all," Fizzlewink said while glancing at Nana. "Now that you've added some Rube Goldberg contraption to the mix, I'm more than stretched thin."

Nana nodded in agreement and continued putting things away. "Why don't you boys run along and get outside for a change. You've been cooped up in that room for weeks, and it'll be winter before you know it."

Gary and Colby looked at each other as though being told to go outside, and play was for little boys, but then they smiled as the same thought occurred to them both.

"It's nice outside. The fresh air will do you both some good." Nana pointed her finger toward the door. "And you stay here, cat-man."

"Ooo, the master is in trouble," Shelly said. Receiving the wagging finger from Nana, Shelly decided to follow the boys outside. "Hey guys, mind if I tag along?"

The three of them left the house and headed toward the "L" train stop a few blocks away. Shelly's car was still in the shop getting the windows replaced and computer fixed. The insurance covered everything, writing it off as a surge in the electrical system though they did not fully explain the windshield and side windows busting out.

They headed downtown toward the old warehouse district off of the Chicago

River. While they rode the train, Colby reprogrammed Shelly's phone by removing her SIM card and putting in a different one to boot from. Once done, he replaced her SIM and restarted the phone. "Looks the same, right? Only now you have a new app, and it will work with a voice command as well."

Shelly reclaimed her phone and started to open the app before Colby stopped her.

"Not here, Shelly," he said, looking around at the passengers. No one was paying them any mind, but he certainly did not want any accidental magic to start a riot.

When the train arrived at Chicago Avenue and State Street station, they transferred to a westbound #70 bus headed toward Halsted Street.

"Where are we going anyway," Shelly asked.

"Hooker Street on Goose Island. There is an old empty warehouse that was closed down then abandoned. Perfect place for some practice with plenty of space." Colby shared a devious smile with his fellow pupils of the paranormal.

When they arrived at the warehouse, Colby took them around back to a spot where the grating over a ground-level window was loose. With a word to his phone's voice recognition.
#RemoveGrateOpenWindow.

A rune construct appeared, and he directed it to the grating. He stood back as the screened covering disappeared, and the window opened. Colby stepped inside, followed by the others.

"This place is kinda creepy," Gary said. "You think it's haunted?"

"Until recently I would have said there is no such thing as ghosts, but now… I'm not so sure," Colby answered.

"There are ghosts," Shelly said, much to the boy's shock. "Not here…I mean they exist. I've been able to see them for years, but I don't sense any in the warehouse."

Colby looked at Shelly. "Why am I just hearing about this? I mean, I knew from eavesdropping, but you never admitted it openly."

Shelly shrugged her shoulders and kept walking into the open space of the abandoned building. "Haven't thought of it lately, and was told not to say anything unless you developed talent. You have to admit there have been many more interesting things going on, besides I haven't been bothered by any for a few weeks."

"What ghosts bother you? Do you see dad?"

"No, I've never seen Dad. Mostly just Ma, Nana's mother…Crazy old bat," she said.

"So dad is not dead because if he were, you'd probably see him, right?" Colby was pleading for confirmation of his aspirations to one day see his papa again.

Shelly looked at her brother, understanding his desire to hear what she often thought. "Maybe," she said. "I'm not sure how it all works, really. Most of the ghosts I've seen either ignore me or pester me with non-stop talking. Others want me to pass on a message or something."

Colby held onto his new hope and followed the others into the warehouse with a bounce in his step. "So I think we should stick to things that won't cause structural damage, such as fire would," he said, directed to Shelly.

"Seriously, I'm not the one who had a thing for fire growing up. I remember it being you that set my Barbie camper on fire and rolled it down the street," Shelly said. "And what about all the action figure funeral pyres you two held. There are more torched and twisted plastic dolls and figures buried in the back yard-"

"Never mind," Colby said, turning red. "Let's just start with the simple stuff."

The three practiced several simple constructs over the first twenty minutes before moving on to more complex spells. They made things appear then disappear. Shelly created a pool of water while Gary formed a miniature twister above it to make a water spout. They soon progressed to creating energy balls and shooting various discarded cans and bottles off of a half wall.

"This is kinda cool but also-" Shelly started.

"Boring?" Gary finished.

"So what do you suggest," Colby asked.

Shelly gave a wicked Goth-girl smile and entered a hashtag, **#Invisibility.** Shelly disappeared. "Now find me." The clomping of her boots echoed through the open space as she ran off to be found.

"Hide and seek," Colby said. "Really, who's the kid now?"

"Shut your trap and just see if you can find me," she snapped back. Her voice echoed off every wall, distorting the location of its source.

Colby rolled his eyes at Gary, who just smiled and began to turn and go look for Shelly.

"It's magical hide and seek dude." Gary stopped mid-turn to find himself inches away from a creature, unlike anything he had ever imagined and screamed. It was something like a seven-foot goblin.

Colby turned to see the monster and smirked. "Very funny, Shelly, you look better that way."

Relieved, Gary stopped screaming and slugged the creature in the arm playfully. "You had me going there for a minute Shelly." He turned to laugh with Colby, but his breath cut short. He lifted his hand and pointed behind Colby.

Colby turned around to face two more of the creatures and dropped his phone. The screen cracked, and as he stepped back away from the creatures to meet back-to-back with Gary, his phone crunched below the foot of an advancing beast. "I don't think this is Shelly doing this," Colby said.

"Are they Shizumu?" Gary asked.

"I don't think so, they have no red glow, but they sure look pissed."

Gary tried to hashtag a construct to help, but nothing was happening. "I can't do a spell."

Colby looked over at his smashed phone. "My phone is dead, hand me yours."

Before Gary could toss Colby his smartphone, it was knocked out of his hand and whirled through the air into the hands of one of the creatures.

The monster looked at the phone with interest and then tossed it aside. "You are one of them?" it asked.

"One of who?" Colby said.

"The makers," the creature said as it moved closer. "You glow with power like they do, but it is different."

"I don't know what you are talking about. I'm just a kid from the North-side." Colby backed toward Gary until their backs were touching, and they were surrounded by five of the beings.

"I sure wish I had my phone. Maybe I could call someone to help straighten this out. What do ya say, fellas or ladies," Colby said. "Whatever you are," he muttered under his breath.

Colby reached behind him to make sure Gary was still there when he felt an object slide into his hand. Shelly's phone. He tried to think of a construct, but his emotions took hold, and the Emassa burst forth in a sphere of light that surrounded him, Gary, and the now visible Shelly.

* * *

"Get us out of here," Shelly screamed.

Colby could not speak. His fingers were frozen out of fear, and he could not move them. He closed his eyes to block out terror the way he did as a child. "If I can't see you, you can't see me," he whispered. He opened one eye and still saw the creatures. He dug deeper into his psyche, hoping to find a way out. In desperation fueled by fear, he muttered the first clear thought that came to him. "There's no place like home." A sudden jolt and he found himself on the floor of his bedroom. Gary and Shelly were beside him.

It took a few moments to realize where they were. Gary was the first to speak.

"That was SICK!"

Shelly smacked him on the back of the head. "Ya, right. Colby, what just happened, and what were those things?"

Colby shook his head as he gained his feet. "I have no idea, on either account."

Fizzlewink ran into the room before anyone could say another word. "Where did you just come from, and why did I just feel like the sun exploded in this room?"

Colby did his best to explain where they were and what they were doing. It was difficult to get a word in while both Nana and Fizzlewink were yelling and ranting over the stupidity of what they did. Colby resigned to eat his licorice and wait until they stopped shouting before he continued. By the time he managed to tell his tale, with support from Shelly and Gary, Fizzlewink was in a state of worry that had him pacing the floor.

"Oh dear," Fizzlewink said over again. "They looked like tall goblins, you said. That would mean that the Dreggs have returned."

"Dreggs?" Colby asked. "Just what is a Dregg, and why were they asking about the 'makers'?"

"They are the result of an experiment gone wrong, well right…then wrong. A curse of sorts."

Nana sat down and took a piece of licorice for herself and started gumming on in. "Which is it? Right or wrong?"

"Both actually," Fizzlewink said. "My maker attempted to cure a plague centuries ago. They succeeded, but there was a slight side effect." Fizzlewink glanced over at Colby before looking back at the floor. "The plague was cured sort of since it no longer attacked their bodies, but it mutated and well…It mutated the people as well. The disease was gone, but the Dregg remained. We tried to find a use for them, but that didn't work out for more than bruce force in the wars with the Shizumu."

"So your people created these goblin things that look like they should be playing for the NBA, and you didn't think to mention this?" Shelly asked skeptically. She was starting to pick up on when Fizzlewink was twisting the truth. "Any other surprises, Dr. Frankenstein?"

"No, but if the Dreggs are here, then they will be looking for the promised cure for their mutation. We never could figure it out since they were all chased off by others that were frightened of them." Fizzlewink sat down. "This is not at all good."

"Ya, and they have my phone," Gary added.

Colby got up and sat at his desk. He pulled up the app and sent a command. "Well, at least they can't access the Hashtag Magic app. I've remotely deleted it and set the phone lock." He pointed to the map on his screen. "Now we can track them until the phone dies or they…"

"Or they what?" Shelly asked.

"Remove the battery…or destroy it," he said as the red dot on the screen blinked out.

Chapter 23

Gary's lost phone, and Colby's dropped one were both high on the list to address replacing. Though they had tablets, they needed something much more efficient. Colby thought that at the same time, something different might rectify the issue of having his only reliable access to Emassa for the others, knocked or dropped from his hand. He researched on-line and found all the parts required to build what he had in mind. For now, the Hashtag Magic app required a relaying through Colby's device to collect Emassa from him to transfer to the others.

He ordered all the parts and extras for spare. Most of the parts were coming from overseas, so it would be some time before enough arrived to begin building his new toys. So Colby convinced Fizzlewink they needed to practice, and the only place they had was the abandoned warehouse. Except it had squatters.

* * *

Fizzlewink eventually relented to Colby's incessant pestering and prodding, and he visited the warehouse to screen it for suitability and prepare it for use as a practicing center. He went alone; that was his only condition. And after getting his way, Colby agreed. The little blue Nefslama informed Colby he would be gone for several days doing his work and rooting out any Dreggs that may have made the place home. Fizzlewink assured them that if he went alone, the Dreggs would not bother him. He would not explain how he knew they'd leave him alone.

While Fizzlewink was gone, Colby and Gary went about normal lives in school, and Shelly went back to work at her jobs bartending at the Goth club by night and waitressing at the diner by day. They were forbidden from practicing magic intentionally unless to protect themselves outside of Fizzlewink's presence. With the Dreggs around, they couldn't afford to draw them closer.

***

Archeology Club was becoming rather tedious with Darla and Rhea, both complaining about how boring Chichén Itzá was going to be. They spent each meeting pouring over the information everyone found about the site and its history. Darla and Rhea seemed only to provide data for the local shopping and goods that interested them. Then there was Rigel with his passive-aggressive attempts at getting his hands on unknown journals belonging to Colby's father.

"Is there anything not related to shopping that you two have to add?" Colby asked in a fit of frustration. "Seriously, this is about a trip to ancient places and uncovering mysteries and clues to the history of these civilizations, not who has the best jewelry." He walked over to the portable speaker on the front desk and stopped the music from Darla's phone. "And enough of this baby-baby music crap."

"What evs," Darla said. "It has to be fun for everyone, right? While you guys are digging around in the dirt, what are us girls supposed to do?"

Colby had enough, and his already tense mood over the things running through his mind got the best of him. Between believing his father was somewhere out in the world, likely in trouble, and the Dreggs and Shizumu, his boiling point was reached.

"You will dig, or you will not go." He turned to the professor and pointed. "And you, Professor, can stop pestering me about my father." Colby grabbed his backpack and stormed out of the room, placing his hands in his pockets to mask the glow of Emassa.

***

For the next several days, Colby avoided Darla and Rhea though they were persistent. He walked around the school, growling at anyone who approached, especially Jasper Bodine.

"Jasper, what is it you think you're proving to your little mindless friends by bullying me or anyone else for that matter. You have nothing, I repeat NOTHING, to offer this institution beyond your father's money and your overpowering smell of cologne." Colby began to pull his hands from his pockets but was stopped by Gary.

"Dude, chill out," Gary said. He turned to Jasper. "Piss off, Jasper."

Gary pushed Colby down the hall and out of the school. They walked toward the parking lot where Colby parked his sister's car since she started letting him use it for school a few days a week. "CJ, what has gotten into you?"

Colby breathed hard and shouted to the sky. After calming his breathing, he looked at Gary. "I just can't hold it in anymore, Gary. I've held so much in for longer than I can remember, and I just want it all to stop."

Gary stood there, waiting on Colby to elaborate, but he shut down. "Colby, I can't imagine what's jumping around in your skull, but you can't keep taking it out on everyone around you."

Colby looked at Gary for several moments before relenting. "I know, and I'm sorry, but I just can't help it. Every day I feel more and more pressure and anger and resentment. It is all building up like a thermal pocket below a supervolcano, and I just want it to explode and be done with it."

"We need to talk to Fizz," Gary said.

"Or let it all go on that ass-hat, Jasper. He annoys the piss out of me. Do you think Fizz would let me just-" Colby started?

"NO," Gary said. "Let's go home."

***

Fizzlewink was in the kitchen when Colby and Gary arrived back at the Stevens' home. He was sitting on the counter eating fish while Nana mixed a noxious pot of something on the stove.

"I really hope that's not dinner, Nana," Colby said.

Nana slapped the spoon down on the counter and spun around. "No, you little smart ass, it's a potion to make you more agreeable."

Colby stared at his grandmother in silence before starting to laugh. "Good one, Nannie." Colby started to leave the kitchen, but Gary stopped him.

"I don't think she's joking CJ." Gary watched the look pass between Nana and Fizzlewink and cringed.

Nana crooked her finger and then pointed at a chair beside the island. "Sit your temperamental little ass down and listen."

Fizzlewink finished wiping his face of fish flesh and took a seat next to Colby. "I'll take it from here, witch," he said. After glaring at Nana, he turned to Colby. "First, you need to empty your head of this senseless anger you carry around, or you're going to hurt someone."

* * *

Colby started to protest, but Fizzlewink stopped him.

"Do not deny how you feel; you can gain strength from it. You do need to come to terms with it, however, or you will burn yourself out."

"What are you talking about, Fizz?" Colby asked.

Fizzlewink shared his theory to Colby's lack of control and unexpected manifestations of Emassa when his emotions were heightened. His power was getting stronger and building as he began to accept it within him. He agreed that Colby would need to begin releasing the buildup of power he withholds until interrupted by an outburst. "You are going to burn yourself out. I think if we don't start some controlled release of power."

"Controlled, how?" Colby asked. "We tried going to that warehouse to practice, but you know what happened."

Perking up, Fizzlewink smiled at Nana and looked back at the boys. "We've been chatting about that, your Nana and I. We think that the warehouse can still serve that purpose…but I will need to finish my work. I checked it out and warded it against unwanted visitors."

Confused, Colby scratched his head and began pulling on his ear, an old habit that returned. "And what did you do to ward it? I thought your strength in Emassa was weakened when your home disappeared?"

A wicked smile formed across the face of the part-time feline. "That's where you come in, my boy. Since your ability returned, the Emassa has been flowing into this realm at an increasing pace. I think because of a little jolt I got from you after one of your outbursts, I was able to channel enough power to form a protection ward around the entire warehouse. But I need to head back now and finish up a few details." Fizzlewink winked at them and trotted out the door.

***

Several days passed before Fizzlewink was satisfied with the ward of protection placed around the warehouse. Using the power access gained from Colby, he directed constructs all around the outside of the building, both imparting an obscuring spell and a barrier to keep out unwanted guests. The obscuring was placed to prevent drawing attention to the building and would deter those with heightened senses from feeling any Emassa radiating from the location. The barrier was a secondary defense against those strong enough to dispel the obscuring.

"I thought that the use of Emassa attracts the Nefslama, Shizumu, and Dreggs," Colby asked.

"Yes it does, but we are only worried about the Shizumu really. The Dreggs will not get past the obscuring, and any Nefslama will be too cautious or paranoid to investigate." Fizzlewink seemed confident in his statements.

The rest of the gang was not convinced but only grumbled their misgivings.

Over the days that followed, Colby, Gary, and Shelly worked with Fizzlewink in the warehouse on practicing the fundamentals of the runes. Colby would call upon specific runes and allow them to float in the air so Fizzlewink could explain its place in the hierarchy of crafting Emassa magic.

"You must first learn these rules and applications in order to understand them better," Fizzlewink said. "Perhaps expanding on what you have already learned will identify the faults in your little computer application."

Colby admitted there were some issues with the Artificial Intelligence routines and the way the constructs were built. He could no longer pass the small ripples off as weak or inadequate hashtags after a failed conjuring resulted in Gary having breasts and long blond hair for an afternoon.

"You make a really ugly chick, dude," Colby laughed.

"He just needs the right dress and make-up," Shelly offered to Gary's horror.

The three pupils spent many days finding out the groupings of runes. Everything they were taught, Colby took copious notes and transferred the information into the backend server for Hashtag Magic. Fizzlewink insisted they studied the long and tedious way as his people did, no electronics allowed during the lessons.

"Do we always need the runes?" Colby asked. "I caused things without knowing these symbols already."

"You have no control or proper understanding yet, Colby," Fizzlewink answered. "It took my people years to learn to control the smallest amount of Emassa without the runes. You need them to focus your intent. For the foreseeable future, you will need to use your '# Magic' app or write them from memory."

Colby's head was aching at the end of each day, but things were beginning to make sense. The only problem he encountered was figuring out how to adjust his #Magic app and the AI daemon. He decided to figure that out later because the parts for his new project came, and he needed to get that started.

***

The following weekend, Colby spent his time in the garage banging and molding, assembling and cursing, and perfecting his new devices. He knew his mother might be upset at how he used some of the money he saved, but this was important, and hopefully, she would understand in a sober moment. He did not see much of his mother of late since she started going to the office early and working late. Some mornings his only indication she came home the night before was the empty vodka bottle on the kitchen counter.

Back when Aria had remembered his long passed birthday, she attempted to make up for missing it by making dinner and giving him an envelope of money. Just an envelope of money without a card. He wasn't even surprised that she forgot a card. Happy belated birthday hastily scratched on the envelope in a half dried-out marker. If she was upset with what he spent the money on, well, he just didn't care. The new watch phones were way too cool to ask permission, and his mom simply wouldn't understand anyway.

Chapter 24

The day came when Colby could present Gary with a new phone to replace the one that was taken by the Dreggs. This new phone, however, was so much more. After a few adjustments and a new construct that Fizzlewink helped create without knowing the ultimate use, they were ready.

Gary arrived at the Stevens' home early to meet Colby before heading out, as became part of their new everyday routine. They would practice a bit every morning over breakfast. After the encounter with the Dreggs and knowing that Shizumu were out there getting stronger, no one took chances.

Shelly came stomping into the kitchen after Nana roused her from bed at Colby's request. "There better be coffee ready, I worked until four this morning, and I am not happy about being woke up."

"You should probably wash that gothic look off before you go to bed, my dear," Nana said, handing her a cup of Joe. "You look like the bride of Dracula without the fangs, but the dead eyes."

Shelly glared at the old woman but accepted the coffee all the same. "Out with it cheese-curd, I want to go back to bed."

Colby reached into the box he left sitting on the counter. He pulled out two pouches and handed one to each Gary and Shelly. "They are new phones built into watches and programmed with my HMOS, Hashtag Magic Operating System. My HMOS will not go into a blue screen of death. There is another notable difference. Once you put them on, someone else will not easily remove them, and they can not be used by another." Colby grinned and stepped back to view their reactions.

Gary opened his pouch and pulled out the watch phone and whistled. "This is a watch phone that works without a handset, like the ones that are just coming out on the market. Where'd you get the money for these?"

"I just bought the parts and made them myself for a fraction of the market price."

"Awesome, you made mine with silver and onyx band, my favorite combo," Gary said, putting on his watch. "Thanks…whoa, what was that," he said, catching himself on the counter before falling.

"That is the binding construct that makes it yours and next to impossible to remove by anyone else," Fizzlewink offered.

"How could you tell, Fizz?" Colby asked.

Fizzlewink shrugged and winked. "The eyes of a cat, though I am not a cat. They allowed me to see the runes just before they took hold. Besides, you asked me for a similar spell a few days ago. Nice modifications."

* * *

Shelly took out her phone watch and admired the leather finish with metal studs. "Very Goth, I like it." She put on her watch and almost spilled her coffee in reaction to the binding. "That was wicked…thanks." She gulped her last bit of coffee and handed the cup back to Nana. "I'm going back to bed."

Colby and Gary headed for the back door but were stopped by Nana.

"Take these packed lunches with you. I have a feeling you'll be gone most of the day."

The boys looked at the brown bags, wondering what horrid and stomach-wrenching experience awaited inside the lunch sacks.

"Don't pull those faces. I didn't make them. Shelly prepared them last night, knowing you would be headed out for the day."

"How does she do that?" Fizzlewink asked as he followed the boys out the back door. "I think she has more ability than she lets on."

"Experience with people refusing to eat her food, combined with the turned-up noses, does not make her a mind reader," Colby said.

Colby stopped halfway through the yard, observing the repaired lawn for the first time. "Thanks for fixing this Fizz…but, would you mind not following us today. I really don't want to explain my cat following me to the park."

Hiding his feelings about being excluded, Fizzlewink shrugged and began walking off ahead. "Not to worry, boy, I have other things to attend today." He transformed into the scruffy old tomcat and stalked off through the bushes.

"I think he was upset," Gary said.

Colby shrugged and tilted his head toward the gate. "He'll get over it. Let's go."

The boys took the leisurely walk to the park, and while they continued, Gary couldn't help but notice the change in Colby's gait. Not so long ago, Colby walked head down and slumped. He avoided looking people in the eye or acknowledging passers-by. Now he held his head high and nodded at anyone they crossed. He carried new confidence that rivaled the shine of the sun. He liked his friend's new attitude.

As they approached the park, Colby stopped, then stepped in front of Gary and faced him. "You need to promise not to interfere today."

"Dude, relax. I promised I wouldn't mess with your matches anymore...unless you ask." Gary smiled. "Besides, I suspect you tweaked your HMOS to give an assist here and there."

Colby squinted and smirked. "You know me too well, my friend, as though we were one mind." Colby turned, and they continued into the park.

"That I do, my friend. That I do." Gary patted Colby on the back.

In the park, the boys made their way to the open space that contained permanent tables and chairs designed for chess but mostly used for Runes. The tables were already half full at mid-morning. By early afternoon, there would be full tables and onlookers waiting for a spot to open.

Colby wondered at how many Emassa gifted people came around to find others such as themselves and how many were simply addicted to playing the game. He admitted to himself, even though he was not very good on his own, Colby was drawn to the game by the mundane aspects of strategy and skill.

He did not dismiss the draw of the runes themselves and what they represented to his abilities, but the game was a honey trap. Like a bear that craves the sweet taste of that golden, gooey sweet treat, people got hooked on Runes and always sought out more. He only begged to find out how much the runes directly influenced addiction.

As he looked over the players and tables, Colby smiled at the nod he received from a familiar face. The old man sat alone at a table, dismissing the offer of a challenge as his eyes met Colby's. Jenkins opened his hand to the chair across from his own, inviting Colby to take a seat.

Colby joined his new friend, leaving Gary to find a game for himself, which he did soon after they parted. Though Gary's game was nearby, Colby was relieved that his friend would be facing away and unable to interfere, being busy with his own match.

"Have you come back to teach this old man new tricks, my young friend?" Jenkins asked.

Colby laughed and smiled. "I think you mean 'teach an old dog new tricks', don't you?" Colby thought he saw Jenkins wince at his words.

Jenkins smirked. "Not a dog person myself. Horrid breath and slobbery things, dogs are. Anyway, I'm glad you have returned." Jenkins began sorting his tiles and placing them on his tile racks to begin play. "What about new tricks, though. Are you going to share more of your wonderfully advanced runes today?"

"We shall see my friend."

Colby went first once the match started. To his relief, the park was not yet filled with spectators. Part of the reason he chose to arrive so early in the day was to avoid a crowd watching. He did not want to fail at playing without Gary's help in front of a bunch of people. Losing miserably to Jenkins would be bearable as he felt at ease with the man. There was something comfortable and familiar about his presence that Colby enjoyed.

Their rounds passed with no great advantage to either side. Colby sensed the old man was going easy on him for some reason, but he held his own. Only a few times did Colby rely on a hint pulled from the enchantment he added to his phWatch. They had finished after the game pieces ran out, with Colby winning by only a few points when Gary showed up.

"Look who I ran into," Gary said and winked at Colby. Behind him stood Darla and Rhea.

* * *

Colby looked past Gary and into Darla's long-lash surrounded eyes. He stared into them and blinked. 'Nope, your magic doesn't work on me', he thought. "What a surprise." Colby knew better.

Darla shrugged and batted her eyes. "Rhea and I were walking past and saw Gary. We figured you would be nearby and thought we'd see what you were up to."

Jenkins cleared his throat. "Why don't you ask these lovely girls to join us?" he said to Colby.

Colby looked first at Jenkins and then back at the girls. "You don't happen to play Runes, do you?" Suddenly a thought occurred to him. If he wanted to know for certain what the deal was with Darla and Rhea, he could test them with the runes.

Darla shrugged and nodded. "A little. I don't play much, mostly at home."

Rhea nodded as well, and each girl took a seat across from Colby and Gary, who sat at the now-free table beside. The boys laid out some runes for the girls.

Colby leaned over to Gary. "I think Darla uses Emassa. I'm not sure about Rhea. Let's find out."

Gary nodded and smiled.

The two tables played back and forth in a friendly and non-aggressive fashion while Jenkins watched on with a curious look upon his face. Colby glanced at the old man on more than one occasion, wondering what was going on the Jenkins' head. By the look on his face, Colby felt like he was assessing the girls as well.

Since his test was going nowhere, Colby decided to be more direct. He began to lay out a sequence of runes in a construct using the practical rules for focusing the Emassa. As he began to place the action and subject runes, he deliberately moved them back into reverse order. This was not done to prevent him from activating the spell exactly; it was done to see how Darla would react. Nothing. At least not from Darla

Jenkins cleared his throat, and Colby looked at him. The man looked back and smiled. "A bit dry today, the air." He leaned over and picked up his bag. "I think this old man has had more than his fair share of fresh air for the day." He stepped back from the table and bowed his head toward the girls. "Ladies, it was a pleasure to make your acquaintance."

Colby began to stand up. "Are you all right, Jenkins?" Colby looked the man over, concerned that he was leaving so abruptly.

"Oh, I am quite fine, lad. I just need to go home and get some rest. I am feeling suddenly drained. I do hope to see you again." Jenkins shook Colby's hand and then Gary's before heading off down the path and was gone from view past the hedges.

"He seems nice," Rhea said. "He reminds me of my papa."

Colby looked at Rhea and then back to where Jenkins went. "Me too," he said softly.

Colby looked back at his construct, noticing that it was a spell for power draining. He looked back to Jenkins, but the man was already gone.

Darla screamed.

Colby turned back to find a scraggly old bluish cat sitting in the middle of the table, batting rune tiles around.

"Fizzlewink. Where did you come from?" Colby said, pushing the cat off the table. "Go home."

The cat growled and then turned around and ran off through the park toward the Stevens' home.

* * *

Darla regained her composure and offered a tissue to Rhea, who was sneezing. "He just jumped on the table out of nowhere." Darla looked at Colby. "Your cat is weird." She stood up and helped Rhea to her feet.

"Is she all right?" Colby asked.

"She's allergic to cats." Darla pulled Rhea out from behind the table and stepped onto the path. "We should be going. See you tomorrow, guys." Darla raised a hand and wiggled her fingers then winked.

Rhea waved while sneezing and blowing her nose.

Colby and Gary gathered their things and began to head back to Colby's house when they stopped near a bench where Colby saw a man staring at his laptop, swearing. When he approached, he discerned the man's screen had gone into the BSOD, and it had the beginnings of runes forming.

Colby rushed over and pushed the screen closed. "Best remove the battery. When you put it back and reboot, it should be fine."

The man looked at Colby oddly and then snapped out of what seemed like a trance.

"Are you okay?" Gary asked the man.

"Um…Fine. I was just um…Working on something, and I think I dozed off or something." The man put his computer in his bag and got up and walked away. "I need some rest," he muttered.

Colby looked at Gary and shook his head. "This doesn't look good. I thought they were isolated to the school and our homes, but this is spreading." Colby looked around and then up. He patted Gary and pointed up and a large antenna on the roof of a nearby cafe. Affixed to the metal tower were a cellular array and a wireless hotspot. It could spread through the web like a virus. "We better check this out where it started, at school."

Chapter 25

The halls of the school began to hold less terror as Colby walked them. He no longer saw torture chambers and cells when he looked at the rooms and lockers while he walked along the corridors with a new air of confidence. He was also working on calming himself and maintaining an even mood. His temper was one of the biggest hurdles he had to master his power. Concentrating so hard, though, had a tendency to give him headaches.

Gary walked along beside him, talking on his new phWatch. After putting his replacement SIM card in the device, it activated, and he was now strutting around, making sure everyone saw the new accessory every chance he got. He disconnected a fake call from a fake friend. He had no friends besides Colby. Besides, he was just doing it to show off his gadget. Gary turned to Colby as a hand wrapped around his arm.

"What have we here, fellas?" Jasper said, turning Gary around. "Looks like someone got a new toy, and it looks very much like the new model my dad's company hasn't even released yet."

"Hardly, Jasper," Colby said. "I happen to know these are nothing like anything MacroTech could produce."

"And how is that cheese-poof?"

"Because they work."

Jasper began to loosen his grip on Gary's arm, which started to slip down his wrist. He moved toward Colby when his hand came in contact with Gary's phWatch. "Ouch, what the…" he pulled his hand back and prepared to strike at Gary when he found his arm in a vice-like grip.

Rigel held Jasper's arm firm. "Is there a problem here, boys?" He let go of Jasper's arm and watched as he and his friends sulked away, muttering empty threats.

"Thanks, Professor Stark," Gary said. "I'm glad I didn't have to let loose on that ass-hat!"

Rigel chuckled and looked at the watches on both the boys' wrists. "Nice gadgets." He nodded to them and gave a wink before turning and walking back down the hall. "Better get to class."

Colby turned along with Gary and headed toward homeroom. While settling into his first class, Colby began to develop one of those new headaches. He sat down and dropped his bag on the floor so he could rub his temples.

"You all right?" Gary asked while pushing Colby's book bag under his seat.

Colby continued to rub his temples and grumble. "Just a sudden headache again, but it's going away."

Gary continued to look at his best friend, doubting that it was as simple as a sudden headache. Nothing of late was anywhere within the same state as simple. "Ah, huh."

The teacher instructed everyone to put away their things and prepare for a surprise quiz. She walked the aisles, handing out tests to the rhythm of grumbles and groans with a hint of a smile.

Colby took his test and began answering the questions first in rapid succession, and then slowing as the words and numbers began to blur and meld together. He looked around the room to witness twisting faces and forms blending into a darkening background. While his vision went black before him, his peripheral picked up a blue light that began to swallow him from behind.

Runes began to slip past him from somewhere beyond his sense of direction as he spun in circles to get his bearings. They twisted and turned into a vortex around him before sailing off and arranging into a construct too small to read.

Moving closer, Colby began to read the runes in an attempt to understand their meaning. He reached out to touch the construct only to find it recoiling from his own energy now flowing freely from his hand. Colby looked down at his hands to realize the color of Emassa was a deep purple. As he wondered at the change in his manifestation of Emassa, the runes broke forward and split into countless copies of the unknown construct, spreading out in a spider web configuration.

Each collection began to glow brighter, revealing the outlines of a face on the other side. The faces lost all expression as the eyes rolled back into their sockets. Streams of red energy shot forth from high above, each converging upon a construct and attacking the faces beyond the display of runes.

The faces contorted and bellowed sounds of pain, regret, horror, and shock. Most went quiet an instant later, except the ones that screamed from the flames that burst out from inside them.

* * *

Colby tried to race toward them but was blown back as the runes rejoined and pushed him out of the vision. Colby fell backward out of his desk from the impact of being ejected by a force that felt somehow vengeful.

The room erupted in gasps and shouts of surprise when Colby fell backward with a sudden burst of light that only one other in the room noticed.

Gary shot from his desk to the aid of his fallen friend. "CJ-"

Colby had looked up to Gary for only a moment before his eyes fluttered, and he lost consciousness. He woke in the nurse's office, surrounded by Gary, Shelly, and Nana.

"What happened?" Shelly asked. There was care and concern in her eyes that Colby had seldom seen before. "Were you attacked?"

All eyes were on Colby, but he drifted to the figure standing in the doorway.

"Everything sunny in here?" Rigel asked, leaning against the doorframe. "I heard someone had an episode, nothing about an attack."

Shelly turned to locate the alluring sound that caused her to shiver when her eyes fell upon its source. She smiled but found that her tongue refused to cooperate.

Colby and Gary watched the exchange between Shelly and Rigel and wrinkled their noses.

"It was nothing, Professor. I had some headaches and then a dizzy spell. I skipped breakfast this morning." Colby was selling excuses, and he could tell that Rigel was not in the market to buy. "Can we go home now?" he asked Nana.

"I'm driving," Nana proclaimed since no one was in any shape to argue. "Come along, Shelly, and stop drooling, my dear." She pulled Shelly along past Rigel and looked him up and down more closely. "Hubba-hubba, you got a granddaddy?"

Rigel blushed.

* * *

Gary helped Colby up and walked him toward the door. "Looks like we won't be in the club today after classes, Professor." Gary walked Colby out.

Rigel tilted his head and smirked until he caught Nana looking at him more closely. He looked away and stepped aside.

***

"Where's Fizz?" Colby asked as they piled into the car. "I figured he'd be here with the amount of Emassa that was let loose as I was thrown from my own vision."

"What a vision," Shelly said, looking back at Rigel, who stood at the school entrance watching them leave.

"Earth to Shelly…We're talking about what happened to CJ," Gary said.

Shelly snapped out of her trance when Nana threw the car from reverse to drive and hit the gas. "What the hell? Who let her drive?"

The ride back to the Stevens' home was filled with more action than a theme park roller coaster. The car swerved and swept through traffic and blew through stop signs. Not one pothole was missed, and neither were any traffic cones spared. When they pulled into the driveway back home, the exit from the car was equally erratic. The jarring ride made for gaining balance a bit challenging.

Shelly snatched her keys back from her grandmother and stomped into the house, followed by the others.

Fizzlewink was in the kitchen waiting. "What happened? You all look ghostly pale."

"Just our lives flashing before our eyes from the old battle-ax driving home," Shelly said. "I've gotta get ready for work, so spit it out, little brother. What happened in this vision of yours."

* * *

"I think I was inside the Internet," Colby started, "or at least some part of it."

Colby relayed what he saw, heard, and felt while he was in his vision. The focus was held on what he felt more than anything else. The overpowering sense of helplessness, dread, and doom being fueled by hatred, anger, and vengeful intent was still coursing through Colby's system. The red ribbons of energy carried with them all that was negative, transferring it into the faces beyond the runes. The faces transformed, and their eyes glowed red, except for the few that burst into flames.

"Something bad is going to happen. I can feel it somehow."

The remainder of the day and into the early afternoon was spent further discussing what Colby experienced. Fizzlewink remained oddly quiet during most of the discussion, while Gary offered more outlandish theories than sensible deductions.

"Maybe you entered an alternate dimension, or you got sucked into the MacroTech OS and brought it to life."

Colby shook his head at Gary's summation negatively. "I was somewhere between the computer and reality; I could…feel it. It was like I saw and felt the intentions of the Shizumu and what they are doing." He exhaled and ran his fingers through his mussed hair. "They discovered me there, and they were pissed."

"You are absolutely certain that they sensed you?" Fizzlewink asked, raising his fluffy white brows. "Because if that is the case, it was no premonition, you were somewhere they dwell when not hosted within a body." Fizzlewink began pacing the floor, moving his stubby legs in rapid motions that defied his stature. "I'm afraid what you saw has already occurred. Worse still…they know you exist."

"What do you mean that I exist?"

Colby began to press for more information but was interrupted by the doorbell.

"What now?" he mumbled as he made his way to the front door. He looked out the side window and staggered back. "What the hell are they doing here?"

"Who?" Gary asked.

"Darla, Rhea, and Professor yummy pants!" Colby took a deep breath and let go of his frustration. He rested his hand on the doorknob and opened the door. "Hello, girls…Professor," he said. "What are you doing here?"

"We heard about your seizure and wanted to make sure you were okay," Rhea said.

Darla nodded to her friend with approval. "And since we were going to come and check on you, the Professor thought…since we would all be together-"

"If you are up to it, that is," Rhea interrupted.

"We could just have our club meeting at your house." Darla smiled and stuck her head past the doorway, searching around and scoping out the Stevens' home. "Can we come in," she said, pushing past Colby.

Rhea followed Darla in as she walked straight past Colby and into the living room.

"Can we get some snacks or something," Darla said to Nana.

Nana smiled her gums at Darla and turned with a curtsy. "You'll get something all right," she said under her breath and went to the kitchen.

Colby led Rigel in and offered him a seat. He looked around the room to find Fizzlewink absent, much to his relief. Fizz was already acting strange though Colby was unsure what peculiar meant for a multidimensional traveling little blue man that lived his life as a mouse chasing, fur ball hacking, ass-licking cat. He saw Gary watching him and shrugged back as they both thought to locate the odd little man.

* * *

"I hope we are not intruding master Stevens…Colby," Rigel began and corrected his use of formal names during private meetings. "Our primary purpose was to see after your well-being."

"It's fine, Rigel. Please have a seat, and we can begin the meeting." Colby sat near the fireplace at the front of the room where he could see everyone. He watched Darla snooping around the room and cleared his throat, indicating she should stop being nosey and sit.

The subject of the meeting centered around the topic of fundraising. They would need at minimum two big events to bring in the dollars required to fund their trip to Chichén Itzá. The first would be in a few weeks during Halloween.

"All hallow's eve," Nana squealed, dropping a tray of lemonade and cheese flavored crisps. "How exciting, we could do a haunted house complete with monsters and vampires and-"

"Witches?" Gary asked.

Nana winked at Gary and sat down on the arm of the couch, nearly on top of Rigel's lap. "What do ya think, Professor yummy pants?"

Rigel blinked and stammered. "I beg your pardon?"

"What she means is that we could host a haunted house party, here at Stevens' Manor," Shelly said, walking into the room. "You'd be there, wouldn't you, Professor?"

Colby was mortified. His grandmother and sister were both falling over themselves to elicit a response from the dark and handsome man. Well, at least Nana pretended to be. There seemed something else was behind her interest in the Professor. Her interest appeared to strike a chord with Rigel as well.

Rigel only nodded the affirmative before standing and straightening his jacket. He cleared his throat before turning to Colby. "Well, that being settled, I think it is time I am going." He turned and headed for the door before turning back to the room. "Will you be returning to classes in the morning?"

"Yes, Professor. I will be in school tomorrow." Colby smiled at the vision of the usually commanding professor, all flustered. Colby turned back to the room to find four women staring at the backside of Rigel exiting the house. "Pathetic, the lot of you."

"Yes, they are," Gary said. Gary sat by the television half-listening during the exchange between Nana and Rigel. When he saw the news break into the programming, his full attention was grabbed and waved Colby over. "You need to see this."

Multiple reports were coming in from all over the city of people falling unconscious or having seizures before eventually recovering. Investigators are stumped as there are yet no indications of any causes or connections between those fallen ill. Several reports of spontaneous combustion have surfaced as well. Uncertain of any connection to the victims of burning, the incidents are being investigated as accidents. The only common thread was that each person was sitting before a computer moments before becoming affected.

The field reporter stood near an ambulance, where she spoke to a recovering woman outside her home. While answering questions, the woman turned to the television camera. Her aura was clear to any with the ability to see it; she radiated a red glow of the Shizumu.

"It actually happened," Colby whispered.

Chapter 26

Fizzlewink returned days after the incident with Colby at school, and the news of mass BSOD broke. His mood and manner changed over the past several weeks as events began to spiral. When asked where he has been or what he was doing, his answers were short and divisive to the point that others looked forward to his absences. Today was no exception; he arrived in Colby's room with an air of urgency and a face that could scare the claws off a real cat.

Colby glanced at Fizzlewink and returned to his computer screen. "You wear the face of a pissed off wolverine, Fizz. What has your tunic in such a bunch lately?"

Fizzlewink leaped from the bed and knocked Colby away from the computer. He stood upon the desk, grimacing at Colby, but there was sadness in his eyes. "You need to stay off this contraption until we know what is going on, Colby. You are too important."

Colby pushed himself back up from the floor and righted his chair. His little blue friend has finally lost his marbles. "Fizz, chill out, dude. My computer is protected. And I should be immune to Shizumu, right?"

Fizzlewink pulled back his head and dropped his tightened expression. As his jowls sagged into relaxation, he lowered his brows and turned toward the PC. "You placed a rune construct on your computer?" Fizzlewink squinted at the screen, looking for signs of the Emassa powered spell work. "I don't see any magic about the device."

"That's because it's inside. I recompiled my Emassa OS and built a new startup routine in the computer that buffers the operating system and hardware from 'outside influences'. It acts as an anti-virus program of sorts." Colby sat back at the computer and cleared his throat so Fizz would move aside. "You mind getting off my keyboard. What is it with cats and keyboards anyway?"

Embarrassed at his cat-like behaviors, Fizzlewink moved, but slowly and deliberately to make it seem as though it were his idea to move. "You feel this will prevent the Shizumu from attacking you? You may be immune from possession, but not an attack on your person."

Colby looked at Fizzlewink without expression. "No."

"What do you mean, no?"

Colby pushed his hand to the computer and watched Fizzlewink's eyes widen as the power of Emassa flowed from his palm and wrapped around his fingers. It was no longer the blue with hints of red tendrils, but a substantial yet pulsing purple light that flowed from his hands.

The Computer screen reacted to Colby's touch, and the pixels began flashing and coalescing at the center of the display to then form a circular symbol. Within the circle was another small one that centered with a dot. Two ellipses spread from the center to the inner edge of the outside circle in a vertical and horizontal position. Between each ellipse were three waved lines spreading from the inner eye to the outer ring.

"The Wheel of the Year, or Wheel of Time," Colby said. "I think I am beginning to understand that it has significance, and if I am correct, this symbol was planted somehow to protect me."

Fizzlewink turned to Colby with a look of pride, and his recent tension melted away. "You are a very clever young man, Colby."

Colby turned his hand around and looked at the purple light emanating from his fingers and palm. "What do you make of this?"

Fizzlewink shrugged and hopped down from the desk. "I expect it is your other gifts awakening and mingling with the part of you that is Nefslama."

Colby let go of the Emassa and released a deep breath. "I feared as much. What if there is Shizumu taint in me?"

"Do not feel so defeated, my boy. This could be a good thing, a very good thing indeed. You are more than the sum of your parts, boy." Fizzlewink offered Colby some licorice and returned it to his pocket when he refused. "Suit yourself. Not all the Shizumu were nasty, vengeful creatures as I have heard, but that is not my point. You will be who you wish to be, and do not let anyone tell you otherwise."

The mood lightened slightly, Colby proceeded to pull up charts of the latest runes he remembered seeing in his visions. He tried his best to assemble them into a construct, but it seemed incomplete. After repeating his experience to Fizz aloud for the umpteenth time, Colby and Fizzlewink shared theories of what everything meant.

"One thing is for certain," said Colby. "These Shizumu are using this BSOD for the purpose of finding hosts, but why are they using the computers? I thought they could just jump from one body to the next?"

* * *

"They can, but something tells me these body-snatching bastards have been lying in wait or being held somewhere for some purpose. It seems to me they are staging a massive campaign of some kind." Fizzlewink twirled his long eyebrows.

"Why the runes, though? I thought only the Nefslama used them, and it is your ancient language, isn't it?"

Fizzlewink looked up in surprise though he tried his best to hide it. "Oh, indeed they are my people's runes, but little is known how and when the Shizumu learned to channel the power. They are not corporeal, and beyond the science of existence, even my people understand. Perhaps they are attempting to twist our own methods to add insult to their goals."

"Or maybe they are just trying to send a message." Colby stood and stretched, cracking his neck and other joints. "I need to go downstairs and check on lunch. Gary is coming over, hoping we might head to the warehouse today?"

Fizzlewink broke from his enthralled stare at the computer screen, where the circular symbol still glowed. "Oh yes, indeed we should, but I'm not going to be the one to wake the 'Mistress of the Dark' in the other room."

Colby laughed and headed for the door. "Chicken shit." He hesitated at the door to Shelly's room and looked back at Fizz. "You don't happen to have any holy water in those pockets, do you?"

***

Colby found Gary in the kitchen when he came downstairs after waking the dead. He gave Gary a thumbs up when Fizzlewink followed in behind him. "I hope there's coffee ready."

Nana got up from the table and waddled to the pantry as quickly as her aged legs could move. "It's too early for her to be up."

Shelly stomped into the kitchen with her hand out, ready for a cup of Joe. In place of her standard dark and dreary goth garb, she wore a simple gray tracksuit and sneakers. Her hair was pinned back from her face, which was free of makeup.

Colby tilted his head to the side and chuckled. "Who are you, and what have you done with my sister?"

Shelly snarled and drank her cup of coffee.

"False alarm, it's Shelly," said Nana. "You kids be careful at that playground of yours."

Fizzlewink huffed and headed for the door. "Playground indeed. I should like the 'kids' assessment of that description at days end."

***

The warehouse interior was transformed from the garbage-strewn abandoned factory, into a full-fledged training facility. Fizzlewink was busy in his time away, creating a space where he could properly instruct the humans on ways to produce simple and effective spells for protecting themselves. There were obstacle courses, target ranges, and various objects strewn throughout the vast area once littered with old machinery and trash.

Colby looked around from the center of the once wide-open space and whistled. "How did you manage all of this, Fizz?"

Fizzlewink shrugged and blinked while waving off the compliment. "This is a mere trifle using the power of Emassa. Your little boost helped, but as your power grows, so does the flow of Emassa into this realm. You are capable of this and much more, and so will the 'others' gain in strength. They have the advantage of knowledge and experience that you lack."

Shelly feigned interest and being impressed. "Wow-wee! Now can we get on with this? I have plans for tonight."

Training began with a quick but thorough review of the basic runes and second level constructs. Once Fizzlewink was satisfied, he began drills of creating the runes for the five elements and holding them for different amounts of time before pulling them back without releasing them.

"This proves to me you can withhold releasing the power once you have conjured it, thus allowing yourself the option of changing your mind."

"You mean in case someone turns out to be a friend, not foe?" Gary asked.

"Sure…" Fizzlewink's lower lip pushed up the top one as he raised his brow. "I suppose that could happen, but I was thinking of a case when you needed to alter the attack if you misjudge an opponent."

Using the various mannequins Fizzlewink mysteriously obtained for target practice, the three new Emassa wielders began thrusting attacks at the dummies. Fizzlewink would tell them an attack, and that is what they would hurl at their approaching enemy. With more misses than hits, it was apparent to them all that they had much to learn about control once they released the magic.

Frustrated with the poor results of attack spells, Fizz moved them along to defensive magic.

"Dismal. Let us move on, shall we."

The construct for the defense shields was simple enough, but as Fizzlewink explained, they may be required to change their shields and rotate them based on the attack.

"Not all attacks can be held off by the same counterspell."

A grueling and intense regime continued as Colby, and the others were led through countless rune constructs and exercises to use them for the purpose of defending against Fizzlewink's attacks. As they created their shields in varying sizes and strengths, they learned from their failures, and Colby adjusted the database in his server through a secure connection to the home system.

* * *

Fizzlewink quickly located and exploited every weakness in their defenses. He watched through squinted eyes and forward-tilted head as the shields were spelled into reality. His tell was slight, but it showed in the quick quiver of his lip just before launching a strike.

Fizzlewink required no phWatch or computer to pull upon the source of magic, Emassa. His people were ancient practitioners and nearly married to its magic. Only since Colby started to break free of what hobbled his natural ability to draw that power, did the Nefslama cat have a strong conduit available to access the power since his ancestors' city disappeared?

Frustrated and beginning to anger, Colby began to ignore the systematic use of his #Magic app and let his instincts fuel the burning rage that the Emassa caused to churn deep within his mind. The purple glow of deliberate yet unconscious channeling of Emassa emanated from his hands as Colby's eyes darted from one object to the next. He needed something to throw Fizz off his game. A smile crept across his face when Colby's eyes leveled on the target dummy behind Fizzlewink.

Colby struck with a viper's speed. The flash of light hit Fizzlewink and wrapped around him harmlessly.

"You stray from the lesson at your own peril, pupil." Fizzlewink lifted his hand to launch a return volley, not understanding the distraction that Colby's attack was.

The target dummy became animated and transformed. As its plastic arms reached toward the exposed back of Fizzlewink, they warped and twisted into tentacles that glowed with Colby's signature color of Emassa. The mannequin lurched forward on legs that split and became six more sucker-covered arms while the head and body morphed into a monstrous octopus-like creature, it wrapped around Fizzlewink taking him completely unprepared. Two more tentacles wrapped around the little blue man and began to squeeze.

A yowl screeched and echoed throughout the warehouse, a sound that caused the others to lose concentration and drop their defenses.

* * *

The surprise that caught Fizzlewink was nothing compared to what was felt when his shrieking call began to grow louder to the point of disorienting the three young humans left helpless by the attack Fizzlewink intended. The tentacles dropped from around Fizzlewink and disintegrated as Colby's spell lost cohesion.

Colby knelt on the ground holding his hands over his ears against the audible onslaught of a thousand cats yowling in the buffered space of the empty warehouse.

Gary and Shelly were likewise assaulted and buckled over from the pain to their ears until, following a final burst of screeching, the place went silent.

Fizzlewink stood upon a table holding his midsection as he laughed at the three of them stumbling to stand. "A game, much like chess, you have to always think ahead and never let down your guard."

"How did you do that?" Colby rubbed his aching body. "That beast had you wrapped tight."

Fizzlewink chuckled and winked. "When you have no need to call forth runes, with a focused mind, that is, you will understand. The mind is capable of much, but not if you allow yourself distraction. The trap you contrived, though rather ingenious, was only attacking me on a single front. Had it also blinded, muted, and deafened me, I would have had less capability to resist or fight back."

Shelly huffed and glared at Fizzlewink. "Next time you oversized alley cat…you won't get off so easy." She turned to Colby. "Can you zap us back home now, I'd like to soak in the tub for a few hours before my date?"

"I don't know how I did it and have not found the rune construct to replicate the spell. Besides, we drove here, remember?" Colby shrugged and headed toward the exit at the rear of the warehouse, where there would be no foot traffic. "Fizzlewink, could you transport us if we hadn't driven?"

"I am afraid that is something I have never done for more than myself and never heard any of my kind achieving without a large gathering, successfully, that is."

Gary grimaced. "I'd rather not hear about what unsuccessful looks like."

"You said 'there's no place like home,' Dorothy, and then we were home. Add that to the hashtag database," Shelly said.

"Runes don't work that way, Shelly," Colby said. "They aren't even English."

"So. We don't know the language really, just words… symbols really. That's all they are."

Colby took what Shelly said to heart. They were just symbols or something to focus a particular thought on. "Maybe you're right."

Fizzlewink twirled his eyebrow and smirked. "It matters not anyway. I have other business to attend." Fizzlewink disappeared without explanation, much to the confusion of the others, leaving them to drive home on their own.

***

The three weary magic users arrived back at the Stevens' home, all grumbling and achy as they slowly walked through the back door.

Nana raised her eyebrow but said nothing as she got up and laid a package of licorice on the island and pointed it out to the worn-out warriors in training.

Once washed up and fed, Colby and Gary stayed upstairs to work out some rendering and construct issues that were revealed during training.

"When you transformed that mannequin, you used the Emassa directly, didn't you?" Gary said.

Colby turned and raised his right brow. "Yes, how could you tell?"

"Besides the fact that everything was purple, which is normally blue when using hashtag magic, you seemed to block off my access to the Emassa through the phWatches."

"How is that possible?"

"I don't know, but when you tapped into your power, I could barely feel the Emassa, and when I tried, I couldn't reach it. And if I couldn't, do you think others were affected as well?"

Colby seemed puzzled but did not dwell on it, thinking it better left to explore with Fizzlewink's wisdom. Instead, he decided to try something that occurred to him on the drive home from the warehouse. "Gary, what do you think would happen if I built a bridging app to connect hashtag magic to a 3D modeling app? I mean, everything is just symbols, why can't we make our own focal points and expand the use of the app?"

Gary perked up and shared a conspirator's grin.

Colby smiled back. His thoughts kept drifting back to wondering where Fizz went off to in such a hurry. Then his mind began to focus, and he started another vision.

Chapter 27

As Colby grew stronger and channeled more of the Emassa, so did Fizzlewink. No longer was he restricted to shifting into the form of an old blue cat, keeping watch over the boy. When he reappeared into reality from departing the others at the warehouse, he took the shape of a blue jay and stretched out his wings.

Fizzlewink shook his glossy feather-covered body and relished in the added power that being in the proximity of Colby afforded him. A sudden leap and flap of the wings sent Fizzlewink into the air as he darted off toward downtown. While he flew, Fizzlewink glided on the wind and dove through the air, chirping out to the world.

Fizzlewink flew through the city streets, dancing on the flow of the wind that gusted between the tall buildings. He conserved energy by riding the flow through the wind-tunnel effect and carefully choosing which streets to turn down toward his destination. Fizzlewink needed all his physical strength to make the climb high up to the top of the building. Limiting the use of Emassa allowed him to avoid detection, although he sensed as though his presence was being felt.

He was busy with his secret disappearances, tracking down where the Shizumu were congregating. Today Fizzlewink felt he finally knew where to end his search, but he had to be careful. The Emassa he now had access to was easy to detect if used too generously.

***

Colby lay on his bed, shaking his head from the images that flashed behind his eyes. He set down his tablet and began rubbing his temples while tightly squeezing his eyes shut. The boys had been working for days on alterations on Hashtag Magic and extending its capabilities and were exhausted. He felt a hand on his shoulder.

"Hey, are you okay?" Gary asked.

Colby waved his friend off. "It's nothing, just one of those weird headaches except I'm having flashes of buildings and cars and people." He looked up at Gary. "It's like I'm flying when I close my eyes."

"What, like a dream or something?"

Colby shook his head and closed his eyes. "No, this feels real."

Gary sat down next to Colby. "Tell me what you see."

Colby described his flight through the city, riding on the wind and gliding between buildings. He pushed and pumped his wings until he reached the top of a tall building where he finally landed on the roof outside a vent. The world around him began to grow and divide into a kaleidoscope of images that caused his head to pound harder. He nearly gave up and opened his own eyes when the image merged, and he was surrounded by darkness and shadows, moving through what appeared to be a ventilation duct.

He scurried along with the vents until he came upon a grating that looked down over a dimly lit room, pulsing red light, breaking the obscurity of the dark space. There were shadows of people sitting in a circle around a table. In the center of the table was the source of the red light, a glowing orb of plasma. Below the orb was a network of cables that disappeared below the table and ran along the wall to a bank of computers at the far end of the room.

Hushed voices echoed through the room over the hum of electronics and air-conditioning pumping cool air into the computer filled space. Colby strained to hear the words when his vision split again into a shattered display as though he was watching eight televisions tuned into the same show from slightly different angles. The voices grew as his vision zoomed in, and he seemed to drop down above the figures.

Colby could understand the voices now. Familiar. The red glow did not reach their faces.

"Access to Emassa has increased, but it is not yet enough," a voice said. "And it gets cut off at times."

Colby heard that voice before.

"Everyday it grows stronger, and soon we will have the power within our reach to complete what we started eons ago my friends," another, more feminine voice said.

Mumbling filled Colby's ears, and his vision spun around as the source of his insight peered around the table. Seven figures held places at the meeting.

"So it is the boy who is linked to what intrudes upon the natural flow of power from the Emassa," a third voice said. "We should end him now and be done with it."

* * *

"No," the female voice said. "You would destroy that which holds the key to our desire. He must first break down the barrier and bridge the divide. Right now, it is through him that the Emassa flows."

"So he is the Gatekeeper?" a man asked. "Are you certain of this?"

"There can be no doubt. It is no coincidence that this child has access to power with a thought that takes us ages to store."

"Then why not simply bring him here and channel him?" an old and raspy voice said. "I do not understand this waiting and watching."

"We have all waited and watched, old one, time has no meaning to us." The woman sounded impatient and short. "There is no need to kill him; he is not to blame for our situation."

"Collateral damage, as the aggressive military types of this world tend to express. How do we even know he is the one, this Stevens boy?"

The voices were distinctly different from one another, but Colby was most focused on the old man and the woman he picked out.

The woman spoke again. "It is true that there is another possibility, the Connor's child. I, however, have seen no signs of adequate Emassa use within him, but there is something strange about the boy."

"I have signs of his use of magic," the old man said. "I think we require a test of his ability."

The female slammed her hands on the table. "You would risk destroying our chance, now that we are so close?"

"You have stated that time has no meaning for us. What are a few more centuries if something should go wrong?" man number four said.

The female began to glow, but her face was still shadowed. "A few more decades and these barbaric humans will likely reduce this world to ashes. Have you not paid attention to the last fifty years? Always on the edge of annihilation, building weapons of mass destruction and little men waving around their rockets like an erect-"

"Enough," the old one said. "I have seen both these boys and admit I am not resoundingly clear on which may be the key to our desires. I suggest we send an agent."

"I thought we had an agent already in play?" man number three said.

"We do, but we are not sure of said agent's motives and alliance," man number four said. "Some of our family have made it clear they enjoy the borrowed lives they lead on this dismal plain."

"Flesh is weak, but it has its uses, and some of them are…Enjoyable," a second female voice said.

"Be that as it may, I have only been escaped and returned to flesh for a decade. Having avoided said prison yourselves, you have no clue what it means to be wasting away so soon." The old man was sounding more tired with each word. "I need Emassa to restore completely."

The voices continued to bicker and argue over what to do. Meanwhile, Colby related all he heard and observed to Gary, who remained silent.

"I say we call on our spy and agent to hear from him. He is closer to the subjects in question, or at least more objective than some on this council." It was the old man speaking again. He seemed more and more familiar the longer Colby listened.

The group then began arguing about the sudden return of the Dreggs. The halflings created by the Nefslama, using Nefsmari as a weapon to exterminate the Shizumu. The one thing that the council agreed upon was the threat the Dreggs injected into their plans. These beings were long ago thought extinct, driven back by their makers when something went wrong.

* * *

"Let the Nefslama keep their own house in order. I say the Dreggs are a welcome distraction to keep the fleshlings busy. Both Nefslama and their hybrid abominations will have more to attend than our little incursion," the second female said. "Besides, how many can there actually be?"

"Unknown. We have both, Shizumu and Nefslama alike, neglected to attend our affairs and keep house. It is time to change that." The old man sounded forceful and commanding now. "I want a test on the boys. We will know at once if our hope lies in one of them or make changes immediately."

"A seeker, is that what you are eluding to?" the first woman asked, her voice now faint and subservient. "Is that wise?"

"It is necessary, and it is what I command. With the power one of those creatures can siphon, I can stabilize my magic and change form more freely."

Before Colby could hear more, the multi-imaged view of the room faded as his source of access withdrew. The pulsing ache in his head grew tenfold. He opened his eyes and took in a deep breath just before heaving all over the floor.

Gary jumped back. "Gross. Dude a little warning next time."

"Sorry," Colby said as he spit out the remaining bits left on his tongue. "That was intense, more so than last times."

Gary pushed Colby back and looked in his friend's eyes. "Last times? As in plural? What you talkin' 'bout Colby?" Gary said in his best Gary Colman impression.

Colby looked up at his friend and snorted. Soon Gary joined him in a hearty and welcome laugh.

Colby described the time in the basement of the school, where he at first thought he stumbled upon a secret room. Now he felt it was the beginnings of waking visions, and he became confused by the overlap with his physical location and actions. There was also what happened at school and other times as well.

"It's a bit overwhelming, to say the least. It's like straining to watch pirated cam movies. You squint to focus on the action while people's heads pop up and down; meanwhile, the sound is raspy and hard to grasp." Colby began cleaning up his mess while holding his head away and looking to Gary for help.

"Oh no, bro, that's all you," Gary said. "So, what do you think all this means?"

Colby let out a breath that sounded as though he was coming to terms with long-running trouble. "It means we watch each other's backs and be careful who we trust." Colby looked at Gary. "You heard what I repeated? It's you and me, and then there are the spy and some agent."

"Who is the spy, do you think? Darla? Oh no, I got it, that Professor guy. He's always talking about your watch and stuff."

"Creepy though he maybe, I'm not so sure. It could be anyone." Colby dumped the vomit filled towels in the trash and walked across the room to the ensuite. "We can trust our families, I suppose, but anyone else is to be considered suspect."

Gary started to nod. "What about Fizz? He is always disappearing and running off on 'other affairs'. What's that all about?"

Colby snorted and walked back into the room. "Fizz has lived as a cat for so long he practically is one. They are independent, finicky, and unpredictable. Besides, he's been with me most of my life. Fizz is family."

Gary scratched his head and grabbed Colby by the shoulders. "Family," he said. He stared at his friend for a moment until it became uncomfortable for both of them. Letting go and turning back toward the computer, Gary changed the subject. "So what do you make of this 'seeker' reference?"

Colby took up his tablet and went back to work on their plans for Halloween and the addition of 3D modeling to Hashtag Magic. "I don't really know. I guess we'll find out sooner or later. I'm more troubled by the familiarity in some of the voices I heard tonight."

"You know who they were," Gary asked, turning around in the swivel chair at Colby's desk.

Colby shook his head. "No. Their voices were familiar, but it wasn't really the sound, more the way they spoke. Anyway, we need to get back to our little project. Those old-time decorations in the attic are not gonna cut it if we expect to make this the best-haunted house ever."

Chapter 28

Nana was in her element as everyone pitched in to decorate and transform the Stevens' home into a ghastly and ghostly haunted house for the Archeology Club fundraiser. She supervised and ordered everyone about, mentioning where everything's place is and how things were not up to her standards. "This fake spider web nonsense simply will not do. It's far too time-consuming to get it to look real enough."

Nana moved around the room, moving decorations and adjusting things. "This is my second favorite time of year. All the spirit realms in proximity, the stars aligned, and the juices of power are flowing. It's the one time of year an old witch-like me can take out her broom and-"

* * *

"Sweep?" Colby interrupted. He received a dark look for his effort at keeping the subject off magic.

Nana didn't care who was around when she started talking about witchy stuff. Colby wasn't in the mood for more stories, and with Darla and Rhea there helping along with Rigel, he wanted to keep the stories to a minimum.

"You used to like Halloween a great deal too until you were nine or so," Shelly said a devious grin on her face.

Colby was not going to take the bait.

"Ya, that's when you stopped going trick-or-treating. What changed?" Shelly asked, smiling.

"You know damn well what happened 'Smelly', that was the year I had to wear one of your old costumes because mom forgot to get me one." Colby dropped a box of decorations and began unpacking them. "You know how fun it is dressing in a plastic costume and on top of it be that of Cinderella? Oh, and to add insult to injury, your big sister running around telling everyone who is behind the mask." Colby was fuming, and his hands began to show signs of Emassa.

"I bet you were an adorable Cinderella," Darla said. "I was Cinderella once myself."

Colby groaned and rolled his eyes. How is it every conversation can be turned into an all about Darla conversation. He tried to block out her voice as she droned on about all the costumes she wore over the years and how lovely she looked.

"Easy now, Sparky," Nana whispered. "Calm yourself, that was a long time ago, and you turned out all right. It was much more fun hanging out with your old Nana and passing out treats to the little ones who came to our door."

Colby looked over at Darla and squeezed his eyes shut while plugging his ears.

* * *

Nana patted Colby on the head, understanding his annoyance, and then watched as his hands continued to glow. "Besides I think the little prank we pulled on Shelly with the fake poop on her bed more than made up for it." She hoped to distract him, and derailing Darla's rant might help.

Colby smiled and began to laugh. "Poor Fizzlewink got the blame for that one. Hey, where is Fizz anyway?"

"I haven't seen him. Most likely he doesn't want to help decorate this place and is hiding somewhere. Speaking of decorating, let's get our collective backsides moving." Nana walked over to the stove and stirred some concoction while shooing the others out to get started.

Rhea leaned into Darla as they went to the other room. "Why would their cat help decorate?"

Darla shrugged, but she leaned down to peer under the furniture to look for the cat. "There is something strange about that cat."

***

Colby's mother, Aria, who spent much of her time at work these days, was home, and jovial helping to set up for the big day. She dismissed the reminder of yet another moment in her past that she was not there for her family. She was determined to make this Halloween a good one.

"We still have another day, mother; it will be perfect." Aria's jovial mood lifted as much as her glass. Though she drank less on account of the fact she worked more, she still spent her time during days off tipping the cup. "I'll just go up to the attic and collect all the old decorations up there, gathering dust."

Nana glared at her daughter, looking for a hidden flask or ulterior motive. "Don't be long, dear, we have much to do and need the extra, though tipsy, hands."

Aria waved her mother off in a less than ladylike manner before heading up to the highest floor of the home. As she approached the last landing, Aria stopped before the final flight of stairs. She avoided this level just as her sobriety since her husband left. The locked room at the end and across from the stairs was Jarrod Stevens' personal study. It was kept locked, and Aria held the only key. Opposite to the study were the stairs leading up to the attic. Aria clutched the key hanging from her necklace and turned toward the attic door.

The attic was organized chaos. Stacks of books and boxes filled space in towers that formed a labyrinth of the history of the Stevens family.

Aria made her way past several such stacks, gliding her fingers lightly along and feeling the memories through her fingertips. Her eyes glistened as she sniffled and pulled her hand back to her side. She stopped and steadied herself before taking a deep breath and moving quickly to a secluded section near the back of the room.

Several large boxes and trunks sat in a corner. The disarray of garland, plastic pumpkins, and strings of lights broadcast the location of a holiday decoration dumping ground. Layers of dust and cobwebs coated the containers revealing the disuse over the years. The Stevens family did not regularly decorate or signify the holidays with glitter and lights as they once did when Jarrod Stevens was still home.

More deep breaths, and Aria was prepared to sort through the old collections to find anything appropriate for the All Hallow's Eve fundraiser that her son was organizing. It was important to him, so Aria made it all that more important to herself. She found many pumpkins, ghouls, ghosts, witches, and the like, piling them to the side. While sliding a large tombstone decoration over, a bundle fell out from behind and landed at Aria's feet.

Aria tilted her head and wondered about the paper-wrapped object. She squatted down and pulled the twine free, allowing the paper to unfold. Beneath the dust-covered old parchment lay a leather-bound book with a raised area and faded impression of a symbol upon the cover. Aria gasped. She raked her fingers across the indent and caressed the cover while her eyes moistened at the sight. This was the book Jarrod used the night he disappeared.

* * *

A flood of memories raced through her mind and assaulted her bottled up emotions. She had halted her fingers before she opened the old book when she heard footfalls on the stairs to the small attic space. Aria hurried to wrap the tome back up in the paper but had no time to replace the string. She shoved the book below a pile of garland and lights before wiping her eyes and standing to face whoever followed her path.

"What on Earth is taking so damn long, Aria?" Nana stood near the small window, hands on hips and looking down her nose over the edge of her glasses. She noticed the glistening eyes of her daughter. "What's wrong with you, woman?"

Aria wiped her eyes and fumbled to push the book further below the pile as she bent to gather Halloween decorations. "Nothing mother, there's just too much dust gathered on these things. They've gone too long without use, but we'll take care of that now." Aria rushed past her mother for the stairs. She stopped and turned. "Are you gonna help? Grab those others and come along."

Nana collected the remaining items and glanced at the pile of garland where the edge of the wrapped item protruded. Raising her eyebrows, she immediately understood what had made her daughter upset. "Nothing wrong, my fat fanny." She turned to her daughter with her arms full and knowing grin on her face. "Coming, dear."

Downstairs the decorating was in full swing. While Colby and Gary helped Rhea and Darla with making the spider webs to suit Nana's liking, Shelly created dark corners with vampires and gothic themes. Rigel lent his hand anywhere that Nana was not while avoiding Shelly's overtly suggestive looks and movements.

Colby and Gary laughed at the flirting that passed between Shelly and bounced off the Professor but went silent when Bruce showed up.

"Hey, Bruce." Colby drawled out his name loudly as he answered the door. "What are you doing here?"

Shelly ran to the door and pushed Colby out of the way. "Ya Bruce, what are you doing here?"

Bruce pushed his way in and glanced around the room until his eyes fell upon Rigel. "I thought you might need some help with making this place a bit more authentic." Bruce's eyes never left Rigel's while he spoke. "Who's the old guy?"

Shelly closed the door and pulled Bruce over to her latest corner of horror. She spoke to him with daggers in her eyes and venom on her lips, but too softly for any of the eavesdroppers to hear.

Nana entered from the kitchen with a pitcher and cups. "How 'bout some special brew kids." Nana looked at the faces of everyone in the room as they stood still, attention drawn to the same spot. She followed their line of sight to see the show playing near Dracula's boudoir. She began to cackle, knowing what triangle that was plainly developing. Nana poured the pitcher into a small caldron on the table and stirred it up, adding some dry ice.

"A witch stirring a potion. Now that would make a scene," Rigel said. He was changing the unspoken subject of everyone's attention. "Would you be willing to play a part on the night of our big event?" he asked Nana.

Nana cackled even louder. "You betcha yummy pants. Though it wouldn't be an act." She winked at the befuddled Professor.

Rigel gazed at Colby with a questioning look.

"She used to tell us she was a witch when we were little to get us to go to sleep," Colby hurried to explain. "Not that telling little kids such nonsense makes for easily falling asleep."

While raising his left brow, Rigel's eyes moved back to Nana. "Well, she certainly has the aura of a witch."

Before Colby could dissuade further discussion on the subject, Nana took over the room as usual.

* * *

"Sit children, and I shall tell you the history of the Prokof Witches." Nana took a seat as she passed out cups of her punch to all who gathered around.

Only Colby, Shelly, and Aria stayed back, although Aria took a cup of punch and proceeded to liven it up from the liquor cabinet.

Chapter 29

"The witches in my family go back many generations, back to the time when Halloween actually meant something other than rug-rats begging for candy at your door, and yard-apes toilet papering your trees." Nana had their attention as she spun her tale.

Eva Mariel Prokpa hailed from a long line of a magically touched lineage. Her family had a long history of being able to channel spirits, read futures, make potions, and cast spells, according to Nana's telling.

Her story told of how long ago the first Prokpa witch was born after a spirit visited her in the night. The spirit told her of eternal power that it could teach her how to harness and use to make a better life for herself. There was something in her family line that would allow her to use it. Long ago, a member of her family was possessed by a demon that seduced her ancestor. It left behind the ability to use magic, and the spirit could teach her to use it.

Night after night, the spirit returned, teaching her secrets of the power within her, and soon she was able to begin casting spells and having visions. One of her visions told her that her family line would one day be very strong, so strong, in fact, that others would seek to destroy them.

From one generation to the next, the power was passed down to those who showed an ability. The secret of their power had to be kept, so those who had no ability were never told of the family gift. Through that first coupling and consequent teaching of the gift, a long line of magically endowed women proceeded the first Prokpa witch.

When the first of Nana's ancestors came to America, they moved deep into the territories and away from the main settlements, only visiting them when necessary. They knew the hearts and fears of men. If they could not control you when they sought power, they would label you. If they feared you out of ignorance, they condemned you.

Condemnation led to persecution and death.

"That is how my family survived the witch trials in Salem," Nana said.

The girls giggled while Rigel looked on, listening intently.

Colby rolled his eyes at the story and watched his mother drink.

"Was it just the girls who had magic?" Darla asked. "Didn't you have any warlocks in your family?"

Aria snorted. "Warlocks? Oh, don't be daft, girl. That word has lost any meaning. A male witch has graced the Prokpa bloodline from time to time, however."

Nana glared at her inebriated daughter. "We had some men born in the family with power though few could use it well and none in five generations. Not until our Colby here was-"

Colby rushed in front of his flappy-gummed grandmother and began ushering everyone out. "Well, we have had a full night, and I think it's time for Nana's medication." He winked and alluded to her mental state being off-balance with a twirl of his finger to the side of his head. "We'll see everyone here tomorrow a couple of hours before showtime." He pushed the last of the guests out the door, catching Rigel's odd wink.

Once the door was closed, Colby took a deep breath and turned to his family and Gary. "Nana, what the hell?"

"Oh, relax fart-blossom, the more strange a truth I tell, the less likely anyone believes it." Nana waved off Colby's worry. "You used to be more fun."

Colby maintained his look of consternation. "Would you please stop calling me fart-blossom, I am not a child who farts in your lap anymore." He stormed up the stairs and slammed his door.

Gary got up from the couch and headed for the stairs. "I better go check on Sir smelly pants. For someone who isn't a child anymore, he sure can stomp around worse than one." He smiled as he went up the stairs.

Aria and Shelly remained in the living room, sipping their punch.

Shelly handed her cup to her mother. "Mind sharing that hooch you got there? I think it's gonna be a long night finishing this decorating."

Aria poured some whiskey into Shelly's cup, her own, and Nana's that was also shoved her direction. "Mother, you really shouldn't have brought up our history in front of strangers."

Nana huffed at the weak attempt at a scolding. "At least I didn't speak of his father's heritage." Nana watched as Aria's face went stiff and white. "Thought that might get your attention. What do you really know of Jarrod's background anyway?"

Aria sat transfixed for a moment before taking a rather large gulp from her glass. "In what respect? He came from a small family somewhere in the south. He never spoke of them much, and I never met them."

Nana tasted her spiked punch and grabbed the bottle of whiskey from Aria, pouring a more healthy serving into her cup. "Horse shit. I don't believe any of that, and I think you don't either. Colby has far too much power to be endowed only from our line."

"I thought that his being the firstborn male in five generations is what made him unique?" Shelly asked.

Nana nodded and took another drink and then hiccuped. "Oh, he is special, yes, but there is more to this than a single-sided gift." Nana watched Aria for a reaction and stared until she finally saw her tell.

Aria absently clasped the key she wore on her chain beneath her blouse.

"Spit it out," Nana said to Aria. "What have you not told us?"

Aria set her glass down and waved off Nana's attempt to fill it with more booze. "Of his family, I know little to nothing. Of his heritage, I know only that he was gifted in magic that is older than recorded history, and he was much older than he appeared. Jarrod never shared all the details with me directly. But the few times I saw him do magic, it had similar properties to what Colby has shown."

Nana nearly choked on her drink. "You think he was more than a male witch?"

The clearing of a throat spooked the women.

"I think that you should not jump to conclusions," Fizzlewink said as he hobbled in from the kitchen.

Shelly moved to Fizzlewink and shoved her finger in his face. "What do you mean sneaking up on us like that. And where have you been? Just when we could use some help, and the others showed up, you disappear."

Fizzlewink pushed Shelly's finger away and hopped up on the couch. "I don't like to be around so many people, besides what if one of them saw me for who I really am?"

"You mean one of them has the gift?" Nana asked. "Who?"

"I did not say that. I simply said, what if..." Fizzlewink grabbed a cup off the table and sniffed its contents before placing it back on the table, holding it away with a look of distaste. "Back to your little theory about Colby's father, I think it best not to speculate and deal only with the facts."

"And what facts are those," Colby said appearing from the staircase. "What are you all talking about down here?"

Fizzlewink caught off guard, fumbled to change the subject. "Nothing really, just wondering where your father went off to so long ago. But since we do not know, I said it was best not to speculate."

Colby saw the lie as if every word took form and warped into a dark mist before evaporating. "Right." Colby would not press the subject at present since he had other matters to take care of first. "Anyway, Gary and I have just finished some adjustments on Hashtag Magic and creating a bridge to another app to build new constructs."

Fizzlewink sat up, displaying his curiosity that was normally reserved, Colby noticed. Odd for a cat-man, he would say of himself while denying being any part cat. After all, it is said that curiosity killed the cat. Colby imagined that somehow Fizzlewink was responsible for that old saying.

"What have you managed with your contraption this time?" Fizzlewink said.

"Everyone stand over here by the front door and watch." Colby waited until everyone was out of his way, and the house was clear from the foyer on through.

He lifted his tablet to eye level and began a panoramic scan of the space with the built-in camera. After he finished the photo, he opened it in a separate application used for 3D modeling and set the photo as a background. With a few strokes, he overlaid several objects that appeared as large blobs on the screen.

"What are those things?" Shelly asked. "Do you plan on filling the room with smoke as well?" She pointed to several objects on the tablet.

Colby pushed her hand away. "It hasn't rendered yet. I need to bridge the rendering to Hashtag Magic and let the runes merge with the objects. Watch this."

Colby's eyes beamed with delight mixed with mischief as he pushed the command button on his screen that connected his 3D app to the runes program #Magic. As the apps bridged, Colby's hands began to glow with purple light and swirls of runes, and the constructs assembled and spread throughout the space when he typed in **#HauntedHouse**.

As the constructs settled into position, they began to grow in brilliance and pulsed until they flashed into form. The room immediately transformed into something out of a classic horror film. Spider webs stretched from one end of the room to the other. A layer of dust settled on all the chairs, tables, and sofa that transformed into antique looking furnishings from some vampire's lair. A fine mist settled on the floor and swirled around as though creatures moved below the foot high fog bank. The stairs to the upper floors expanded into a grand yet aged staircase with dusty old red carpet and rails that took on the shape of carved serpents. The light fixtures became gas lamps that fluttered in a nonexistent wind.

Shelly screamed as the moaning began, and apparitions started flying through the room and then disappeared through walls. "Holy Crap, I thought they were real for a second there. Last thing I need is a bunch of Casper's wanting to phone home and me being the operator."

Fizzlewink patted Colby on the back as he climbed to his shoulder to get a full view of his pupil's massive construct and display of power. "This is well done, but does it have an off switch because I for one will not get any rest tonight with that moaning going on.”

Colby pulled back the Emassa he used to create the effects, and everything returned to normal. He did this without the use of #Magic or any part of his electronics collection.

“That was well done also. I would like to see you do more of that without the aid of your mechanics.” Fizzlewink nodded and pointed to Colby’s tablet and watch. “One day, they may fail you, and you’ll have to learn to control the Emassa without their help.”

Colby shrugged and went up the stairs. “Well, that day isn’t today.” Colby shivered after his words. He knew that something was coming. A seeker, if his vision was to be believed. Without being completely certain, he and Gary decided not to share this information. Besides, tomorrow was a big day, and they didn’t think this enemy agent would risk exposing itself before a crowd of people.

Chapter 30

Colby woke with a start. He had visions again in his sleep. "Gary, you awake?" he asked his friend sleeping on the futon. "Pst…wake up"

"I'm awake. What time is it?" Gary rubbed his eyes and forced himself to sit up. "Damn, man, it's like still dark out."

"It's nearly six; I'm getting up. You hungry?" Colby jumped up from the bed and started to get dressed. He turned on the lights and fumbled through the pile of clothes on his desk chair. "How about some pancakes?"

Gary moaned and pulled the covers over his head. After a few minutes of Colby's rummaging around, Gary got off the futon and reached for his clothes.

"What's up? You don't normally get up this early even when you have too."

"I had a vision about tonight."

That had Gary's attention. "What's gonna happen?"

Colby wiggled his head back and forth. "I'm not sure anything is going to happen, really."

"Remind me then why we're getting up before the damn chickens?"

Colby shrugged his shoulders and pulled on his Henley. "Let's discuss it over breakfast unless you'd rather wait for Nana to wake and make breakfast?"

Gary dressed in seconds. "Not a chance in hell."

Colby and Gary made their way to the kitchen and were assaulted by a stench that brought tears to their eyes. "What the hell is that?" they said.

Nana was in the middle of the kitchen. The island was gone, and in its place was a large cauldron sitting on a fake fire being heated by electric coils. The noxious fumes melted the hairs in their noses while Nana hummed and stirred a large spoon that once hung on the kitchen wall. Bubbles erupted from the green-grey sludge she mixed.

"Fire burn and caldron bubble, if that's for breakfast…we're in trouble," Colby said while Gary laughed nervously.

"Good morning, boys, what a lovely surprise…you awake and here to help me with my brew." Nana smiled and winked. "Have a seat at the table by the window, and I'll fix you up some breakfast."

"Please tell me it isn't what's in that?" Gary said, pointing to the caldron.

Nana chuckled and pulled her teeth out of her pocket to put them in her mouth. "Oh, heavens, no."

* * *

Gary and Colby sighed with relief.

"This won't be ready until dinner time."

Nana faced the stove, but her eyes were watching the reactions of the boys. She laughed to herself. She wasn't cooking a witch's brew for dinner. The truth was she was setting up the caldron as a prop for the evening festivities, but it didn't stop her from having a little fun teasing the boys.

"Relax, I'm just setting up the kitchen to be a witch's den. I found this hidden upstairs behind some Yule decorations…and other interesting parcels."

"You were up in the attic this morning?" Colby asked.

Nana nodded and started breaking eggs in a pan, not paying much care to the shells that fell in along with the insides. "Just sorting through some things your mother left upstairs yesterday."

Nana finished making scrambled eggs and shells with a side of carbon log sausage and burnt toast. She plated the slop and set the dishes in front of the boys and squeezed in next to them, staring until they started to eat. "So…"

Gary bit into a sausage and made a yum sound. "Delicious Nana," he lied.

"Horse crap. I know my cooking is worse than bad, but it's the thought that counts." Nana chortled and poured some milk for them. "I'm talking about the dreams you had last night, grandson."

"How did you…Never mind you're a witch. I really have to get used to that," Colby said.

"Nothing to do with witchy business, my boy, I have ears. I heard you grunting and carrying on in your sleep."

Colby continued to force down his breakfast after picking out the shells from his eggs and scraping off the soot from his toast. The sausage was beyond saving. "I kept seeing images of the Dreggs chasing us from the warehouse, but they were here at the house. It was odd, though; they seemed to be running for us, not after us. But there was something else…a presence was there that I could sense but not see, and it gave me the willies."

"What kind of presence?" Fizzlewink said as he straggled into the kitchen. "Got any tuna?"

Nana got up from her seat and went to the pantry. "You will use a fork this time to eat, at least?" she pointed out to Fizzlewink.

"Sorry, I was stuck in cat form for an awfully long time, old habits, and some such drivel." He turned back to Colby. "Now, about that presence you felt, was it a stinging or itching?"

Colby looked at Fizzlewink with shock. "How did you know? It was both actually. At first, it itched, and then it stung the back of my neck."

Fizzlewink slowly shook his head back and forth. "Interesting…"

"Meaning what?" Colby asked as he leaned forward.

Nana placed a plate of tuna in oil before Fizzlewink and shoved a fork into his hand.

Moments had passed before Fizzlewink responded. "Not sure," he answered and began shoveling food into his mouth. "Could mean nothing…" he started as food fell from his mouth. "Could mean you are being searched out…" he spat more food and slurped and burped. "Could mean you are being watched over." Fizzlewink wiped his mouth with his sleeve and jumped down from the chair then walked to the door.

"Where are you going?" Colby demanded.

"I'll be back, just got to see an alley about a mouse."

* * *

Nana was back at her cauldron, stirring the brew and cackling. "Getting into character."

Colby sat at the table, worry crisscrossing his face. "This is all just too weird and heavy. What I would give just to be back to normal."

"Normal, what is your problem, CJ? You got mad skills, dude. I mean you're a true computer wizard and shit." Gary rolled his eyes at his best friend.

"I mean with dad gone and mom…Well, mom. Then there is that ass-hat Jasper and his bullying. I have a whacked-out family and only one real friend." Colby slid back in his chair and closed his eyes.

"Seems you got a pretty solid caldron, Colby," Nana said.

Colby and Gary turned to Nana, and both said 'huh' in unison.

"Life is like this cauldron and casting a spell. You can add all the choicest ingredients and stir all you like, but if you got a leaky cauldron, that magic potion will never work. You have a solid caldron in your friend there and this family, such as it is. Add to the spell what you choose and stir it up, so long as that caldron holds firm, you'll get out what you put in." Nana winked at Colby and turned back to her stirring. "Just avoid using eye of newt. It's hard to get and adds a taste like licking a cat's ass!"

Fizzlewink chose that moment to return from outside and faced a roar of laughter aimed in his direction. "What?" he said, spinning around looking at his appearance?

***

The day was spent adding finishing touches to the house and yard. Colby and Gary did the yard early in the morning while Shelly and Aria were still sleeping. The odd dog walker would pass by, but with the help of an obscuring spell, no one stopped to watch the goings-on in the Stevens' yard. While most of the decorations were mundane items from the attic and several items dropped off the night before by Rigel and the girls, there were several adjustments made by using the #Magic app with bridged 3D modeling.

"Will they last long enough?" Gary asked.

"Fizz said they'll continue as long as we want. They are fully self-sustained constructs, and unless someone were to understand and then reverse our spells, we will have to turn them off ourselves when we're done with them." Colby sat on a tombstone admiring his work when he heard the telltale giggles of Darla and Rhea walking toward the house. He turned just in time to see them waving hello and picking up their pace toward them.

"Gary, did you take down the obscuring spell?" Colby asked.

"No, why?"

"Because Darla and Rhea just waved at us."

"So what has that…Oh, shit? They were in the computer lab when that blue screen of death thing happened." Gary realized.

Colby groaned and turned to his friend. "So was Jasper Bodine."

"Crap on a cracker," Fizzlewink said, sneaking up behind them. "Time to go into character then." Fizzlewink abruptly waved his hands over his body and transformed into a scrawny black cat. He leaped up on top of a headstone and yowled and shared a toothy grin before leaping off into the rendered mists and spooky trees.

"OMG!" Darla said as she closed in on the boys. "You guys must have been up all night. This is like totes amaze-balls!"

Rolling their eyes, the boys hugged the girls hello and showed them into the house. It was already past noon, and the other volunteers would be there soon to set up the ticket booth while a local vendor would be setting up carnival-style games and a few rides courtesy of Rhea's father. Darla's father used his political connections to have the road blocked off. Luckily the neighbors were all Halloween lovers and happy to see the Stevens' household rekindling their long missed enthusiasm for the holiday. Cars were already clearing the road in preparation for the evening of fun and fright.

"Is that a dry ice machine making the fog?" Rhea asked. "It's so eery. I love it." The tone in her voice warned Colby that she might be suspicious of the changes in the home.

The rest of the afternoon was spent organizing the street vendors and volunteers. Darla performed all the organizing while Rhea chased after her, and the boys stayed out of the way. When all was at ready, the kids returned to the Stevens' home and prepared for the first visitors to the Archeology Club's House of Horrors.

The girls used the guest room to don their costumes that they refused to reveal until they finished. They wanted the full dramatic effect.

Colby and Gary retired to Colby's room to prepare their disguises while Nana, Aria, and Shelly all raced around between their rooms, helping one another get dressed and made up as witches.

Darla and Rhea were the first to arrive in the living room setup as their staging area. Darla dressed as Medusa and Rhea as a lady vampire. They watched and whistled admiration as the Graeae, three 'grey witches', of Greek mythology crept down the stairs.

Nana led the way, holding their shared eye. "Ah, don't look at Medusa sisters lest ye be turned to stone," she cackled. "And be wary of the bite of the dark mistress for fear of waking as a creature of the night."

The five women milled about the living room preening and waiting impatiently for the boys to appear.

"Come on already, you two, time is a-ticking, and the yummy professor will be here any minute to act as the undead butler," Shelly yelled. "I bet he still looks delicious as a zombie."

The ladies all agreed and nodded until Rhea screamed. They all looked up at what she was pointing at the top of the stairs.

Nana swung the shared eye toward the top of the staircase. "By the pricking of my thumbs-"

"Some stinky cheese goblin, this way comes," Shelly finished.

Two wicked-toothed demon-like creatures crept down the stairs. Each was barely clad in torn cloth bearing wart and boil covered skin that festered and oozed green puss. Their long, curled ears were topped with tufts of matted hair while blood dripped from their fangs.

"Funny Smelly, especially coming from your dry rot looking self," sounded Colby's voice with a lisp caused by the assumed 'fake' teeth.

"That is so scary! I love it," said Rhea. Her eyes squinted as she looked them over.

Darla, usually the center of attention, feigned interest. "Very nice. It will do, I suppose."

The sound of knocking on the door charged the air like the three youngest of the women fought to be the one to open the door for Rigel. Shelly won the race, mostly from intimidation, a slight growl, and a lot of pushing.

"Open the locks, whoever knocks," Nana sang.

Colby moaned. "Cool-it Nana, save it for the paying guests."

"Welcome, do come in and make yourself at home Professor Stark," Shelly said and smiled, forgetting she wore rotted-out false teeth.

* * *

Rigel raised his right brow and crossed the threshold. "Indeed," he said. "I must say this place is amazing compared to last night. Simply…Magical would be the best way to describe it."

The twin goblins looked at each other concerned. "Has anyone seen a black cat around?" Colby said.

"Fizz? He was out back last time I saw him," Nana said. "Are we all ready, then? Places everyone the first show is in five minutes."

"I thought Fizzlewink was a Russian Blue?" Rhea asked.

"Um…we dyed him black for the occasion," Colby said.

Everyone took their places in various parts of the house. While Gary pretended to flip some switches, Colby cast the runes to turn on the rest of the interior effects, including moans and creaks, ghostly howls, and witchy cackles. Everything was set for fright night.

***

The fundraiser was in full swing by 8:00 PM. A steady stream of visitors flowed throughout the Stevens' haunted house. They made their way from the front door through the first level, starting with the 'un-living room' where they encountered ghosts sailing around and appearing from nowhere. Vampires and zombies jumped out from behind furniture and walls.

The next stop on the tour took them through to the kitchen, where the three witches stirred their potion and waited upon unsuspecting victims to serve for dinner, the witches' dinner.

Jasper Bodine was among one group that made its way from one room to the next. He sneered and joked about the lameness of each prop spouting off about how fake they were. He decided to veer away from the group he was in and snoop around upstairs. His ultimate purpose was to find Colby's room and wreak havoc upon his nemesis' sanctuary while stealing something special. He was unaware of the reason he was compelled to follow this command. He didn't even remember the Professor whispering in his ear as he entered the Stevens' home.

The stairs creaked as Jasper took them two at a time, attempting to avoid notice. As he looked to the top, the staircase seemed to stretch further away and higher than he expected. Confused but undeterred, Jasper picked up his pace, looking down to keep from tripping. When he thought he had reached the top, he looked up again to find the stairs stretching away again. He looked behind him to find he was still on the bottom step.

"What the…there must be something in that foggy mist making me high."

He picked up his pace, but this time kept his eyes on the landing above him. This time he reached the top and did not look down until his feet were firmly planted beyond the staircase. Jasper looked around to make certain he wasn't followed, for the hairs on the back of his neck were at full attention to an unseen pair of eyes he felt upon him.

Every door on the floor was locked and would not budge, but Jasper found another set of stairs and decided to check them out. Slowly, he took each stair without taking his eyes off the uppermost landing above. Once he reached the top, Jasper found two doors. One door was locked; the other stood ajar.

"Guess that decides that," he whispered aloud.

Pushing the creaky old door open, Jasper made his way up the stairs and into the musty old attic. "What a mess," he decided and turned to leave, but the door slammed shut, locking him in the room.

Jasper pulled on the doorknob while kicking and shouldering it in a vain attempt at forcing it open. It would not shift, so he looked around the room for anything that he could use as leverage or a pry bar. Jasper rummaged through boxes and trunks, knocking stacks over in the process. Finding nothing that might help, he began to panic. Jasper did not like feeling trapped or out of control because it made him imagine horrible things, and he was already beginning to hear noises.

* * *

A shuffling and scraping sound broke the silence as Jasper stood in the center of the attic, holding his panicked breath for fear of being discovered. The sound grew nearer... Thump, thump, thump... Scrape. Thump, thump, thump... Scrape, he heard as the sound drew closer still. Jasper began to slowly back into the shadows and out of the open moonshine radiating in through the lone window. Thinking himself safely hidden, he chanced to take a slow and steady breath. His breath cut short as he saw the shadowed form of something emerging into the glow of moonlight.

He could make out the shape of a tall and lanky figure, with a rounded head and long pointed ears protruding to each side. The eyes, shining and menacing, focused upon his position. Jasper backed farther still into the darkness; the air was stolen from his silent scream as he felt a set of arms wrap around him from behind.

Chapter 31

The grounds around the house were set as a swampy dead forest and graveyard shrouded in mists. A slim covered stone walkway marked the path for the patrons to follow as they made their way around the house to the front porch.

Colby and Gary lurked in the mists, poised to scare the crap out of anyone they could, raising their angst before they entered the house for act two. The two of them prepared their grotesque goblin forms for the attack as they heard the voices of approaching victims.

The voices stopped, followed by a moment of still silence before the screaming pierced the night. Thundering footfalls echoed through the misty graveyard as several teenagers barreled down the path, ignoring the two creatures hanging across their path. The kids kept running without stopping to look behind them.

As the swirling fog settled, Colby and Gary looked to one another for answers before turning to peer through the dense air in the direction the others approached from. Nothing seemed out of the ordinary, but they climbed down from their perches to investigate all the same.

"Did you add something to the start of the path and forget to tell me?" Gary asked.

Colby shook his head no. "I was gonna ask you the same thing. Do you suppose the girls came outside instead of staying in the house?"

Gary scratched his goblin head and raised his boil-covered brows. "Maybe the witch Nana tried passing out some treats, and they tasted the food?"

The boys laughed and tossed funny scenarios back and forth until Colby's last joke passed with no reply.

Colby peered into the mist ahead and blinked then rubbed his giant yellow eyes, thinking he saw something, but there was nothing there.

"Did you just see anything, Gary?" he asked. Silence. "Hey baboon face, I said did-" he started before turning around. His voice lost its air.

Gary stood frozen in a pose of agony, his facade of a goblin melting away. Behind him stood, no floated a hazy outline of a being without full form. It had piercing red glowing orbs where the proximity of eyes would be.

The thing's shadowy clawed hands grasped and held Gary firm where he stood, unable to move. As the illusion was ripped from his body, the Emassa construct of runes melted and crumbled while the power flowed from Gary along the arms of the shadow man. Its eyes pulsed with every drop of power that it appeared to be siphoning off of Gary's spell.

Colby dropped his own goblin form and called up his #Magic app to send an attack at the beast. Before he could raise his arm to call up the construct, a powerful hand gripped his shoulder from behind and pulled him off the path, into the fog.

"Do not attack the seeker," the Dregg said. "It will realize its mistake."

Colby struggled with the monster but could not break free. He looked down at his hands in an effort to force his Emassa to protect him, but it would not ignite. "What-" his words were cut off as the Dregg covered his mouth, and another approached and pointed toward Gary.

"You must save your friend, but not with that easy magic in your toy. Use what you did when you fled from us in the old building."

Colby was frightened by the creatures that surrounded him, real monsters. Something registered, however, and fear for his friend fueled a spark within him that cause his magic to flare as soon as the Dregg holding him let go.

The Dregg smirked as it watched the purple energy flash around Colby's hand.

Concentrating on Gary, Colby focused on what he wanted more than anything, his friend safely by his side. Colby could see another dark figure approaching the seeker attacking Gary, from behind. It was not a shadow, Colby realized. Another Dregg was sneaking up on the shadowy seeker, and it wrapped its arms around the thing sapping energy from Gary. The seeker let go of Gary then turned against its attacker.

Colby refocused his mind, and through the force of instinct and emotion, power and will, Colby pulled on Gary's body with his mind and released the Emassa from his hold. Gary disappeared in a flash of light and instantly reappeared next to Colby. Relieved but still weary, Colby looked back at the monsters in the yard.

The seeker screeched, forgetting about Gary, who now laid listlessly to the ground next to Colby, goblin form completely gone. Only his underwear and t-shirt remained. He lay helpless at the feet of the two things fighting for dominance behind him.

* * *

Colby tried to get up, but the Dregg held him fast.

"You wait until the seeker has gone. I will remove my hand, but stay quiet." The Dregg let his hand fall free of Colby's mouth and lifted a finger to his lip.

Colby held his tongue, though he fought within to hold back from finding the Dregg's soft spot and introducing his knee. When he realized the screeching abruptly stopped, Colby turned back toward Gary to find only the Dregg there, lifting Gary from the ground and approaching. The Dregg holding him let go, and Colby lurched forward as his feet took a flight of their own accord.

"Put him down," Colby demanded.

"It will be fine, your friend will recover," the Dregg said but did not lower Gary. "We must take him inside."

Colby glared at the Dreggs and searched for their motives. "I suppose you want me to invite you in so you can come and go as you please? Attack us while we sleep or something?"

The Dregg that held him back earlier laughed, a deep and resounding laugh from the gut. "You watch too much television young maker. We are not vampires. We do not need an invitation to enter."

Colby was unsure if he was being mollified or threatened. He hesitated a moment, but his decision was made for him when the Dregg began carrying Gary toward the back of the house. "We can go in through the kitchen and take the back stairs to my room."

Colby did not wish to interrupt the fundraiser since they assured him Gary would be fine. "Take the stairs up between groups and put him in my room."

Before following the Dreggs around back, Colby set a few constructs to make up for the absence of him and Gary. They would not be as effective, but at least there would be something to fill the void before the guests made their way to the front and into the house.

Opening the back door, Colby stood aside and pointed the way for the Dreggs to head for the back stairs up. He need not have bothered as he watched the first beast make its way past the three witches and up the stairs without a sound. The other Dreggs followed after Colby moved to lead the way to his room.

There were no wandering guests on the back stairs, but once on the second level, Colby used his sudden appearance to scare some kids down the stairs past him without them lingering to notice Gary in the arms of the creature. When he turned back to them, he found they already entered Colby's locked room. Colby ran to his door and entered, closing the door behind just as a scrawny black cat followed inside.

"What are these…things doing here?" Fizzlewink said as he morphed into his natural blue cat-man form. "What did they do to Gary?" Fizzlewink jumped up on the bed next to where Gary lay unconscious. He lifted the boy's eyelids and peered into his eyes and mouth, pulling out his tongue and examining the rest of his body. "He's been siphoned," he determined and glared at the Dreggs. "How?"

Colby moved between Fizzlewink and the Dreggs. "It wasn't them. Some dark thing with red eyes wrapped around Gary and started sucking all the Emassa from him."

Fizzlewink eyes went wide, and he began shaking his head. "Not good…Not good at all. Oh, dear, this will not do."

The lead Dregg, or at least what Colby assumed was their leader, stepped out from behind Colby and approached Fizzlewink. "You understand what this means, do you not, little blue cat-man?"

Fizzlewink nodded and put his hands in his head. "I had hoped there would be more time, but I misjudged their abilities."

"It is their desperation, not their abilities that drive them," the Dregg said.

* * *

Colby stood, listening to the conversation confused. "Would someone kindly tell me what the hell this is all about?"

Realizing his mistake, Fizzlewink pulled Colby into the conversation. "The shadowy creature you saw tonight is a semi-conscious construct of Emassa called a Seeker. It carries a portion of a Shizumu. While the thing is not entirely corporeal, it is able to track and then absorb Emassa from anyone or anything it finds."

Rubbing his temples, Colby sat next to Gary and looked at his friend's helpless form. "The whole house must have been like a torch in the night."

"Precisely young maker. You begin to understand," said the Dregg.

"But why did it single out Gary, the entire graveyard would have fed the thing. The mists, the trees, everything was built from multitudes of constructs that emanated from our link to the source."

"Because it was likely looking for that source and Gary was the first man-creature it found. He was surrounded by a spell, yes?" asked the Dregg.

Colby began to put the pieces together. Though the entire property was emitting Emassa born power, this seeker was on the search specifically for a living person. He was emitting a vast construct, thanks to his link to Emassa and the phWatch. He just happened to be on the path that would have ultimately led to Colby himself. Even the limited intelligence of the Seeker allowed it to unravel the construct around Gary and consume the power.

"But why did it try to kill him, rather than inhabit Gary?" Colby asked.

Fizzlewink explained how it was only powered by part of a Shizumu, not the full manifestation of one, and, therefore, incapable of possessing his young friend's body. "More than likely, it was sent to identify the source of Emassa and, if possible, immobilize it and then take him back to its masters. Gary should be immune to infestation at any rate."

* * *

The pain in Colby's head increased, and his hands began to glow. "Why could I not call the Emassa then when it mattered?" His emotions were raging. The ebb and flow between anger and failure fed the Emassa in his hands as the purple glow intensified. The light began to pour from his hands and brighten the room to near blinding brilliance before ceasing in a sudden final pulse. Colby felt the hand of the Dregg upon his shoulder.

"That would be due to my contact with you, young Colby Stevens." The Dregg removed his hand and stepped back. "One of the effects of our creation was that we cancel out the Emassa, making us of no use to our makers when we refused to remain tools in their war with the Shizumu." The last few words dripped with bile and aimed toward Fizzlewink.

Fizzlewink sat back, insulted look on his face. "I had nothing to do with that, so you can aim your hatred elsewhere, Dregg."

The Dregg's angered look did not soften, but he looked back at Colby. "You are lucky the Seeker was chased off before it discovered the truth of its mistaken identification. But rest assured, they know where to find you now." The Dregg made its way to the window and motioned to its companions. Before following them out, it turned back to Colby. "You have an unwelcome guest found snooping in your attic. I suggest you free him. And learn to control your emotions, boy. They imprison you, and if you wish to truly be free, you must control how you feel to control what you may become."

Colby only then noticed the name stitched on the army jacket the Dregg wore. It read 'Conrad'. "Conrad?" Colby said to the surprise of the Dregg. "Is that your name?"

The Dregg nodded and leaped out the window. "We have no quarrel at the present young maker, try to keep it that way. We will be watching and will see you again." The words echoed through the night as the Dreggs headed out into the mists and disappeared from view.

Colby stared out the window. "What do you think that means?" he asked but did not wait for an answer as Gary began to wake.

"What happened?" Gary asked as he looked around the room and met the worried yellow eyes of Fizzlewink. He pushed back from the cat-man and sat up. "Someone want to explain why I'm out of costume and in your bed?"

"You were attacked," Colby said as he approached. He explained the events of the night after the Seeker attacked. As Colby finally reached the current state of events, he remembered Conrad saying something about an intruder.

Gary finished putting on some different clothes as he hopped behind Colby and Fizzlewink, heading to the stairs to the attic level. As they reached the foot of the steps, they were pushed aside when Jasper Bodine came barreling past them, ashen-skinned and sweating. The slight odor of urine wafted on the breeze caused by his passing.

"You will regret this, Colby Stevens," Jasper whimpered as he passed. "When my father hears of this, you will pay."

Colby poked Jasper in the chest with his index finger; eyes narrowed and lips tight. "You don't scare me anymore, Jasper Bodine. The days of me cowering to the likes of you and your bully brigade have ended."

Jasper looked at Colby wide-eyed and sniffled before he ran down the remaining stairs.

"And your dad can just stuff it," Colby said to Jasper's retreating back.

The three turned to one another with looks of surprise and restrained laughter when they heard footsteps on the landing above them. They turned back up toward the upper level to see a shadow flowing over the steps and stretching down toward them.

Colby and Gary started backing away as the shadow stretched further down the steps toward them. Colby chanced a look up top and let out a relieved huff when he saw Medusa standing above looking down.

* * *

"What are you doing up there?" he asked Darla.

Darla began the climb down, clutching her Grecian style dress away from her feet. "I heard weird noises up there while chasing some visitors down the hall. When I got up there, I heard crying from the attic door and thought someone got locked in. Imagine my surprise when Jasper Bodine knocked me over on his way out." She passed Colby and Gary without winking at Colby as she passed. "What a big cry baby, he turned out to be."

Darla reached into the folds of her skirt and withdrew an object. She handed the watch to Colby. "Here, Jasper dropped this on his way out. Isn't this yours?"

Colby took the watch and thanked Darla. He couldn't imagine why Jasper would have wanted to steal Colby's watch, the one his father left behind. He put the watch back on his free wrist.

Colby looked at Gary. "You think she saw anything?"

"Probably."

"What should I say to her?"

"She wasn't freaked out so we can assume she has knowledge of magic. Let her come to you."

Colby shrugged in agreement. "You want to go back out there and scare the pants off people?" Colby asked.

"You think it's safe? You didn't admit to knowing about the Seeker."

"They only sent one, and I don't know yet who we can trust with knowing about my visions getting stronger."

Gary sighed. "OK. I'll go with you on this one time. But if you get a preview of those things coming back. We have to tell somebody."

* * *

Colby agreed and pointed to the door. When Gary didn't move, he pushed his friend out to the porch.

"Something tells me it will be fine. The Dreggs are probably still nearby, and I'm hoping some of Jasper's buddies are as well."

They shared a devious grin and cast their spell, **#GuiseOfGoblin**.

The boys ran through the house and outside after the fleeing Jasper Bodine. They laughed and made ghoulish noises as they scared the visitors who remained.

Colby felt a lifting of weights off his shoulders after facing Jasper in his home, crying and smelling of soiled pants. His one time dreaded bully and reason for hiding from being himself was no longer a threat. He stood up to him, if only a little, but it was a start. His friend Gary was safe. These new creatures the Dreggs were perhaps new allies against the unknown. He was in a good place emotionally, and that was something he hadn't felt in a very long time.

When the night was over, and he and Gary waved the girls off as they left, Colby felt a bond beginning to form. There was something drawing him to those girls and closer to Gary, but he felt that there were missing pieces yet to find. He needed more than anything to understand what was happening to him, but the one person who would be able to give him the answers he now needed, it seemed, was missing.

He had a way to go, but with his emotions coming under control, he was learning to manifest his power through #Magic. Colby would use this and anything he could muster to help find his father. No matter what it took, he would learn this new magic thing and do what he had to in order to bring his father back home.

***

Rigel stood on the front porch as the boys jumped off and into the yard, his face obscured by shadow. His posture sagged as the skin of his hand-aged beneath the moonlight. He smiled in spite of himself at the joyful mischief the two lads shared. Rigel was reminded briefly of a time he once shared the same carefree glee of magic and freedom he felt with his brother long ago in a forgotten world. He was beginning to become attached to his nephew. The Professor's attitude soured. He was running out of time, but he had no idea exactly how much time remained before the bargain giving him flesh dissolved with his borrowed skin. He needed access to Jarrod's things, but the spell giving him the flesh of his brother prevented him from taking liberties with belongings that were not attached to his soul. Rigel looked at one of his seekers approaching from beyond the boundary of the Stevens' yard.

Rigel reached out and held his hand just over the glowing skin of the seeker. Energy surged from the creature and surged into the man, replenishing his power. The seeker relinquished the magic it absorbed from the many spells around the property.

"I'll get what I need, as long as time allows me to play this game." Rigel looked at the rejuvenated hand raised before his borrowed eyes. "I'll not go back there. I'll not give this up." Play along, Rigel reminded himself before relaxing into a confident stride and walked off into the rising mists of the magic-infused yard.

Chapter 32

A heavy mist still hugged the ground and shifted around the artificial tombstones and mausoleum staged in the side yard of the Stevens' home. Hours quickly passed since the last of the guests departed from the block-party style fundraising festival Colby and his club organized. Beyond the rows of houses and trees that obscured the view of Lake Shore Drive, the barely audible motors of few passing vehicles was the only noise breaking the stillness of the early morning darkness.

A strained squeak followed by a hushed click echoed around the yard. The noise was soon followed by a muffled padding in the grass. The mists began to swirl as the fur-covered question mark cut through it, forcing the ground clinging fog to separate before folding back in its wake. Two glowing yellow eyes caught the moon's light as it floated down past its midpoint of travel across the star-filled sky.

The Russian blue cat leapt up to perch atop one to the tombstones and moaned deeply before releasing a single abrupt yowling call. He waited.

Minutes passed in silence, the only noise a slight buzz followed by a muted pop as Fizzlewink transformed into his blue-skinned small statured self. He twirled his favored eyebrow in time with his eyes that darted around, scanning the darkness.

"I have wondered how long it would be until I heard from you," a voice called as his shadowy outline stood out against the rising fog behind him.

Fizzlewink jumped at the sudden voice. He was surprised because he did not sense the man's approach.

A chuckle escaped the man's mouth. "You are slipping old friend."

Gathering himself in a feeble attempt to compose his dignity, Fizzlewink shifted around but remained seated. "We have never been friends."

"Regardless of our working relationship, you have failed to contact any of us as expected. Why now?"

"I have been rather occupied with the boy."

The man was not convinced. "I can see that. He has progressed dangerously fast."

Fizzlewink sat up defensively. "That is not my doing. He is more powerful than we calculated."

"A turbulent child with a temper is dangerous with a weapon of magic. You will teach him to control his emotions, or he will be dealt with by the others." The dark tone of the man's voice left little to interpret.

"He will be controlled and malleable as promised." Fizzlewink jumped down from his perch and started to walk away. His steps halted at the sound of the man clearing his throat. "Was there something more?"

"Are you certain you have the stomach for this Fizzlewink? You were quite vocal in your protests when the child was discovered."

"There are other variables at play that we did not account for," Fizzlewink protested. "There are Shizumu out of bounds and congregating everywhere in the area." Fizzlewink heard no response from the man, which meant he already knew. "Then there is the arrival of the Dreggs."

That got the man's attention. Fizzlewink, though he couldn't make out the features of the man from the way his shadow stiffened, could tell this was news to his late night visitor.

"When?"

"They were here last night," Fizzlewink paused as he watch the man's obscured head dart around, looking for signs of the beasts. "This was the third or fourth time they showed themselves to the boy."

"The boy has been working with them?"

"Heavens no, but they are drawn to him like a moth to the flame for some reason. And lucky since there was a seeker here tonight, and it wasn't normal."

The man said nothing for several moments. When he did speak, there was a tightening to his tone and a hastening in his words. "You have a job to do; that hasn't changed. I will inform the others, and they will deal with the Dreggs and discuss the seeker."

Fizzlewink stood, blinking. "I will do as I agreed."

"Then you are prepared to prove your worth?" the man asked.

Fizzlewink did not speak but nodded slowly.

"You will retrieve something for me. A small token to prove you will do as you are told."

Fizzlewink noticed the man said 'me' and not us. He wasn't sure what it meant but filed it away for later consideration.

"What would you ask of me beyond what part I have already conceded to play?" Fizzlewink attempted to conceal the worry, but his voice betrayed the sinking of his emotions.

"I have come to know that a certain object, a watch, has come into the boy's possession. Something once belonging to that traitor Jarrod." The man paused, but only long enough to see the understanding in Fizzlewink's eyes. "Good, I see you know what

I'm referring to. You will go and fetch it for me. Now."

Fizzlewink didn't like being in this situation, but he had little recourse. "Wait here."

He didn't bother changing form as he sullenly walked around the back of the house, shoulders sagging and head down. As quietly as he exited earlier he doubled his efforts at silencing his actions this time. Fizzlewink entered the house and with slow, stealthy, deliberate steps, making his way through the first floor to the stairs. He paused only long enough to make certain he hadn't disturbed the old witch sitting in the living room chair.

Nana sat with her head back and mouth wide open, taking in deep nasally breaths and exhaling with a vibrating rattle that would rival a buzzsaw.

Fizzlewink shook his head and proceeded to ascend the stairs, careful to avoid those that creaked. Once at the top of the first flight, he picked up his pace at the sound of a low howl outside. He took that to be a signal to hurry along.

The second door on the right, slightly ajar, was his destination. As he crept along and stayed in the shadow along the wall, Fizzlewink slinked into the room and scanned around for the watch. Colby had not been wearing it lately, but it wouldn't be far from him.

As he suspected, Fizzlewink spied the watch on the nightstand beside a radio alarm clock. In a silent burst of movement, Fizzlewink shifted position to stand over the watch, hand poised to snatch it up, but he hesitated. Another howl in the yard raised the hairs on his neck.

* * *

With a wave of his hand and a mumbled word, Fizzlewink dashed off and exited the room, shoving his hand in his front pocket. In his haste, he failed to notice the door just before the stairs open, and a robed figure step out into his escape route.

"What are you doing, lurking around at nearly three in the morning?" Aria asked while yawning and rubbing her eyes.

"Off to see a man about a mouse," Fizzlewink said as he rushed past her and bound down the stairs.

"Don't mess in my garden!" Aria hissed. "Why can't he use a toilet like any normal person?"

Fizzlewink heard her but chose to ignore the comment. He had to get outside before his visitor made any more noise to draw attention.

Once outside, Fizzlewink found the man where he left him, only his hand escaped the shadow of the tree he stood beside.

"Excellent," the man said as Fizzlewink slowly handed over the prize. "We've searched for this a very long time."

"It's just an old watch," Fizzlewink said though he suspected different. His eyes never left the timepiece as the man fondled and rotated it in his hand.

The man placed the watch in his pocket. "We'll be in touch." The man turned and disappeared into the darkness leaving Fizzlewink alone and glaring.

Once he felt it safe, Fizzlewink let out a long held breath and smiled. He turned to head back to the house when he heard the muffled scream and sounds of struggle. He dashed below the closest bush as he transformed back into his cat façade.

The moments dragged on as he peered into the darkness and sniffed the air. There was no more noise, not even the buzz of cars on the drive nearby could be heard. Fizzlewink cautiously eased out from under the bushes when a rough hand took hold of the back of his neck and lifted him off the ground, dispelling his guise.

Feet dangling far from the ground, Fizzlewink felt the hot and foul breath of his assailant. The stench was unmistakable, and only one thing could catch him by surprise when being right on top of him. He opened his eyes to stare directly into the cold, and depthless glare of the Dregg that Colby called Conrad.

"What have you done little man?" Conrad asked. He lifted his other hand to dangle the watch by its band as he held it between his fingers.

Before Fizzlewink could answer, steam began to rise from the place where Conrad held the watch. The face of the timepiece began to glow. As the intensity grew, both the Dregg and Shizumu tried to keep watching the item against the protest of their own eyes wanting nothing more than to retreat behind tightly closed lids.

In a flash, the watch was gone.

"That was unexpected," was all Fizzlewink could think to say.

"I think it past time we took a more active interest," Conrad said. "You will tell me what is happening."

* * *

Fizzlewink wiggled to get free, but it was no use. His skin burned where the Dregg held him. "I will tell you nothing."

The Dregg laughed, a deep and low rumble. "You forget what the Dreggs were created to accomplish and what we can do. We shall see who has the cat's tongue before we are satisfied."

Conrad shoved Fizzlewink into a sack he pulled from his shoulder. Cinching it closed, he swung the sack around to his back then added a satisfied grin to his hard featured face when he heard the grunt from inside the bag.

***

Colby woke suddenly and with a jerking start as he felt a pull from him. Not a physical pull, but one that reached into his being and yanked slight and quick as though plucking a stray hair. As his eyes opened, he thought he saw a flash or reflection, but couldn't find the source once his eyes adjusted to the light pouring in from the moon through the window.

He looked at the clock on his bedside table. Seeing it was not yet four in the morning, he grumbled but smiled a bit when he caught a glimpse of his father's watch next to the clock. Its crystal face was reflecting the blue-green light of the digital display of his alarm clock.

He fluffed his pillow and nestled back under the covers before closing his eyes and drifted back to sleep. He had a full few weeks at school ahead planning for Mexico, and he needed his rest. Soon it would be Thanksgiving break that was the start of several holidays that ushered in winter, the last season before the upcoming spring trip.

Author

Hashtag Magic
Blue Screen of Death
Control+ALT+Delete
Web of Trolls
Open Source
Selfie Sacrifice (2021)

Chronicles of Aurderia
The Balance
River of Souls
Queen of Shadow

Follow on Facebook and Twitter:
http://fb.com/Author-JStevenYoung
@jstevenyoung
Website: http://jstevenyoung.com